浙江省社会科学界联合会社科普及课题"舟山海洋神话英汉对译读本"(22KPD29YB)成果

本成果受到浙江海洋大学外国语学院学科建设经费资助，
在此致谢。

浙江海洋大学海洋应用语言与文化系列研究专著之一

舟山海洋神话故事英汉对译

周　敏　等　著

浙江工商大学出版社
ZHEJIANG GONGSHANG UNIVERSITY PRESS
·杭州·

图书在版编目(CIP)数据

舟山海洋神话故事英汉对译 / 周敏等著. —杭州：
浙江工商大学出版社,2022.6
ISBN 978-7-5178-4958-2

Ⅰ.①舟… Ⅱ.①周… Ⅲ.①神话—作品集—舟山—
英、汉 Ⅳ.①I277.5

中国版本图书馆 CIP 数据核字(2022)第082959号

舟山海洋神话故事英汉对译
ZHOUSHAN HAIYANG SHENHUA GUSHI YINGHAN DUIYI
周　敏　等著

责任编辑	张莉娅
责任校对	林莉燕　李远东
封面设计	浙信文化
责任印制	包建辉
出版发行	浙江工商大学出版社
	(杭州市教工路198号　邮政编码310012)
	(E-mail:zjgsupress@163.com)
	(网址:http://www.zjgsupress.com)
	电话:0571-88904980,88831806(传真)
排　版	杭州朝曦图文设计有限公司
印　刷	杭州高腾印务有限公司
开　本	880mm×1230mm　1/32
印　张	9.25
字　数	236千
版 印 次	2022年6月第1版　2022年6月第1次印刷
书　号	ISBN 978-7-5178-4958-2
定　价	78.00元

序言

党的十八大以来,习近平总书记围绕建设海洋强国发表的一系列重要讲话、作出的一系列重大部署,形成了逻辑严密、系统完整的海洋强国建设思想。建设海洋强国对推动经济持续健康发展,对维护国家主权、安全、发展利益,对实现全面建成小康社会目标进而实现中华民族伟大复兴都具有重大而深远的意义。建设海洋强国战略中,我们外语学科应该做什么,能够做什么,一直是我们努力探索的问题。习近平总书记致2019中国海洋经济博览会的贺信中指出:"海洋是高质量发展战略要地。要加快海洋科技创新步伐,提高海洋资源开发能力,培育壮大海洋战略性新兴产业。"其中"提高海洋资源开发能力"中的"海洋资源"必然包括海洋自然资源和海洋文化资源。海洋文化资源的挖掘、整理、保护、研究、阐释和国内外传播,是我们外语学科教师们能够做的事情,也是责无旁贷的事情。因此,浙江海洋大学海洋应用语言与文化研究院自2021年5月成立以来不断推动海洋法律翻译、海洋文化、海洋文学等主题的研究,并制定实施每年出版1—2部主题专著的计划。

周敏老师2010年7月硕士毕业于四川大学英美文学专业,来院任教后科研方向顺应国家、地区以及舟山市发展大势,从广泛的神话故事研究聚焦到舟山海洋神话故事对外传播,实现了科研对接国家战略的转向,显示了把握学校和学院的学科方向开展特色研究的洞察力。

　　作为学院"海洋应用语言与文化"学科特色科研与教学的推动者,我接过周敏老师题为《舟山海洋神话故事英汉对译》的书稿,既欣喜又感叹。欣喜的是,她快速地从多元化渠道把碎片化的舟山海洋神话故事,梳理有序、阐述有道、评析有据;感叹的是,她有效地把学院的几位老中青优秀译者团结起来,协力完成汉英翻译任务,凝聚力大,团队意识强。周敏老师的这部作品作为学院特色教学与科研的标志成果之一,纳入了"浙江海洋大学应用语言与文化系列研究专著",获得了资助出版,为我们的学科建设做出了贡献。我在此表示热烈祝贺,并期待更多成果接踵而至。

浙江海洋大学外国语学院院长

2022 年 4 月 6 日

目
录

一、创世神话

　　创世神话,即释源天地起因万物由来的神话,代表着人们感知认识世界的最早想象,也能反映出人们认识过程中的思维意识发展,以及一种文化的发展过程。中国神话中的创世神话繁多,不同的民族和地方都有自己的创世神话或创世文化英雄,但从其释因的角度来看,主要有:自然形成说,即天地是自然演化而来的;躯体化生说,即天地是由巨兽或者巨人的躯体演化而生的;卵生说,即天地是由巨卵孵化而来的;神人制造说,即天地是由一位神或者男女二神创造而出的。在流行的中国创世神话中,以盘古开天地的故事最为出名,之后又有女娲补天后续,作为天地开创这一壮举的想象和描绘。北京师范大学杨利慧教授在《中国神话母题索引》中对书中所采用的神话有这样一个定义:"人类表达文化(expressive culture)的诸文类之一。它通常具有这样一些特点,是有关神祇、始祖、文化英雄或神圣动物及其活动的叙事(narrative),通过叙述一个或者一系列有关创造时刻(the moment of creation)以及这一时刻之前的故事,解释神祇、宇宙、人类(包括特定族群)、文化和动植物的最初起源,以及现时世间秩序的最初奠定。"❶杨利慧教授所采用的神话定义虽与本课题研究中所采用的神话广义定义不同,但很好地阐释了创世神话的特点,即神话故事中的叙事对象经历着某一个创造时刻,这个创造通常是会成为宇宙天地,某一种神祇、人类始祖、神圣动物或者神圣风俗的最初起源。本课题中收集和整理的舟山神话故事符合这些特点,较为完整地描述了天地初分、日夜交替、造人等起源问题,也有故事讲述了舟山(舟山最主要的岛或舟山最早发展起来的地方定海)是怎么来的,东海里的鱼虾是怎么来的。虽故事的叙事主角和主要神祇虽稍显凌乱(女娲氏、女娲、玉帝和吕洞宾),且故事之前并无明显的连贯的内在体系,有的故事内容甚至带有明显的近现代修改痕迹,但仍可见其在流传的过程中被本地化和融合的文化特点,在传播过程中的各种差异都极具研究价值。

---

❶ 杨利慧、张成福:《中国神话母题索引》,陕西师范大学出版社总社有限公司 2013 年版,第 7 页。

1. 兄妹分天地

老早老早以前,天地是合拢的,混混沌沌。那时有个天皇氏,有个地皇氏,还有个女娲氏。他们是三兄妹。三兄妹统想做帝:天皇氏想做帝,地皇氏也想做帝,女娲氏也想做帝。这样,三兄妹就争起来。争来争去,谁也勿肯让,互相狠性命地打起来。七打八打,结果把天捅出个大猛大猛的洞,外面的光亮漏进来,亮猛亮猛。这样,天地便分开了。

天帝晓得天被捅破了,交关生气,命他们把天补好。三兄妹只得躲到山里去炼石头。炼呀炼的,炼了好几千年,才用炼好的石头把天补好,补得圆圆的。所以,直到现在,天还是圆的。

天帝为了防三兄妹再争再打,就把他们分开了:天皇氏分到了天上,地皇氏分到了地上,女娲氏呢,就分到天与地的中间。女娲氏便是最早的人,人不是住在天与地的中间吗?

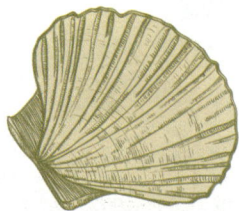

The Siblings Partioned the Sky and the Earth

Long long ago, the sky and the earth remained undivided and everything was in a state of chaos. By then, there was an immortal named Tianhuang, who had two siblings named Dihuang and Nvwa. Each of them aspired to become a heaven. Then they began contending with each other, but none was willing to concede and all disregarded their lives during their fight. They fought for several rounds, only to find a gaping hole torn in the sky due to their actions, through which the bright light from outside came in. That was the time when the sky and the earth became separate from each other.

The Supreme Lord discovered the split in the sky, extremely irritated. He commanded the three to mend what had been broken. They then had no alternative but to retreat to the recesses of mountains, where they started the refinement of stones. It was not until thousands of years later that they had completed the mending process with what they had been refining. The patches then helped round the sky, and its orbicular shape has not changed ever since.

The Supreme Lord dispatched the three to different places, for fearing that they would again compete and fight with each other. Specifically, Tianhuang was sent to the sky, Dihuang the earth, and Nvwa the middle part between the sky and the earth. The place where Nvwa was sent to is exactly where the humanity lives, and that makes her the earliest human.

一、创世神话

2. 女娲补天

据老辈人讲,老早老早的辰光,这天呀,地呀,海呀,山呀,人呀,统呒没的。天是糊塌塌的一片;地是粘渍渍的一块。后来呢,不知从哪里掉下个大神女娲,传说其是个开天辟地的女神。其炼了三千三百三十万块青石,拼成了天,拼得圆圆的,滑滑的,呒缝呒隙,青光晶亮。

天有了,地呢? 女娲从玉帝那里偷来一只球,一甩,甩在天的中央。这球骨碌碌地滚,把粘渍渍的东西统滚雪球样滚上了,变成个圆圆的地,便是地球。所以,天、地都是圆的。

天有了,地有了,女娲又用五个指头在地上乱七八糟地抓呀,挖呀,挖出蛮多洞眼,溢满水便成了江河湖海;抓出蛮多皱脊,长出草,便成了山岭礁岛。有了山,有了水,有了树,有了草,总得有人来停居呀,于是女娲又用黄泥造了人。人传宗接代,世界便热闹了。

Nvwa Mended the Sky

According to the description of the elderly, there was no such thing as the sky, the earth, the seas, mountains or humans in the remote past. The sky had not presented itself clearly, nor had the earth been given a solid form. As time went on, an immortal named Nvwa, who was said to be a goddess for the separation of the sky and the earth, came down out of nowhere. With thirty-three million and three hundred thousand stones she had refined, she managed to give the sky its external shape. The stones rendered the sky round, fitted it smoothly and perfectly, and lightened it with their light.

The sky had already been in place, but what about the earth? No things as the sky, the earth, the sea, mountains or humans in the remote past. The sky had not presented itself clearly, and it began rolling down at a high speed, divesting the earth of all the sticky substances just like a snowball. Then the earth became "the earth" as it showed its rounded form, and that's why both the sky and the earth are round.

With both the sky and the earth in place, Nvwa then started clawing and digging into the earth with her five fingers. As a result, a multitude of pits and holes formed, and rivers, lakes and the seas took shape with overflowing water; a multitude of low and winding ridges formed, and mountains, rocks and islands took shape with growing grass. Now that mountains, water, trees and grass had been created, it was only natural that this place was inhabited by human beings. For this reason, Nvwa created human beings with yellowish soil, and the world became lively as they reproduced themselves.

一、创世神话

3. 日夜是咋分开的

相传在很久以前,大地一片漆黑,呒没太阳,也呒没月亮。

当时神界有三姐妹,三姐妹心地统交关善良。她们很想为人做点好事,就奏禀帝。帝就把大姐封为太阳神,二姐封为月亮神,小妹妹只因太小,暂时没有封。

太阳神和月亮神受封后,整天不歇息,高高地挂在天空上。这样,大地就亮猛了。但是,人们分不出白天也分不出黑夜,统辛苦煞。这事被未受封的小妹知道了,她便请求帝,让她也像大姐、二姐那样,为人做点好事。帝就封小妹为鸡神。

俗话说:"鸡啼五更。"小妹受封当了鸡神后,每天五更定时定点为两个姐姐啼叫。太阳神和月亮神就按鸡神的啼叫,有规有矩地从东边升起,到西边落下。这样,就有了日夜。

How the Day and the Night Separated?

As legend has it, the world in the distant past was in complete darkness and there was neither the sun nor the moon.

Among the divinities back then, there were three sisters who were greatly kind-hearted and concerned to promote the welfare of mortals. Having received their reports on this intention, the Supreme Lord decided to appoint the eldest sister as the God of the Sun, and the second eldest the God of the Moon. As for the youngest one, she at that moment was too young to be included.

Upon their appointment, the two gods had been working around the clock, hanging themselves high above in the sky; accordingly, the world became brighter than ever. However, this also meant that it was impossible for people to distinguish between the day and the night, which made all the efforts in vain. When the youngest sister learned of the situation, she pleaded with the Supreme Lord to allow her to play her own role in bringing happiness to the mortal world, just as her two older sisters were doing; and she then was appointed as the God of Chicken.

As a Chinese proverb goes, "The crow of a rooster suggests the approach of dawn." Upon her appointment, the youngest sister had been crowing at the fifth watch of every night without failing to remind her two older sisters. In line with her crows, the God of the Sun and the God of the Moon regularly rose in the east and sunk in the west; then there were days and nights to call.

　　　　　　　　　　　　一、创世神话

4. 天狗吃月亮

～～～～～～～～～～～～～～～～

一户人家,有三姐妹。老大生得难看勿过,老二勿难看也勿好看,老三顶好看。

这三姐妹,统要抢着做太阳神和月亮神。抢的结果呢,生得难看勿过的大阿姐,做了太阳神;生得勿难看也勿好看的二姐,做了月亮神;生得顶好看的老三,没抢着,只做了只天狗。

大阿姐做了太阳神后,因为自己生得难看勿过,觉得惶恐猛,怕羞不过,怕人家看清其面孔,总要放出刺一样戳眼的光,让人白天勿敢看其。生得勿难看也勿好看的二阿姐,做了月亮神,夜里荫风凉凉,舒舒服服,高兴猛,整夜含着笑脸,望着地下子民百姓。生得顶好看的老三,做了只天狗,恶煞了。她奔到太阳神面前说:"侬呀,生得介难看,咋好做太阳神,侬也没惬意,叫太阳把侬晒煞。"她又奔到月亮神面前,看月亮神最惬意,气狠狠

The Heavenly Dog Eating the Moon

There were three sisters in a family. The eldest one was born unusually ugly, the second eldest just plain, and the youngest particularly attractive.

The three sisters were all scrambling for the positions of the God of the Sun and the God of the Moon. The result of their fight was that the eldest sister who was uncommonly ugly was appointed as the God of the Sun, and the second eldest who was hardly prepossessing the God of the Moon. As for the youngest, who was far more comely than the other two, failed in this fight and only was granted the position of the Heavenly Dog, or "Tiangou".

Since the eldest sister assumed office, glare had been her invariable resort to preclude people's stares at her in daylight. This was because she was so self-conscious about her appearance that any attempt at discerning her exterior would daunt her. In contrast, the second eldest sister with better looks found her time working as the God of the Moon hugely comfortable and delightful. Throughout every night, she enjoyed the cool and gentle wind blowing over, beaming at the commoners below her. The youngest sister that looked the best, however, was discomfited by her position so much that she rushed up to the God of the Sun, to whom she said, "It seems to me that you are far from being qualified for the job of the God of the Sun, given how hideous you look. Still, I can see that you are bending over backwards to do some whitewash here." With that, she then rushed up to the God of the Moon, whose

一、创世神话

地说："有朝一日,我咬侬煞。"从此以后,天狗总想咬月亮神,所以会有糊月,糊月便是天狗吃月亮。

天狗要吃月亮,月亮神一点也勿怕。其忖:"侬要吃我,子民百姓会救我咯,会打侬、吓侬、用烟熏侬咯,侬弄我勿煞。"百姓喜欢月亮神的笑脸,只要一出现糊月,就会马上拿出铜锣、脸盆"咚咚"地敲呀,拿出炮仗"嘭嘭"地放呀,点起柴火用烟熏呀,就是敲天狗、吓天狗、熏天狗的。天狗呢,听到"咚咚"的敲声,"嘭嘭"的炮仗声,吓煞了;烟熏得难熬煞了,嘴巴合勿拢,鼻头水都呛出来啦,只好逃啦。

leisurely conditions made her so indignant that she declared, "Watch out, because someday my mouth will find its way to you." And from that day on, this idea took root in her mind. If the moon should begin to wane, that is when the Heavenly Dog has managed to get the better of the God of the Moon; and it is no wonder why the moon has phases.

The God of the Moon appeared not in the slightest frightened when threatened by the Heavenly Dog. After deliberation, she responded, "You can threaten all you want, but you should know the commoners below me will come to my rescue. It would better for you to shake this idea, otherwise those people may treat you with aggression, intimidation and acrid smoke." The commoners cherished the gracious expression of the God of the Moon. For that reason, they tended to take targeted steps to scare off the Heavenly Dog as soon as the moon began to wane, such as pounding on gongs and basins, letting off firecrackers to create noises, and igniting firewood to give off pungent smoke. The Heavenly Dog, their target, tended to be horrified by the cacophony and succumb to the acrid smoke, her mouth unable to shut and snot oozing from her nose; she then had no option but to take flight.

5. 开天门

相传,很久以前,每年农历八月十六的晚上,天就会裂开一条缝,缝中露出七彩的光,一直照到地上,这就是开天门。

开天门时,天上还会放下一个梯子,这个梯子一直通到月亮,人们还可以登着梯子到月亮上去呢。月亮里有山,山坡上长着一株三个人才能抱拢的大树,叫娑婆树。娑婆树树叶交关茂盛,结的果子多勿过。每当人们上去玩的辰光,娑婆树会摇来摇去,表示人去玩其欢喜猛。

后来,地上有人看中了这棵娑婆树,想把它搬到人间。有人拿着斧头砍它,有人用锯子锯它。砍呀,锯呀,可每当娑婆树要断掉的辰光,就会有只喜鹊飞来,停在人带来的饭桶上,吃饭桶里的饭。人怕饭被喜鹊吃光,就放下斧头、锯子,奔过去赶喜鹊。喜鹊被赶走了,但娑婆树的斫口也随着合拢了。人就这样拼命地砍呀,锯呀,又赶喜鹊呀,砍砍锯锯,奔奔赶赶,这样反反复复,这株娑婆树一直呒没被弄断。

到了八月十六的晚上,娑婆树被人砍得难熬煞。难熬得

The Heavenly Gate Opened

According to legend, in those far-off days, a crack would turn up in the sky on the evening of the sixteenth day of the eighth lunar month, through which iridescent light would beam down to the earth, indicating the opening of the Heavenly Gate.

Other than the opening of the Gate, there would be a ladder coming down on that occasion, which led all the way to the moon. People who chose to climb it could finally reach the moon, where they would find hills, as well as a huge tree growing on the hillside, which could only be encircled by three people hand in hand. The tree was known as the Suopo Tree. It was endowed with incredibly exuberant foliage and plentiful fruits. It would always sway to and fro, when seeing people from the earth enjoying themselves on the moon; that was a gesture to express its delight on their arrival.

Then, some people on the earth had their eye on this tree, and were scheming to move it to where they lived by means of axes and saws. But every time the body of the tree came near to breaking off, a magpie would fly over, alight upon the rice bucket those people brought along and nibbled at the rice within. The fear that the entirety of their rice could be robbed of would then provoke those people into a scurry to chase the magpie away, with their axes and saws left behind. However, as this was going on, the Suopo Tree was recovering itself, and all that had been sabotaged was restored. Axing, sawing, driving the magpie away, then proceeding with axing and sawing—those people had been caught

一、创世神话

哭起来，人听到了，吓了一跳，放下斧头、锯子呆呆地立着，娑婆树对人说："你们不要再伤害我啦，我会给你们好处的。每年的今日晚上，你们在地上等着，我会把娑婆树果掉落一颗，谁得，谁就会发大财。"

人一听，就下来啦，不砍啦，直等到八月十六的晚上，才抬着头，望着月亮，盼望着掉落娑婆果来，但是不管人如何地等，如何地望，一年一年，一代一代地等呀，盼呀，始终不见有娑婆果掉下来。而天门呢，再也没开过，天梯也不再放下来啦。

in this cycle, shuttling back and forth with sweat on their brows, only to find the Suopo Tree had survived all of it.

On an evening of the sixteenth day of the eighth lunar month, the Suopo Tree had had enough of taking all this lying down and began wailing. The sound of its wail petrified those people, their axes and saws let down, when the Suopo Tree said unto them, "Could you please stop treating me like this? In return, I will give you something that redounds to your benefits. On the same evening every year since now, I will shed one of my fruit, and you all could just wait for it down on the earth. The finder, if there is any, strikes gold. "

Hearing this, those people instantly called it quits and turned back from the moon. They started waiting, until the evening of the sixteenth day of the eighth lunar month; then they would look up at the moon, expecting the descent of the fruit of the Suopo Tree. The wait had lasted for years, and expectations for generations, but no matter how long they waited, and how wishful they were, none of the fruits was seen fall from the moon. As for the Heavenly Gate, it had stayed shut ever since then; and the ladder coming with it was withdrawn.

6. 人狗成亲

　　传说盘古分天地以后,地上本来呒有人,是天上放落许多虫子,虫子变成了人。这些人繁殖得交关快,不久,地上的人就多得像蚂蚁。人多呒没东西吃,连草根和树皮统吃光啦,就开始偷和抢,天帝知道后,想用油雨灭绝人类。

　　有一天,天上乌云重猛,雷声"隆隆"响,忽然下起瓢泼大雨,这雨不是一般的雨,而是油雨。闪电以后,油雨变成大火,人呒处可躲,哭声喊声连成片。最后人统被烧煞啦。传说只有一个姑娘,见无路可走,"腾"地跳进自家井里,一只黄狗,看见女主人跳进井里,也跟着跳进。因井里水不深,呒没被淹死,也呒没被烧煞。后来地上的火灭了,姑娘和黄狗才从井里出来。这时地上也呒半点生物了,姑娘伤心地大哭。谁知道黄狗却开口说话了:"女主人啊,何必伤心呢?世上呒没了人,不是更干净吗?别看我狗头狗尾的,心地却比人还好三分呢。让我和你成亲,生儿育女吧。"姑娘看黄狗会开口讲人的话,知它不是一般的狗,而是神狗,就点点头答应了。这样,姑娘就跟黄狗做了夫妻,使人呒没绝种。

　　姑娘跟狗做夫妻,因狗有尾巴,当时生出的人也有尾巴,一节连一节,共有十节。十节尾巴有九节黄啦,人就要死啦,要归位啦。到这时人都懒得生产,勿去做啦。坟呢,自家也堆搭好,一髭水,一髭炒麦粉,统坟里摆进。弄块板,铺搭,坟里

Man and Dog Got Married

It is said that after Pangu divided the universe into the heaven and the earth, there was not a human existing on the earth. However, released from the heaven were a lot of worms, which turned into human beings. These people bred quickly, and soon there were as many people on the ground as ants. There were so many people on the earth that there was not enough food to feed them. As a result, even the grass roots and bark were eaten up by people. So they began to steal and rob one another. Having known the situation on the earth, the Heaven Emperor wanted to extinct the human beings on the earth with the oil rain.

One day, it was darkly cloudy with rumbling thunder. All of a sudden, it rained dogs and cats. Yet the rain was not the general rain, but oil rain. The lightning made the oil rain into a conflagration, which preventing people from finding a shelter to hide themselves. The earth was permeated with people's crying and shouting everywhere. In the end, all the people were burned but a girl. It is said that the girl abruptly jumped into a well when she found no other way out. Seeing its mistress jump into the well, the yellow dog jumped into the well, too. However, both the girl and the dog were not drowned due to the fact that the water in the well was not deep, nor did they get burned. The girl and the yellow dog did not climb out of the well until the big fire on the ground died away. Then there were no other living creatures but the girl and the dog. The girl was so sad that she burst into tears. Just at that time, the

一、创世神话

困进等死。

天帝知道这事后,心里忖:"十节尾巴九节黄啦,只吃勿做,吃得家里东西呒没啦,这样下去活着的人咋办?"天帝偷偷把人的尾巴统给斩落呒啦。这以后人几时要归位,统勿晓得啦。

一场油雨过后,谷也被烧光,种田呒没种子。人要饿煞。这咋弄呢?后来一只麻雀从天上衔来一粒谷,可这粒谷正巧跌落到石板缝里。老鼠知道后,把其用嘴咬出来。这粒谷,老鼠呒没吃,就做种啦。"粒谷种九年,湖广都种遍。"至今已经种遍天下了。因当初稻谷种是麻雀衔来的、老鼠咬出的,所以现在老辈人还说:"麻雀吃谷,呒没罪过;老鼠吃点呢,也呒没罪过咯。"

yellow dog, God knows, began to speak, "My dear mistress, why should you be sad? Doesn't the world become even cleaner without any other people around us? Although I am a dog, I am more kind-hearted than humans. Let me marry you and have children." Having found that the yellow dog could speak like a human being, the girl knew that the yellow dog was not an ordinary dog, and it must be an immortal dog. Thus the girl agreed to the dog with a nod. The girl and the dog became wife and husband. So man did not become extinct.

Now that the dog had a tail, the human beings born at that time also had a tail owing to the marriage of the girl and the dog. At that time people had a ten-part tail which was linked one part after another. When nine parts of the ten-part tail turned yellow, the human being was to die, doomed to return to his original place. When reaching this point, the human being was unwilling to labor and started to build the grave of his own, into which he placed an earthen jar of water, a jar of fried wheat flour. Then he made a bed with a piece of board in the grave, waiting for the approach of death.

Having known what was going on on the earth, the Heaven Emperor thought to himself, "When man finds nine parts of the ten-part tail have become yellow, he stops working but eating. As a result, all the food in the home is eaten up by him and what will happen to the living people without food if things are going on like this?" The Heaven Emperor secretly cut off man's tail. From then on, no one knows when he is going to die.

After an oil rainfall, the rice plant was also burned. There were no seeds to be planted in the field. People must be hungry to death. How could people deal with this situation? Then a sparrow carried a grain of rice from the heaven, which happened to fall down into a crack in the flagstones. After the mouse knew it, it

　　　　　　　　　　　　　一、创世神话

picked the grain out with its mouth. The grain was not eaten up by the mouse, so it was kept as the seed. After nine years of planting, the rice seeds had become so many that they could be planted everywhere in both Hu'nan and Guangdong. And today the rice seeds have been planted all over the world. Since the original seed of rice was brought by the sparrow and picked out by the mouse, no wonder that nowadays the elderly often say like this, "It's of no crime for the sparrow to eat the grain of rice. Neither does the mouse for the eating of the grain of rice."

一、创世神话

7. 人的来由

有一年，天上落油雨。油雨一落，落到各处统着火，人烧死了，房屋烧光了。

有个大姑娘，"扑通"一声跳进井潭里，有只黄狗跟在后头，也"扑通"跳进井潭里。井潭里有水，勿会着火，世上只留下这个大姑娘和这只黄狗了。后来，黄狗和大姑娘生出一个人。这个人，长相像人，就是在背脊骨下面，屁股节骨上生出来根黄狗尾巴。这根尾巴是一节一节的，总共有十节，过几年，尾巴黄一节，过几年，尾巴黄一节，十节尾巴全黄了，人也就死了。这样一来，人的尾巴黄到第九节，就晓得快要死了，呒没多少辰光好活了。这叫作"十节尾巴九节黄"。到了这个日脚，人心冷了，横竖要死了，生活懒得做了，整天困困吃吃，吃吃困困，等死！格末，他下头还有小人，小人勿会做，就要饿煞！

天上晓得了，差观音菩萨下凡来，将人的尾巴统统斫掉。尾巴斫掉了，人啥辰光死勿晓得了，勿会偷懒了，一直做生活做到勿会做为止。从此，人的尾巴呒没了，成了现在这样的人了。

How Humans Came into Being

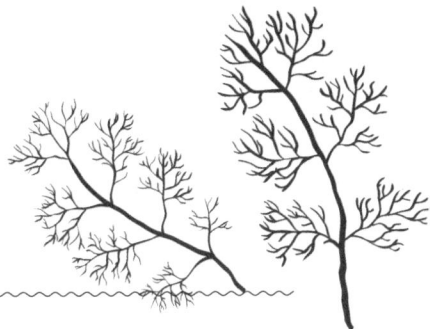

One year, it rained oil rain. As soon as the oil rain fell, everywhere was on fire, with people burned to death and houses burned down.

A young lady jumped with a flop into the well, a yellow dog following her closely and jumping into the well with a flop. The water in the well prevented the girl and the dog from catching fire. Thus in the world were left only the girl and the yellow dog. Later, the yellow dog and the girl gave birth to a person. This person, looking like a human being, had a tail like the yellow dog, growing out of the buttock ganglion just below his back bone. It was a ten-part tail connecting one part with another. In a few years, one part of the tail would turn yellow. Another few years passed, and the second part of the tail would turn yellow. In this way, when one's tail turned yellow in the tenth part, he was doomed to die. Such being the case, when one's tail turned yellow in the ninth part, he would know that he was about to die without having many hours of good life left. This is called "The ninth part of the ten-part tail turns yellow". When this day came, a man's heart felt cold, for he was to die anyway. He would wait for his death by eating and sleeping all day long without doing any work. Then his children would certainly suffer from hunger with no one supporting them.

The Heaven knew this and sent the Goddess of Mercy down to chop off all the tails of men. With the tail cut off, people knew nothing about when to die. They would not be lazy and work until they were too old to work. From then on, man has no tail at all, becoming a person like a modern man.

一、创世神话

8. 女娲伏羲传人种

交关早的辰光,有一年,天上落了九九八十一天大雨,地上发了大水,房屋被冲坍,人和牲畜统被浸死了。

这件事被玉帝晓得后,把女娲和伏羲变成一只南瓜,从天上放落下来,放到海上。南瓜在海里漂呀,漂呀,一直漂到东海洋面。"哗"一个浪头,南瓜碰在礁石上,"嘭"一声爆开,女娲和伏羲从里面跳出来。

伏羲爬上山岗顶,一看四周全是海,只有其和女娲两个人,又看看女娲生得介好看,立时三刻动了凡心,就对女娲说:"天底下呒没人,侬同我做夫妻算了。"

女娲忖了忖,红着脸说:"侬想同我做夫妻,有个条件。""啥条件?""我在前面跑,侬在后面追,如果被侬追着,我就同侬做夫妻。""好咯。"这样,女娲就在前面跑了起来。

女娲跑呀跑,伏羲追呀追,也不知过了多少日啦。这时海里有只老乌龟被惊动了,老乌龟爬上岸来,看到两人顺着山脚团团跑,感到交关奇怪,就拦住伏羲问:"侬这是在做啥?"伏羲就把事情的经过一五一十讲给其听。老乌龟听了哈哈大笑:"侬咋会介笨!这要追到何时呀!"伏羲问其有啥办法,其讲:"侬调个头勿就可以追着了嘛!"伏羲一听,心忖,这倒是勿错的。就马上调转头,朝相反的方向奔去,结果女娲终于被其追着了。

Nvwa and Fuxi Giving Birth to Human Beings

One year, long time ago, it had been raining hard for 81 days, resulting in a flood on the earth. Houses collapsed owing to the flood and people and animals were soaked to death.

When the Jade Emperor knew about this, he turned Nvwa and Fuxi into a pumpkin, which was released from the heaven, landing on the sea. The pumpkin floated on and on until it reached the surface of the East Sea. A big wave splashed the pumpkin, which hit the reef. Open burst the pumpkin, from the inside of which Nvwa and Fuxi jumped out.

Fuxi climbed up to the top of the mountain to see the sea all around him without any other human beings but he himself and Nvwa. He found that Nvwa was so beautiful that his worldly mind was perturbed. He said to Nvwa, "Now that there is no other human being in the world, we two become husband and wife at that."

Nvwa thought for a while and said with her face turning red, "There is only one condition that you have to agree on if you want to marry me." "What condition is it?" asked Fuxi in an anxious way. Nvwa replied, "I will run ahead and you should chase after me. If I am caught by you, I will marry you." "That's great!"

Nvwa ran and ran, and Fuxi chased and chased. No one knew how many days had passed since then. At this moment an old turtle was disturbed in the sea. When he came up to the shore, he saw the two running round the foot of the mountain. Feeling rather

一、创世神话

伏羲和女娲成了亲,女娲怀孕了,后来生下一个像篮球个大的肉团团。伏羲原以为要做阿爹了,交关开心,想勿到是个怪胎,一气之下用刀把肉团团劈成九十九块。可这九十九块肉,见风就长,结果变成了九十九个人。其又把劈落来的一些碎肉撮拢来捏成一团,又变成一个人。

伏羲和女娲把这一百个人,送到各岛各处去安家落户,传宗接代,还一个一个为他们定了姓,这就是百家姓的由来。据说,最后的一个人因是用碎肉丁捏拢的,个头顶小,就姓丁。

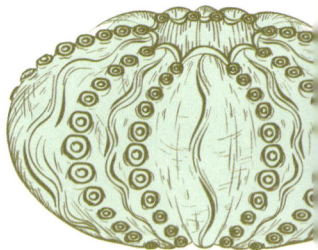

puzzled, he stopped Fuxi and asked, "What are you doing?" Then Fuxi told him exactly what had been going on. Hearing Fuxi's remarks, the old turtle chortled and commented, "How stupid you are! When will you catch up with her if you are chasing after her like this?" Fuxi asked the old turtle what he had to do. The old turtle said, "You have to turn around so that you can catch her then." Hearing this, Fuxi thought to himself that he was right. He immediately turned around, running in the opposite direction. As a result, he finally caught Nvwa.

Fuxi and Nvwa got married, and Nvwa became pregnant, giving birth to a flesh ball as big as a basketball. Fuxi thought that he felt so happy that he was going to be a father. Nevertheless, it was a freak, so he split the flesh ball into ninety-nine pieces with his knife in a pet. But the ninety-nine pieces of flesh would grow quickly when meeting with the wind, thus turning into ninety-nine persons. He then picked up the chopped flesh and pinched it into a ball, which became another person.

Fuxi and Nvwa sent these 100 persons to settle down in different places so as to carry on the family line. They gave each of them a different surname. This is how the hundred family surnames came into being. It is said that the last person was thin and short because he was pinched together with the broken flesh. So he was given surname "Ding".

9. 定海①的来历

　　传说在几千年以前，现在的东海，原是一座交关大的都城，叫东京。那时，皇帝是个昏君，老百姓良心统坏猛。玉帝得知后，说："东京这地方，呒没一个好人，统要其塌掉。"玉帝在讲这话时，正巧被吕纯阳听见啦。吕纯阳大仙说："东京介大座城市，城里有介许多人，一个好人呒没，这我勿信咯。"玉帝讲："我已经查过三年啦，统查清爽啦；东京人统坏勿过。"吕纯阳说："请玉帝暂时甭塌，要是有好人，其勿是委屈煞了！让我再去查查看吧。"玉帝说："好咯。"这样吕纯阳就下凡来啦。

　　吕纯阳大仙下凡来到东京，咕咕忖忖，脑筋动动，最后便用天河水当油，开爿油店。自家装扮成瞎眼老头，店门口写着"三个铜钿，油舀多少，买主自便"十二个字，卖起油来，以此来试人心。起头，一些人只拿小红毛瓶来，装得满满咯；后来，就换更大的。结果，大到咋相貌为止呢？大到用水桶来挑，把屋里厢的缸、甏、罐，统装得满进满出。老头总归是勿话。

　　当时，离城几里外，住着一户人家，姓葛，屋里厢只有娘儿俩，儿子叫葛仙翁，是个读书小囡。有一天，阿娘对儿子说："依去打三个铜钿的油来。"儿子说："好咯。"就拿了只油瓶，到

---

① 定海是舟山历史可追溯最早的人类居住区域，据考证新石器时代就已经有人居住，现在定海指舟山市定海区。

The Origin of Dinghai[1]

Legend has it that the present East China Sea was originally a big capital city, called Dongjing, thousands of years ago. At that time, the emperor was a fatuous monarch, and all the common people had bad consciences. When the Jade Emperor learned of this, he said, "Dongjing is a place without any good people, so it must be destroyed." Lv Chunyang chanced to be there when the Jade Emperor was talking about this. The Great Immortal Lv Chunyang said, "Dongjing is so big a city, where so many people are living. I don't believe there is no good people in the city." The Jade Emperor replied, "It has taken me three years to make a thorough investigation of it. Now I can make a clear conclusion that the people in Dongjing City are all evil." Lv Chunyang commented, "I earnestly request Your Majesty not to destroy the city for the time being in case there are good people there. Otherwise injustice will be done to good people. Let me make another investigation of it." The Jade Emperor agreed. Thus Lv Chunyang descended to the world.

After the Great Immortal Lv Chunyang descended to the world, he thought carefully before deciding to do some business. Eventually a good idea came into his mind that he would run an oil shop by using the water from the Milky Way as the oil. He disguised himself as an old blind man, beginning to sell oil with the following characters written at the shop door, "With three copper coins, a

---

[1] Dinghai, the oldest human living area in Zhoushan, refers to Zhoushan City in the story. Dinghai is a district in Zhoushan City now.

　　　　　　　　　　　　　　一、创世神话

油店买油,他看到别人随便舀,也跟着舀了满满一瓶,掜到屋里厢,对阿娘讲:"我油已经打来啦。阿姆,我跟侬讲,这油店老头,要饿煞咯,拿出三个铜钿,油随便侬舀多少,有的人会用水桶去挑,这样河水变油也会蚀光咯。"阿娘问:"侬舀来多少?""我看别人统舀,也舀满满一瓶。"阿娘心交关好,用手指着油瓶说:"阿拉三个铜钿,只可舀三个铜钿的油。其做生意,再加眼睛又瞎,蚀不起咯。阿拉莫多舀人家,快去还其。"儿子一听,就掜着油瓶到油店,心想让老人家多赚点,把油倒得比阿娘划的痕还下头些。

吕纯阳看在眼里,心忖:"今朝被我讲对啦,这后生良心蛮好。我开油店介许多日子,介好的人只碰见其一个,难得,难得。"随后,吕纯阳对小后生小声说:"东京这地方要塌啦。"小后生说:"老先生,侬讲这话当真?""我咋会跟侬乱讲话。""啥时候塌?""侬这城门外,有爿杀猪场,旁边有座坟,坟头的石狮子嘴出血了,东京就要塌啦,侬就好逃咯!"小后生应声:"多谢老先生。"小后生就走了。吕纯阳看小后生走啦,油店门一关,去天庭向玉帝禀报啦。

从此,小后生每天都去坟前看石狮子,每日都要从杀猪场经过,每日都会遇见杀猪屠王恩。日子多啦,杀猪屠王恩心忖:"这小后生咋啦?每日都来看石狮子。"一天,王恩问小后生:"侬做啥啦?每日都要来看过。"小后生说:"卖油老先生讲,石狮子嘴里出血,东京就要塌啦,我来相相看。"杀猪屠一听,感到好笑猛,心想:"我背其个木梢。"第二天天亮,杀猪屠王恩把猪血往石狮子嘴里"哗"一擦,走回杀猪场。这时小囡又来啦,看看石狮子嘴里出血啦,急忙往家奔。杀猪屠王恩看到,暗暗发笑。

buyer can get as much oil as he likes", attempting to test the people's conscientiousness with this remark. At first, some people only brought their little red flasks, filling them to the brims; later, they would change flasks to bigger bottles. At last, what big carriers people would bring to the oil shop? They even used such big water vessels as buckets, the house vats, earthen jars and cans, and so on so forth, all of which were filled as much as possible. Seeing this, the old blind man always kept silent.

At that time, a few miles away from the city, there lived a family named Ge. There was only a mother and a son in the house. The son was a schoolboy named Ge Xianweng. One day, the mother said to her son, "Go to the oil shop to buy some for the three copper coins." "OK." replied the son. With the words, the boy took an oil bottle and went to the oil shop for the oil. When he saw others scooping oil freely with three copper coins, he also scooped a full bottle, following the suit of other people. Arriving at home with the full oil bottle, the boy said to the mother, "Mother, I've got the oil for you. I would tell you that the old man in the shop will die of hunger. People can get as much oil as they like with only three copper coins. Some people will use buckets to scoop up as much oil as they can. If the things are going on like this, the oil, even turned from the river, would be running short." The mother asked the boy, "How much have you scooped up?" "Seeing other people getting the oil as much as possible, I scooped up a full bottle." replied the boy. Being an honest woman, the mother said to the boy, pointing to the oil bottle, "We can only buy the oil worthy of three copper coins. Being blind, it is not easy for the old man to do business. He can not afford to lose too much. We can not scoop up more oil than the coins deserve. Hurry up to give it back." Hearing this, the son took the bottle of oil with him to the oil shop. Thinking to himself that he hoped to let the old man earn more money, he poured the oil from the bottle into the vat in the shop all the way to the scratch on the oil bottle made by his mother.

小后生奔到屋里,对阿娘讲:"阿娘,勿对啦,石狮子嘴里出血啦,东京要塌啦,阿拉快逃!"说罢,背起阿娘就逃。其刚一逃,地皮真塌啦。"砰咚,砰咚",跑一路,塌一路。原来的房屋都变成大海,海水滚滚向前,总跟其差三步。其奔快点,塌快点;奔慢点,塌慢点。其逃了三日三夜,背酸煞啦,对阿娘讲:"阿拉逃了三日三夜,背也酸煞啦。塌呢,总差三步,这样啥时才逃得出呢?这也是死,那也是死,阿拉还是勿停下吧。"讲完,把阿娘放落,让阿娘坐在山坡上,自己躺在阿娘面前的平坦地方。说也奇怪,坐的地方和躺的地方勿塌,海水只在其和其阿娘的四周流。

后来,人们把其躺的地方叫定海,阿娘坐的山坡叫放娘尖;其阿娘搁脚的地方呢,就是现在的岱山岛和泗礁岛。

俗话说:"塌东京,涨崇明,还了东京地,要过三千年。"塌东京距现在仅一千年,让玉帝还回东京,那还是两千年以后的事呢!

Watching the boy with the tail of his eye, Lv Chunyang thought to himself, "Today I spoke it right that the lad has a pretty good conscience. I have been running the oil shop for so many days, and the boy is the only one I have met, whose conscience is so good. How rare it is!" Later, Lv Chunyang whispered to the young man, "Dongjing is going to be destroyed." Feeling somewhat puzzled, the boy asked, "Do you really mean what you said, old gentleman?" "How could I lie to you?" the old man replied. Then the boy kept asking, "When is the city going to collapse?" "Outside the city gate, there is a pig farm, beside which stands a grave. When the stone lion on the grave yard begins to bleed from its mouth, Dongjing is going to collapse. At that time, you should flee from the city." Having thanked the old man, the young boy left for his own home. Watching the young boy disappearing in the distance, Lv fled from the city and reported it to the Jade Emperor.

From then on, the young boy went by the pig slaughterhouse and met the pig butcher Wang En every day when he went to the grave to see the stone lion. As the days passed by, Wang En, the pig butcher, thought to himself with suspicion, "What's wrong with this young boy? He comes to see the stone lion every day." One day, Wang En could not help asking the lad, "What have you been doing? You have to come here to see the stone lion." The lad replied, "The old man who sold oil told me when the stone lion bleeds from its mouth, Dongjing City is to collapse. So I have to take a look every day." Hearing this, the pig butcher felt so ridiculous that he decided to play a trick on the young boy. At the daybreak the next morning, the pig butcher wiped the pig's blood into the mouth of the stone lion and went back to the pig slaughtering. Just at this time the lad came to see the stone lion once again. Finding the blood in the stone lion's mouth, the young boy dashed to his home in a hurried way. Seeing this, Wang En, the pig butcher, laughed up his sleeve.

The young boy rushed to the house and said to his mother,

　　　　　　　　　　　一、创世神话

"Mum, something terrible is happening. The stone lion's mouth is bleeding and Dongjing is going to collapse. We have to run away from here." With these words, he lifted up his mother onto his back, fleeing. As soon as they began to run away, the ground did really collapse. "Bang, Bang", the sound of earth cracking was heard. The collapse was following them closely all the way when they were fleeing. The original houses had been drowned by the sea. And the seawater was rolling forward, always maintaining three steps away behind them. When they ran faster, the collapse also went on faster; when they ran more slowly, the collapse also slowed down. The boy with the mother on his back had been running away for three days and three nights. Feeling so sore in the back, he said to his mother, "We have been fleeing for three days and three nights, and my back is sore enough. The collapse is always three steps away from us. Such being the case, when and how can we escape? We will die anyway whether we flee or not. We, nevertheless, stop fleeing and stay in this very place." With these words, he put his mother down, letting her sit on the hillside. He himself lay down on the flat place in front of his mother. Strangely enough, the place where the mother sat and the boy lay down stopped collapsing. The seawater was flowing only around them.

Later, people called the place where the young boy lay "Dinghai" and the hillside where his mother sat "Fangniangjian". The places on which the mother rested her feet were called "Daishan Island" and "Sijiao Island".

As the saying goes, "If Dongjing falls, Chongming rises. It will take three thousand years to give back the place of Dongjing." The fall of Dongjing is only one thousand years away from now. Let the Jade Emperor give Dongjing back, and we have to await it for another two thousand.

一、创世神话

10. 女娲填海①

女娲是日头的囡。

其长得交关好看，交关聪明，也交关有本事。其勿愿意老待在日头脚跟过日子，就自家一个人撑着小船到海里去游。

海里风浪大呀，女娲撑的小船被风浪摇得晃来晃去，晃来晃去。一时大浪头压过来，小船被打翻啦，女娲被淹死了。

女娲死后，阴魂勿散，变成了一只小鸟。这只鸟每日勿停地从远处衔来烂泥、石子填大海。可是大海介深，介大，咋填得平？其不管。其只是不停地填呀，填呀，填呀，相信总有一天会填平。

据说现在的海燕就是女娲的后代。越是大风大雨，海燕越要在海面上飞，那是其按女娲的嘱咐在填海呢。

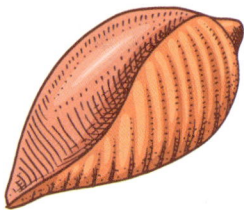

① 该故事与精卫填海的内容情节相似，但主人公为女娲，是一个女孩的泛指。

Nvwa Trying to Fill up the Sea

Nvwa[1] was the daughter of the sun.

Nvwa was very bright with a good look and capability. She was reluctant to stay at home all day long, so she sailed a small boat alone to the sea for a trip.

Nvwa's boat was rocked on stormy waves because of the strong wind on the sea. A sudden huge wave fell over the boat and the boat was overturned. Thus the girl was drowned to death.

When the girl died, her ghost did not go away and turned into a bird. Every day the bird carried mud and stones from a distance to fill the sea. But the sea was so deep and so vast that how the bird could fill up the sea with its mud and stones. However, the bird did not care about the result and was engaged in filling the sea day by day, believing that the sea was filled up in the end as long as it kept on.

It is said that today's petrels were the descendants of Nvwa. They would fly over the sea whenever the wind is stronger and it is raining even harder. Their doing so is just in accordance with the instructions of Nvwa.

---

[1] Nvwa in this story means a little girl, not the goddess in the former stories *Nvwa Mended the Sky* and *How Humans Came into Being.*

一、创世神话

11. 黄帝战蚩尤

　　早起头,中国的黄帝和蚩尤打仗。蚩尤眼痒黄帝的江山,黄帝要保护自己的疆土,双方打得不可开交。盘古氏看老百姓在战争中死的死,伤的伤,交关伤心,便从中调停,叫双方甭打了。蚩尤说:"不打仗可以,但我要同黄帝打一次赌。如果我输脱,情愿把百宝袋相送。如果黄帝输脱,要把江山让给我。"盘古氏说:"可以。"黄帝和蚩尤掷骰子打赌,盘古氏做中间人。蚩尤掷下骰子,得了个廿四点。黄帝看了,脸都吓白了。因为四粒骰子,廿四点是满分。还有啥点数能超过满分的呢?没有法子,黄帝只得硬着头皮,把骰子掷落去。谁知三

Huangdi[1] Fought Against Chiyou

Long long ago, Huangdi fought against Chiyou in ancient China. As Chiyou envied the great territory Huangdi had and Huangdi wanted to protect the motherland of his own, both sides were locked in a fierce fight. Master Pangu, the creator of the universe in Chinese mythology, felt very sad when seeing so many ordinary people died and wounded in the war. He stood out to mediate and asked both of them to stop fighting. Chiyou said, "It is no problem to stop fighting, but I want to take a bet with Huangdi. If I lose, I am willing to send him my treasure bag. If Huangdi loses, he will give up to me his kingdom." Master Pangu said, "That's it." Huangdi and Chiyou played the dice for the bet, Master Pangu acting as their middleman. Chiyou threw the dice first and got 24 points. When Huangdi saw this, his face turned pale with fear, for 24 points were the full mark for the four dices. Were there any more points that could surpass the full mark? With no way out, Huangdi had to force himself to throw the four dices. But each of the three dices got six points, and the other dice was split in half. One half of the dice got six points and the other half got one point, adding up to twenty-five. Huangdi won.

Seeing that he was going to lose the bet, Chiyou took a step

[1] Huangdi is a deity in Chinese religion, one of the legendary Chinese sovereigns and culture heroes included among the mytho-historical Three Sovereigns and Five Emperors.

　　　　　　　　　　　　　　　　　　一、创世神话

粒骰子每粒六点,另外一粒骰子裂成了两半,一半是六点,还有一半是一点,加拢来有廿五点。黄帝赢了。

蚩尤一看苗头不对,拔腿就往东海大洋逃,脊背上还背着百宝袋。黄帝张弓搭箭,朝蚩尤射去。"嗖!嗖!嗖!"一连三只羽翎箭,箭箭射在蚩尤的背袋上。百宝袋射破了,黄金、白银、珍珠、玛瑙、珊瑚、宝石、摇钱树、聚宝盆……从百宝袋里骨碌碌掉落下来,统统落进东海大洋。东海里本来没有鱼。这会儿,金子变成黄鱼,银子变成鲳鱼,蚌壳里有了珍珠,礁岩上生了珊瑚,摇钱树、聚宝盆统统变成了海里的海生植物和海生动物。东海大洋里到处是宝贝,变得富庶极了。

to run away to the East China Sea. On his back he carried a bag of treasure. Huangdi took three arrows with his bow and shot at Chiyou. "Whizzing! Whizzing! Whizzing!" The three feathered arrows all hit the treasure bag on Chiyou's back. Then the treasure bag was broken. Consequentially, gold, silver, pearls, agate, coral, precious stones, cash cows, cornucopia, and so forth, fell down from the bag into the East China Sea. There were originally no fish in the East China Sea. Now the gold was changed into yellow croaker, the silver into pomfret, pearls were contained in the clam shell, corals grew on the reef, and all the cash cows and cornucopia were transformed into plants and animals in the sea. With treasures everywhere, the East China Sea became extremely rich and populous.

二、舟山龙神话

　　"龙龙,鳞虫之长,能幽能明,能细能巨,能短能长,春风而登天,秋分而潜渊。"汉许慎的《说文解字》对龙如是定义,让人们对龙的形象充满了无限想象。龙自古以来在中国文化中就有着重要的意义,袁珂先生道:"古者神人多乘龙。如祝融乘两龙,夏后启乘两龙,蓐收乘两龙,句芒乘两龙,'颛顼乘龙而至四海','帝喾春夏乘龙'(《大戴礼·五帝德》),等等。"[1]并且中国古代天子多以真龙自居,视龙为最高权力之象征,可代表皇权与天地,也可代表华夏先祖。从神话角度来看,龙是中国神话中的神圣动物。与龙相关的神话传说在华夏大地的许多地方传说中都能觅到些许痕迹,作为千岛之城的海中洲舟山,更凭借得天独厚的地理条件和靠海而作的劳动人民丰富的想象力滋养出了许许多多与龙相关的神话传说故事。

---

[1] 袁珂:《中国神话传说词典(修订本)》,北京联合出版公司 2013 年版,第 98 页。

12. 龙的来历

盘古时候，天地间还咹没龙，传说龙是黄鳝、泥鳅跳龙门以后变的。

有一日，天宫正在比赛跳龙门，谁能跳过去就封谁做龙。这龙门交关难跳，鲤鱼咹没跳过去，黄鳝和泥鳅又咹没资格跳，他们急得统哭啦。

哭声传到天宫，守门官禀报了玉皇大帝。玉皇大帝派守门官下凡查看。守门官带天兵来查问，黄鳝和泥鳅对守门官讲："阿拉想上天参加跳龙门。"玉皇大帝晓得后，答应三年以后允许他们去跳。

三年时间到了。跳龙门这一日，天宫里热闹足了。黄鳝、泥鳅苦练了三年，信心足猛，穿着盔甲去了。

旁边人看连鲤鱼也跳勿过龙门，依介笨个黄鳝泥鳅也想来跳，统笑煞啦。泥鳅胆子大，狠性命"嚓"地一下穿过了龙门，变成了一条黄龙。黄鳝见泥鳅过去了，胆子也大了起来，也"嚓"地跳过去，变成了一条赤龙。看热闹的人统看呆煞了，再也勿敢小看泥鳅和黄鳝啦。

The Origin of Dragons

At the age of Pangu, there were no dragons in the world. It is said that the eel and the loach turned into dragons after they jumped over the Dragon Gate.

One day, a race of jumping over the Dragon Gate was being held in the paradise. Those who could do it would be granted the title of the dragon. It was very difficult to jump over the gate, and even the carp failed. The eel and the loach were not qualified to do it, so they cried out of frustration.

The cry reached the paradise. The gatekeeper of the paradise reported that to the Jade Emperor. The Jade Emperor sent the gatekeeper to go down to the mortal world to check it out. The gatekeeper followed the order and went with heaven soldiers to the source of the cry. The eel and the loach told the gatekeeper, "We want to go to the heaven to jump over the Dragon Gate." When the Jade Emperor was informed, he promised that they would be allowed to do it in three years.

Three years passed when the day for jumping over the Dragon Gate came and the paradise was bustling with noise and excitement. The eel and the loach had practiced for three years, so they were confident. They went over in their armors.

The onlookers laughed at them because they thought the eel and the loach were too stupid to jump over the Dragon Gate where even the carp failed. The eel was so brave that he tried his best so that he made it and turned into a yellow dragon. Seeing this, the loach was encouraged so he also made it and turned into a red dragon. The onlookers were all dumbfounded and would not look down upon the eel and the loach any more.

二、舟山龙神话

13. 龙成蜃的传说

很久前,一个深山岙里有个新娘子。她第一天上灶做饭,就被灶间壁上喷出的水珠溅湿了新衣裳。她很奇怪,寻找喷水的地方,看见喷水的小洞不断大起来,水也越喷越多了!她很害怕,又很好奇地看着,过不久,洞中爬出了一只像小牛大小,头中间生一只角,浑身黑色光滑的怪物。新娘子正要大声呼喊,突然想起了老年人常说的蜃的传说,她静下来,慢慢地脱下了穿在里面的一件大红衣服,打开厨房门闩,人靠在正门旁边,等待着怪物的变化。

新娘子早先听大人说过,龙修炼多年以后,就可以变成蜃,可以去跳龙门,跳过龙门就可以得道成仙。

眼下,新娘子看见蜃停止了喷水,慢慢地向她走过来,走到她身边时,她不慌不忙地拿起红衣裳,挂在怪物的独角上,轻轻地默祷着:"愿你早跃龙门中状元!"并向怪物拜了三拜,怪物就头顶大红吉衣,出屋后口喷大水,冒着倾盆大雨,向大河奔去了!新娘子很疑惑,不敢向人讲起这件事,日子一久也就淡忘了!

一年以后的一个早晨,新娘子起来烧早饭,刚引火入灶,突然听见屋里"哐啷"一声,紧接着从烟囱洞里掉下来一件闪闪发光的东西,她拿来一看,是一件用大大小小的珍珠串连起来的珠衣,衣上还系着一张纸条,纸条上写着:

Dragon Turning into Shen

Long long ago, there was a bride in the depth of mountains. The first day when she went to the kitchen to cook, the dews on the wall behind the stove splashed onto her new clothes. She was so curious as to look for the place from which the water came. She saw the hole that squirted water was becoming bigger and the water coming from it was becoming stronger. She was scared but still watched out of curiosity. Soon there was a monster crawling out of the hole. Black and slippery all over, the monster was of the size of a small cow, with a horn growing out of the middle of its head. When the bride was about to shout for help, she remembered the legend of Shen often told by the elders. Therefore, she calmed down, took off her red clothes under the overcoat, opened the bolt of the kitchen door, leaned against the front door, and waited to see how the monster would change.

The bride had heard from the elders before that after many years of cultivation, a dragon could turn into Shen and jump over the Dragon Gate. Once it succeeded, it could become a god.

Now, the bride saw Shen stop squirting water and approached her slowly. When it came to her, she gently held up the red clothes and hung them on its horn, praying in a low voice, "Wish you success in jumping over the Dragon Gate and becoming a god as soon as possible." After she bowed three times toward it, the monster went out with the lucky red clothes. Then squirting large amount of water, it ran toward the big river in the heavy rain. Kind

二、舟山龙神话

红衣助我跃龙门，至今成神来报恩，

吉衣变成珠衣还，只酬心中三分情。

新娘子看了纸条，想起了一年前的事情，拿着珠衣告诉了公婆丈夫，大家也觉得惊奇。年老博古的公公告诉他们：大红吉衣等蜃跳龙门以后，就成了它的护身之宝。蜃为了报恩，找来这件珠衣，这件珠衣也是天下独一无二的稀世珍宝，能夜明、避水、避火、吃墨。

of confused, the bride dared not mention this incident to anyone and almost forgot it as time passed by.

One year later, the bride got up to make breakfast. As soon as she made fire, she heard a loud noise in the kitchen and then something shining fell through the chimney. She picked it up and saw an outfit made of pearls big and small. On the outfit was tied a note, writing:

> Red clothes helped me jump over the Dragon Gate
> and become a god, so I come back to repay the favor.
> The pearl outfit in exchange for your red lucky clothes
> only expresses a small portion of gratitude.

After seeing the note, she remembered the incident that happened a year early. With the pearl outfit in her hand, she went to tell her parents-in-law and husband, who were all amazed. The old and knowledgeable father-in-law told them that the red clothes turned into Shen's juju after it jumped over the Dragon Gate. In order to repay the favor, Shen sent this pearl outfit, which was a unique treasure in the world because it could shine at night and was water-fire-ink-proof.

二、舟山龙神话

14. 三龙会

　　过去天下只有三条龙,一条是天龙,一条是地龙,还有一条是海龙。这三条龙是三兄弟,可性情却完全勿一样。天龙住在天上,心肠顶好;地龙住在地上,一年到头数其顶勤快;而海龙呢,又凶又狠,又懒又馋,良心坏勿过。

　　这三条龙,每年八月十五统要带着老婆到陆地上来相会。天龙带着老婆从天上到陆地上来,海龙带着老婆从海里也到陆地上来。可海龙来到陆地上以后,地上的龙子龙孙就要遭殃了,一年要白白做,种出来的东西统要被海龙抢光。其还想要霸占整个天下,想把天下统变成海。

　　天龙的老婆生得蛮好看,地龙的老婆也生得蛮好看,可海龙的老婆难看猛。每年八月十五海龙来到陆地上,总要调戏天龙和地龙的老婆。这事被天龙和地龙晓得了,统气煞了,决心要想出办法,勿让海龙再到陆地上来。

　　有一年的八月十五,天龙和地龙叫来所有子孙,在海边拦

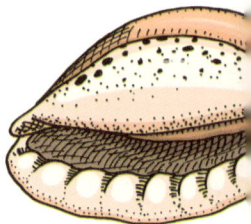

Three-Dragon Meeting

Once there were three dragons in the world, the sky dragon, the earth dragon and the sea dragon. They were brothers but had completely different temperaments. The sky dragon lived in the sky and was benevolent; the earth dragon lived on the earth and was hard-working; the sea dragon, however, was fierce, vicious, lazy, greedy, and very evil.

These three dragons would meet on the earth with their wives on lunar August 15 every year. The sky dragon would come with its wife from the top of the mountains and the sea dragon would come with its wife from the sea. When the sea dragon came, the sons and grandsons of the earth dragon would suffer, and their efforts of the year would be destroyed. The crops they had harvested would be taken away by the sea dragon, who would even want to dominate the whole world and turn it into sea.

The sky dragon's wife was pretty, so was the earth dragon's wife, yet the sea dragon's wife was ugly. Every year when the sea dragon came to earth, it would flirt with the other two dragons' wives. The other two dragons knew about it. Outraged, they were determined to find a way to stop the sea dragon from coming to earth again.

One year, on lunar August 15, the sky dragon and the earth dragon gathered all their descendants to set up a fence with 99, 999 pieces of bamboo at the seaside to prevent the sea dragon from coming ashore. The sea dragon was angry to see so and

二、舟山龙神话

起了九万九千九百九十九根竹篱笆,勿准海龙走上来。海龙看见天龙和地龙想用竹篱笆挡住其上来,发怒了,其使出了所有的劲道冲坏篱笆,奔到了陆地上,抢去了所有的财物,吞吃了成千上万的人。

　　天龙和地龙看竹篱笆挡勿住凶狠的海龙,就叫来所有的子子孙孙,在海边堆起九万九千九百九十九块大石头,用石头来阻挡海龙。海龙见海边有石头挡着,就更加大喊大叫起来,狠着性命往地上冲,这就是八月十五大潮汛。

managed to destroy the fence with all its forces. It ran onto the land, took all the property and devoured hundreds of thousands of people.

The sky dragon and the earth dragon found that the bamboo fence could not stop the fierce sea dragon, so they gathered all their descendants to pile up 99,999 rocks to stop the sea dragon. The sea dragon saw the stone wall at the seaside and became even more outrageous, shouting and slamming itself against it, which formed the big tide on every lunar August 15.

15. 海龙王的传说

　　很早以前的海龙王，非常凶狠，常常兴风作浪，吞没渔民的船只。后来有个叫哲高的渔民，用计斗败了凶狠的海龙王，然后自己做了海龙王。哲高做了海龙王后，大海涨潮落潮有了定规，渔民出海比过去平安多了。聪明机智的哲高是怎样做了海龙王的呢？

　　哲高原来生活在一个海岛上，给一个姓张的渔霸做长工。这渔霸家中原来有兄弟三个，分别是张大、张二、张三。这兄弟三人都非常刻毒，哲高一年干到头，连个蟹脚钳也分不到。哲高心里非常气愤，总想想个办法，惩罚渔霸出出气。

　　有次哲高一年干到头回屋里，因为他年轻力壮，他猜初五这天，张大准又会来喊他去做长工。他从外地买来了当时海岛上的人没见过的芝麻糖和白糖，又抲来一只猫。张大果真来了，哲高装得非常客气，热情地对张大说：

The Legend of the Sea Dragon King

Long long ago, there was a sea dragon king who was very fierce and often encouraged the wind and the waves to devour fishers and their boats. Later, a fisherman named Zhe Gao defeated the sea dragon king with the help of schemes and became the sea dragon king himself. After that, the sea tides waxed and waned regularly, so fishermen were safer in fishing. How did Zhe Gao the clever became the sea dragon king?

In the past, Zhe Gao lived on an island, working as a long-term working hand for a fishing hegemon from the family of Zhang. There were three brothers in the family of Zhang, called Zhang Da, Zhang Er and Zhang San. The three brothers were extremely vicious. After working for them for a whole year, Zhe Gao could not even be rewarded with a foot of the crab. Zhe Gao was so angry that he wanted to find a way to punish them to get relieved.

Once Zhe Gao went back home after finishing the whole year's work. Since he was young and strong, he guessed that Zhang Da would call him back to work on the fifth day of the lunar new year. He bought from other places sesame sugar and white sugar, which people on the island had never seen before, and also caught a cat. Zhang Da did come. Zhe Gao pretended to be very generous, saying, "Mr. Zhang, nice to see you! I want you to eat something really delicious as a snack of the new year. Zhang Da asked, "Where did you get such a delicious snack?" Zhe Gao said, "It was born by an animal." "Born by what animal?" "By this precious cat."

　　　　　　　　　　　　二、舟山龙神话

"张老板，你来了，今天过年我请你吃样好东西。"一边请张大，一边把黑黑的芝麻糖，外面蘸些白糖，拿给张大吃。张大一吃喷香，忙问："介好吃的东西哪里来的？"哲高回答："这是东西生出来的。""什么东西生出来的？""是只宝猫。"猫粪是黑的，和黑芝麻糖很像，张大便信以为真了，想把猫占为己有。对哲高说："哲高，把猫卖给我算了！""不卖，这宝猫撒出东西，拿到街上卖，价钱木佬佬●高。"哲高说得非常坚决。"这你不卖弄不来，我拿去给屋里人尝尝新。"张大左说右说，最后哲高装作被迫同意的样子，猫被张大㧑去了。

张大把猫㧑去之后，为了让猫多撒粪，给猫吃得又好又饱，事先把白糖撒好，让猫把粪便撒到白糖上。这样过了一两天，张大把一家人都叫来，拿出沾了白糖的猫粪给大家吃。一吃这猫粪酸几几，糊塌塌，最臭了。张大知道上了哲高的当，气得把猫打死，找哲高算账去了。

哲高知道张大一定会来，事先做好了准备。张大一进门，哲高说："张老板，吃肉吃肉。"马上切碗白切肉，给张大吃。当时海岛很少吃肉，就是吃肉也只知道红烧，不知道白切。张大一吃，这肉味道非常好，忘掉了生气，忙问："你这肉哪里来的？"哲高说："我有把宝刀，生货切了会变熟的。"张大心忖：上

● 舟山方言，意为"非常"。

The feces of the cat were black, very much like the black sesame sugar. Zhang Da believed it and wanted to take the cat for himself. He said, "Zhe Gao, please sell this cat to me!" "No, this precious cat can produce snacks. If I sell it in the market, the price would be very high." Zhe Gao said resolutely. "This cannot be bought in the market. I want to take home for my family to have a try." Zhang Da pleaded relentlessly. Finally, Zhe Gao pretended to be forced into agreement, so Zhang Da took the cat away.

Back home, Zhang Da fed the cat well in order to get more feces. He got white sugar ready and let the cat pass the feces on it. Then after a day or two, Zhang Da gathered his family together and took out the cat feces topped by white sugar for them to taste. It tasted sour and stinky. Zhang Da realized that he was cheated. He was so angry the he killed the cat and went to Zhe Gao.

Zhe Gao knew Zhang Da would come, so he got things ready. As soon as Zhang Da entered, Zhe Gao said, "Mr. Zhang, please have some meat." Immediately Zhe Gao cut a bowl of white meat for Zhang Da. The boiled meat was rarely known at that time. Zhang Da tasted the meat and found it was very delicious, so his anger disappeared. He asked, "Where did you get the meat?" Zhe Gao said, "I've got a magic knife. If you cut raw meat with it, the meat would become cooked." Zhang Da thought, "Last time, he cheated me. This time he won't. I just saw he cut the raw meat with the knife. With the knife, raw meat would become cooked and very delicious." Then he said to Zhe Gao, "Sell the magic knife to me! I will forget about your offence last time." Zhe Gao said, "How can I sell my magic knife!" "If it is not for sale, then lend it to me please!" Zhe Gao pretended to be helpless, "Fine. You can borrow it." Thus Zhang Da took the knife away.

Zhang Da also bought some meat. He cut it with the magic knife at home and dipped it in soy sauce and invited his family to

二、舟山龙神话

次被他背木梢了,这次总不会吧,我刚刚还亲眼看见他切肉;生的切了会变熟的,特别是肉切了又介好吃。马上贪心又来了,他对哲高说:"把宝刀卖给我吧!上次帐就甭算了!"哲高说:"宝刀咋好卖呢!""你不卖就借我用一场吧!"最后哲高装作无可奈何的样子说:"借你用一场,就用一场吧!"这样刀被张大拿去了。

张大也买了斤肉,回到屋里,用宝刀把肉切了,沾了酱油,给全家人吃,结果晚上一家都拉肚子了,拉得一塌糊涂,气力都没有了,张大知道又上哲高当了,气得直骂。第二天,天刚亮,他就向哲高家奔去。

哲高知道天亮张大就会来,对家里人讲:"张大来了,你们要看我声色行事,我棍子一敲,你们全倒下,吹白泡装死;我再一敲,你们马上跳起来。"

哲高对家里人刚交待好,老远看见张大有气无力地瘪儿瘪儿来了。张大一进门,只听哲高对家里人大吵大骂:"你们这帮畜生,我非敲死你们不可!"只见哲高手拿棍子,一记一记把家里人敲倒了,个个都嘴吹白泡死了。张大见状,忙说:"你大糊了,这是为什么,把他们都敲死了?"哲高说:"我就是要把他们都敲死,前两次你被背木梢都是他们的主意。"张大问:"你把他们都敲死了可咋办?""老板你别心急,吃老酒,吃老酒。"哲高陪张大吃酒。吃到半当中,张大又说:"人敲死了,总得去医医啊!"哲高说:"我有办法。"只见哲高拿起木棍,每人都敲一记,一记一记敲过都跳起来,活了。张大见状,目瞪口呆,惊奇极了。哲高对张大说:"张老板你不晓得,我最近得了个宝贝,叫还魂棍,死了的敲过会活。"张大忖这东西可是最最宝贵的了,就说:"你这东西给我吧!"哲高说:"老板要,我没办

eat it together. That night, the whole family was troubled with diarrhea and felt weak. Zhang Da realized that he was again fooled by Zhe Gao and cursed him with anger. The next day, he ran to Zhe Gao's right after dawn.

Zhe Gao knew Zhang Da would come, so he told his family, "When Zhang Da comes, you should all follow my order. When I strike you with this stick, you should all lie down and pretend to die. When I strike you again, you should jump up at once."

Right after the arrangement, Zhe Gao saw Zhang Da limping near. Entering the door, Zhang Da heard Zhe Gao shouting at his family, "Zhe Gao is coming, and I will strike you all to death!" He saw that Zhe Gao struck them down one by one and they all lay down dead. Seeing that, Zhang Da said in a hurry, "Are you out of your mind? Why did you kill them all?" Zhe Gao said, "I meant to strike them to death. It is their idea that made you suffer so much." Zhang Da asked, "What are you going to do now that you have killed them?" "Don't worry, boss! Let's drink, boss!" Zhe Gao invited Zhang Da to drink. After drinking for a while, Zhang Da said, "You really need to send for a doctor." Zhe Gao said, "I got this." Zhe Gao took the stick and struck each one again. The dead all jumped back alive. Zhang Da was so shocked that he became dumbfounded. Zhe Gao said to him, "Boss, you see, I got a magic stick, called 'soul stick'. A strike with it would return the dead to life." Zhang Da considered this stick the most precious. He said, "Give this to me." Zhe Gao said, "If you want it, I can't refuse, but you should give it back to me." Zhang Da didn't want to see Zhe Gao go back on his word, so he walked out while making the promise.

Extremely happy, Zhang Da thought he got the most precious thing. He called his two brothers, Zhang Er and Zhang San, to come to drink. Half through the drink, Zhang Da offered to show

　　　　　　　　　　二、舟山龙神话

法，但过些时候得还我。"张大怕哲高变卦，边答应边拿着还魂棍往外走。

张大以为自己得到了最宝贵的东西，非常高兴，把两兄弟——张二、张三都请来吃老酒，老酒吃到一半，张大为让兄弟看看宝贝的威力，拿起木棍一个个把老婆和孩子都敲死了，两个弟弟大惊，张大说："没关系，没关系，吃老酒。"张二和张三说："人死了还吃老酒！"张大一边吃老酒一边说："你们别愁嘛，我有办法。"拿起木棍，一个一个敲过去，一次没敲活，又敲一次；一次没敲活，又敲一次；三次敲过，气一点都没了。张大见老婆孩子救不活了，大哭了起来。张二、张三知道了事情真相，恨得要命，兄弟三人连夜赶到哲高家，把哲高拘来了。

哲高被拘来后，就是把他千刀万剐他们也不解恨。最后他们把哲高装进麻袋，背到海边，准备把哲高沉到海里喂鱼。当时正是海水落潮，三人就把麻袋吊在树上，暂时回屋里吃餐饭。

哲高被吊在树上，刚刚这时，张大的老岳父是个驼背，赶着一群山羊从这经过。哲高从麻袋中看到，就说："这办法灵足了，直了直了。""什么东西直了？"驼背听麻袋里有人说话就问。"我驼背吊直了，我从中午吊到现在，吊直了。""给我吊吊好吗？""你驼背倒有些驼背，你要吊我就让给你，你把我放下来吧！"驼背把哲高放下来，哲高从麻袋出来，伸伸腰，挺胸凸肚，背一点不驼。驼背信以为真，钻进了麻袋。哲高扎好麻袋，把麻袋吊在树上，自己赶着羊去了。回到屋里杀羊烤肉吃了起来。

再说张大、张二和张三，回屋吃了饭，估计海水涨潮了，到海边，从树上放下麻袋，三人喊着"一，二，三"一齐使劲，只听

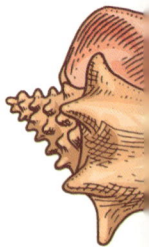

the power of the magic stick. He used the stick to strike his wife and children to death. His two brothers were panicked. Zhang Da said, "Don't worry. Let's drink." Zhang Er and Zhang San said, "Stop drinking! They are all dead." Zhang Da said while drinking, "Don't panic. I got this." He held up the stick to strike them again, but they didn't come back to life. He tried again and again, but in vain. Zhang Da realized that his wife and children couldn't come back to life, and then he started to cry. Zhang Er and Zhang San knew about the truth, and got very angry. The three brothers got to Zhe Gao's home immediately and caught him.

When they caught him, they tried to find the most vicious way to punish him. Finally they decided to put him in a bag, carried him to the seaside, and planned to throw him into the sea to feed the fish. At that time, the tide was low, so they hung him in a tree and went back home to have dinner.

During this period of time, Zhang Da's father-in-law, a hunchback, passed by, driving a flock of goats. Zhe Gao saw him and said, "This way works well, and it got straight." "What got straight?" the hunchback heard someone talking in the bag. "My hunchback got straight after I am hung here from noon till now." "Can I have a try?" "You do have a hunchback. If you want to be hung here, then I'll let you try. Put me down first." The hunchback put Zhe Gao down, and Zhe Gao got out of the bag, stretched himself, and showed his straight back. The hunchback believed him and crawled into the bag. Zhe Gao tied up the bag and hung it in the tree. He drove the goats back home, killed them and started to eat mutton.

Zhang Da, Zhang Er and Zhang San finished dinner and guessed the tide would be high, so they went to the seaside, put down the bag and pushed it down the sea together. They heard the cry coming out the bag while the bag was falling into the sea.

After the three brothers went back from the seaside, they saw

麻袋里有人喊"救命呀",麻袋早被抛到了海里。

兄弟三人从海边回来,忖忖屋里人都死完了,心里气闷,只顾吃闷酒。忽然听见外面"嘭嘭"有敲门声,高声叫:"开门,开门,我来了。"一听声音三人都慌了,忙问:"你是啥人啊?""我是哲高呀!"一听吓煞了,张大战战兢兢地说:"哲高呀,阴归阴,阳归阳,虽然你没命了,我屋里也好几条命丧在你手里,这笔账就算了吧!""你们开开嘛!""你要干什么?""我给你们送羊肉来啦,你们三个人,我只一个人,开开门怕啥!"这样门开了,见哲高端着一盆喷香的羊肉,张大大着胆子问:"这羊肉从哪来的?"哲高说:"老板,你不晓得今天是啥日子! 今天是海龙王生日,凡是今天去海里的人,都有廿只羊好分,羊肉随你吃,现在去还来得及。"这三人对羊肉非常喜欢,忙问:"真的吗?""你们把我装到麻袋,亲自抛到海里,我现在不是好好回来了,端着羊肉,这还有假。"三人忖这是没错。哲高又说:"你们不相信,就一个一个往海里跳,第一个人一摆手,第二个跳,第二个人一摆手,第三个跳。"结果这样定了,张大先跳,跳到海里手一定会摆的,结果老二也跳下去,老二一摆手,老三也跳下去了。贪心不足,三人都葬身于大海。

哲高从海边回到屋里,对老婆说:"明天天亮,会有癞头鼋来,他们问我,你就讲哲高先生给人家看医生去了。"哲高晓得,海龙王抓人,都是先派虾兵蟹将癞头鼋,第一次肯定是癞头鼋来。果然张大岳父、张大、张二和张三一齐向海龙王告了状,海龙王天刚亮就派二个癞头鼋拘哲高来了。

癞头鼋到哲高屋里,见哲高老婆正在纳鞋底,就问道:"哲高呢?""哲高给人家看医生去了。""看啥医生?""给人家看癞头去了。"这两个赤壳的癞头,一听忙问:"会看癞头?"哲高老

the dead family members and felt upset. While drink sullenly, they heard someone knocking at the door. "Open up, open up. I'm back." The three brothers panicked when they heard the voice, asking, "Who are you?" "I'm Zhe Gao!" So scared, Zhang Da said in a trembling voice, "Zhe Gao, you are dead, and then you should leave our world. Though you have lost your life, several of my family members are also dead because of you. Please go away." "Open up!" "What do you want?" "I'm here to send you yummy mutton. There are three of you but one of me, so why are you scared?" Then the door was opened, and they saw Zhe Gao holding a big bowl of mutton. Zhang Da gathered courage to ask, "Where did you get the mutton?" Zhe Gao said, "Boss, don't you remember what day it is today? It is the sea dragon king's birthday. All those who jump into the sea would get twenty sheep and eat as much mutton as they like. If you go right now, you can still make it." The three brothers liked mutton very much, and asked, "Really?" "You put me into the bag and throw me into the sea, but I'm back fine and well with the mutton. Isn't this real?" The three brothers would not doubt any more. Zhe Gao added, "If you don't believe me, you can jump into the sea one by one. When the first waves his hand, the second can jump, and when the second waves his hand, the third can jump." Consequently, Zhang Da jumped first, and he would definitely wave his hand in sea, so Zhang Er jumped and waved his hand, and finally Zhang San jumped too. Out of greed, the three brothers all drowned in the sea.

Zhe Gao went back home and said to his wife, "Tomorrow there will be some scabies-headed men coming to find me. You tell them that I have gone to other people's homes to treat patients." Zhe Gao knew, if the sea dragon king wanted to catch someone, he would always send his lobster, crab and turtle soldiers. The first is surely a scabies-headed turtle. Zhang Da's father-in-law, Zhang

二、舟山龙神话

婆说:"我们民间的癞头都是他医好的。"两个癞头听过商量,我们先让他医好癞头,再把他柯去。

哲高知道两个癞头鼋来了,穿了长衫,戴了礼帽,提着只皮箱,真像郎中先生,进门说:"两个客人来啦?"癞头鼋说:"你这位先生会看癞头?""嗯,我会看癞头!""给我们俩医医吧!""医医可以,但有话在先,人家医癞头非常慢,我医癞头很快,这是硬生活,痛猛。""只要医得好,随侬了。"

哲高把两个癞头鼋绑在矮凳上,拣起竹做的像刀一样的萝叉,对着癞头鼋就削,连血带肉,二个癞头鼋痛得乱叫:"不医了,不医了!"哲高一解绑,两个癞头鼋,抱着带血的头就逃。

两个癞头鼋逃到龙宫,海龙王刚上朝,他俩不敢说让哲高医过癞头,只喊:"大王不行了,我们被哲高打得一塌糊涂。"虾兵蟹将一看,两个蛮有本事的癞头鼋被打成这样,怕得要命,都不敢去抓哲高了。海龙王不相信哲高会介厉害,决定自己出马去柯哲高。

海龙王要来,哲高也猜到了。哲高把铁秤秤砣煨到火里,外面备了一头公牛。海龙王骑着龙卷马,穿着龙袍刚到,哲高就把煨红的秤砣,往公牛屁股里一塞,他马上骑上公牛,公牛被烫得飞一样地逃,海龙王在后面追。龙卷马从龙宫到哲高家路很远,也有些吃力了,追不上猛逃的公牛。海龙王忖,我做海龙王,骑的东西还不如凡人的跑得快,不如凡人的高大,这只东西要能调给我就威风了。海龙王在后面大喊:"等等嘛,不要逃嘛,跟我调调嘛。"公牛开始逃得木佬佬快,后来秤砣慢慢冷了,速度一点点慢了,被海龙王追上了,海龙王问:"你怎么不逃了?"哲高说:"你叫我等等嘛,调调嘛,我就等你啦。"海龙王忖这人硬倒硬,对我还很忠呢,我叫他等等就等

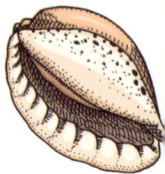

Da, Zhang Er, and Zhang San did go to the sea dragon king to tell on Zhe Gao, so the dragon king sent two scabies-headed turtles to arrest Zhe Gao.

The scabies-headed turtles went to Zhe Gao's home, where his wife was making a sole. They asked, "Where is Zhe Gao?" "He has gone to other people's homes to treat patients." "What patients?" "Scabies-headed patients." These two red-capped scabies-headed turtles asked in a hurry, "Can he cure scabies?" Zhe Gao's wife said, "He has cured a lot of scabies-headed patients." The scabies-headed turtles decided to ask Zhe Gao to cure their scabies before arresting him.

Zhe Gao knew two scabies-headed turtles had come, so he dressed up as a doctor, wearing a long robe, holding a suitcase. He came in and said, "Nice to see you." The scabies-headed turtles said, "Can you cure scabies?" "Yes, I can." "Treat us please." "Sure, but others may cure scabies very slowly, while I can do it very fast. I do it directly, which hurts a lot." "As long as you can cure it, do what you like."

Zhe Gao tied the two scabies-headed turtles up on a stool, held up a knife made of bamboo, and started to peel their heads. Blood and meat came off their heads and they yelled with pain, "Stop, stop, no more treating!" The minute Zhe Gao untied them, they ran away.

When they came back to the dragon palace, they reported to the sea dragon king. They dared not say that they asked Zhe Gao to treat their scabies, but just said, "Bad news. We were defeated by Zhe Gao." The lobster and crab soldiers were all frightened when they saw the capable scabies-headed turtles defeated, so they dared not go to catch Zhe Gao. The sea dragon king didn't believe that Zhe Gao could be so strong, so he decided to go himself to catch him.

等,海龙王提出跟哲高调调坐骑,哲高说要调连衣服、帽子所有的穿戴一起调,海龙王也同意了。

哲高穿着龙袍,戴着龙帽,骑着龙卷马,奔到龙宫,虾兵蟹将一看大喊:"龙王来了,龙王来了,哲高轲来了没有?"哲高说:"轲来了,后头骑着牛来啦。后面来啦。"只见海龙王骑个公牛,穿着哲高的衣服,急得满头是汗,慢腾腾来了。癞头鼋虾兵蟹将一看,早就气煞了,拿出刀斧,不管三七二十一,就把海龙王打死了。从此海龙王就由渔民哲高做了,所以现在的海龙王脱了龙袍,里面还穿着渔民特有的龙裤呢。

Zhe Gao also foresaw the coming of the dragon king. Zhe Gao put an iron weight into fire and got an ox ready outdoors. Wearing his dragon robe, the sea dragon king rode his dragon horse to come. As soon as he arrived, Zhe Gao jammed the red iron weight into the ox's ass and hopped on it. The ox felt so much pain that it ran so fast as if flying. The sea dragon king chased after him. After traveling from the dragon palace to Zhe Gao's home, the dragon horse was kind of tired, so it couldn't catch up with the ox. The sea dragon king thought, "As a dragon king, my horse was even not as fast as nor as big as a mortal man's. It would be great if we could change." The dragon king called behind him, "Wait, stop running. I want to change." At the beginning, the ox ran fast, but when the iron weight cooled off, it started to slow down and was caught up with by the dragon king. The dragon king asked, "Why don't you run?" Zhe Gao said, "Because you said 'wait' and you want to change." The dragon king thought, "This man is stubborn, but he follows orders. When I asked him to wait, he waited." The sea dragon king said he wanted to change the ride. Zhe Gao said he wanted to change clothes and hat as well, and the dragon king agreed.

Wearing the dragon robe and the dragon hat, riding the dragon horse, Zhe Gao went to the dragon palace. The soldiers shouted, "The dragon king has come. Where is Zhe Gao?" Zhe Gao said, "He is behind me, riding an ox." Riding an ox and wearing Zhe Gao's clothes, the real sea dragon king was coming slowly, with sweat all over his head. Seeing him, the soldiers were all so outrageous that they took out their knives to kill him without thinking twice. When the real sea dragon king was dead, Zhe Gao became the sea dragon king. That's why even now the sea dragon king could be seen wearing fishers'dragon pants under the dragon robe.

二、舟山龙神话

16. 绿龙

传说古时候,金塘岛这地方富猛,人们统过着交关富裕的日子。可有一年,突然天上黑云滚滚,落了一场暴雨,把一个好端端的金塘岛,弄得房屋倒塌、田地歉收。

这一年,村西头一间茅屋里,一对年过半百的老夫妻生了个男孩。老婆婆说:"老爹,穷人家的孩子跟富人家一样,总得有个名字吧!"丈夫说:"那就叫金果吧!金果是摔勿烂、跌勿坏的。"老婆婆说:"好咯。"第二天,丈夫早早出门打猎去了,勿小心跌入深沟,从此屋里只有母子俩相依为命了。

金果慢慢长大了,他长得高大魁伟,为人心地善良,种田、打鱼、打猎,样样活计统一好把手。村里人统很喜爱他,大家统亲热地叫他"金哥"。

一年冬闲辰光,金哥告别阿娘上山去打猎。他走呀,走呀,足足走了七天七夜。突然,眼前一片漆黑,在漆黑的天地间,滚着一团蓝蓝的火,火中还有个姑娘在呼救呢。金哥向火奔去,用树枝打开一条路,把那哭得泪人一般的姑娘救了出来。

金哥把姑娘放到大青石上,问:"姑娘,侬是哪里人,叫啥名字?""我叫佘姑,家住蛇山。""侬到这里做啥,我怎样送侬回?""我是蛇王的囡,今天出来游山玩水,勿幸遇到了黑蟒精。黑蟒精想害我。""那黑蟒精住在哪里?""住在金塘岛的仙人山

Green Dragon

Legend has it that in ancient times, Jintang Island was a prosperous place where its people led a rich life. But one year, black clouds rolled in with torrential rain, turning the peaceful island into a mess. Houses were collapsing, and the fields failed to produce.

That year, in a hut at the west end of the village, a baby boy was born to an old couple, who were over half a hundred years old. The wife said, "A child from a poor family is equal to that of wealthy origins. It should have a name." The husband said, "Call him Jin Guo❶ then. A golden fruit is unbreakable." The wife said, "Well, that's it." The next day, the husband went out early to hunt, but accidentally fell into a deep ditch. From then on, there was only the mother and the son left to live together in the house.

Gradually, Jin Guo grew up into a tall, stout and kind-hearted man. He was a master of farming, fishing and hunting. Everyone in the village loved him and called him "Brother Jin".

One winter, Brother Jin said goodbye to his mother and went hunting in the mountains. He walked and walked, for seven days. All of a sudden, everything went dark. In the darkness, there was a blue fire rolling, in the middle of which a girl was calling for help. Brother Jin ran to the fire, opened a road with branches, and saved the girl half submerged into tears.

Brother Jin put the girl on the big bluestone and asked, "Girl,

---

❶ Jin Guo means a golden fruit symbolizing strongness and toughness.

　　　　　　　　　　　　　二、舟山龙神话

上。"金哥听了佘姑的话,站起身,对佘姑说:"请侬自己回家吧,我要到仙人山去斩黑蟒精!""独木难成林,你得找个帮手呀!侬跟我去见我父王,他或许能给侬找一个帮手。"佘姑拉着金哥的袖子说:"如果找勿到帮手,侬就要蛇宫里的小金鸡,它会帮你的。"

金哥跟着佘姑到了蛇宫。蛇王对金哥说:"谢谢侬救了我女儿,我宫殿里的财宝随侬挑。"金哥一件东西也勿要,只指着一只小金鸡说:"如蒙大王恩赐,就把小金鸡给我吧!"蛇王哈哈大笑,答应了:"小金鸡是我的掌上明珠,侬要好好照顾她。"

金哥把小金鸡放到怀里,当夜急急忙忙赶回家,喊:"娘,快开门!"娘听到儿子的声音,连忙开门。门一开,一阵风把豆油灯吹灭了。金哥伸手摸小金鸡,小金鸡已勿知去向了。娘越急越是点勿着火,忽然,一阵金光,把屋里照得通亮。只见穿着金黄色衣裳的佘姑,对着金哥微笑呢。金哥才明白小金鸡就是佘姑变的。佘姑走到娘的跟前,喊声:"娘。"阿娘看儿子带来个介漂亮的姑娘,真笑煞了。

金哥和佘姑成亲了,金哥想到黑蟒精还呒没除掉,第二天就告别娘和佘姑,去杀掉黑蟒精。临走,其解下祖传的龙泉宝剑,对佘姑说:"如果我有三长两短,宝剑会发响。"佘姑和阿娘交关难过地送走了金哥。

转眼几个月过去了,金哥一去无消息。一日,佘姑睡在床上,忽听到墙上宝剑一响,通红的血从剑鞘里流出来。佘姑知道金哥遇难了。第二天,佘姑就把阿娘托付给左亲右邻,背上龙泉剑,向仙人山方向走。

佘姑走呀,走呀,一日走到纺花山脚下。这里住着一位纺棉花的婆婆,佘姑一见婆婆,知道她是一个得道之人,说:"婆

where are you from and what is your name?" "My name is Lady She and I live in Sheshan." "What are you doing here, and how can I send you back?" "I am the daughter of the Snake King, and I came out to play in the mountains today. Unfortunately, I met the black python, and he wanted to hurt me." "Where does the black python live?" "It lives on the Xianren Mountain on Jintang Island." After hearing Lady She's words, Jin stood up and said to her, "Please go home by yourself. I have to go to the Xianren Mountain to kill the black python." "A tree cannot make a forest. You need a helper. Come with me to visit my father, and he may be of assistance in finding you a helper." She tugged on Jin's sleeve and said, "If you can't find help, you should ask for the little golden chicken in the Snake Palace. It will help you."

Jin followed Lady She to the Snake Palace. The Snake King said to Jin, "Thank you for saving my daughter. Of all the treasures in my palace, take whatever you want." Jin didn't take anything but pointed to a little golden chicken and said, "So kind of you to give me a present. I would like the golden chicken." The king laughed, "She is the apple of my eye, and you must take good care of her."

That night, with the little golden chicken in his arms, Jin hurried home and shouted, "Mum, open the door!" When the mother heard her son's voice, she opened the door in a hurry. When the door opened, a gust of wind blew out the bean oil lamp. Jin reached out to make sure if the little golden chicken was still there, but it was nowhere to be found. The more anxious the mother was, the more she could not light the fire. Suddenly, there was a burst of golden light that illuminated the room. It turned out to be Lady She, who wore a golden dress, smiling at Jin. Not until then did Jin realize that the little golden chicken was Lady She. Lady She went up to Jin's mother and said, "Mum." The mother was so delighted to see that her son had brought such a beautiful girl.

二、舟山龙神话

婆,请告诉我金哥在哪里,告诉我怎样能消灭黑蟒精。"婆婆告诉佘姑:"黑蟒精被金哥劈死在仙人山的半山腰里,金哥自己也倒在仙人山了,如今黑蟒精的阴魂正缠着他呢。"佘姑听了婆婆的话,含着泪花说:"我一定要救出金哥。婆婆,请帮帮我!""只要你找到幸福泉,把泉水撒在仙人山上,黑蟒精的阴魂就会散去,金哥就会活转来。"婆婆说着,从屋里拿出一只槐木碗,一双八耳麻鞋,又从纺车上撕下一团棉絮,对佘姑说:"拿去吧,你会交好运的。"佘姑穿上八耳麻鞋,就不怕山陡路滑啦;耳塞棉絮团,就不怕黑蟒精的阴魂作怪啦。佘姑走呀

Brother Jin and Lady She got married. The next day, thinking that the black python had not yet been eliminated, Jin said goodbye to his mother and Lady She, and embarked on the journey of killing the python. Before departure, he took off the family Longquan Sword, and gave it to Lady She, saying, "If anything happens to me, the sword will clatter." In sorrow, Lady She and the mother saw Brother Jin off.

Several months passed in a flash, but no news of Brother Jin. One day, as Lady She was sleeping in bed, she heard the sword on the wall clatter, red blood flowing out of the scabbard. Upon that, Lady She realized that Brother Jin had been killed. The next day, she entrusted the mother to relatives and neighbors, put on the Longquan Sword and headed for the Xianren Mountain.

She walked and walked, and one day she came to the foot of the Fanghua Mountain. An old lady who made her bread by spinning cotton dwelt around here. Lady She could tell from her appearance that she was also a divine being, and she asked, "Granny, please tell me where Brother Jin is. And how can I kill the black python?" The old lady said to her, "The black python was killed by Jin halfway up the Xianren Mountain, but Jin himself also fell on the Xianren Mountain. Now the ghost of the black python is haunting him." Upon her words, Lady She said, full of tears, "I have to save him. Granny, please help me." "If you find the Spring of Happiness, and sprinkle the water on the Xianren Mountain," said the granny, "the ghost will disperse and Brother Jin will come to life." The granny took out from the house a wood bowl made of Chinese scholar tree, a pair of eight-eared sisal shoes, and tore a ball of cotton wool from the spinning wheel, saying to Lady She, "Take them. May the luck be with you." With the eight-eared sisal shoes on, Lady She would not be afraid of the slippery road; and with the cotton wool balls in her ears, the ghost was deterred.

二、舟山龙神话

走,寻呀寻,终于爬上了仙人山顶,寻到了幸福泉。

佘姑用槐木碗盛来了幸福水,轻轻撒在山阴里。顿时山阴吭没了,明亮的山上,金哥迎面走过来,佘姑高兴啊!这时,天空飘下一条黄绢,落在佘姑手里,上面写着:"为民除害,助天有功,封你为奉化绿龙。"佘姑立刻感到头上痒松松的,头上冒出对角,就地一滚,就变成一条绿龙。

绿龙载着金哥从山顶上直飞下来,飞到家门口。娘喊一声"佘姑",小绿龙回一次头;娘喊一声"金哥",小绿龙又回一次头。娘喊了十八声,小绿龙回了十八次头,绿龙穿过镇海关,一直飞到奉化住下来。至今仙人山到大浦口这段河流有十八个湾,据说就是绿龙十八次回头留下的。

After a long journey, Lady She finally managed to climb the top, and found the Spring of Happiness.

Lady She filled the wood bowl, and sprinkled it gently into the shade of the mountain. At once the mountain shade was gone, and over the bright mountain there came Brother Jin. Lady She was so happy! At that moment, a yellow silk floated down from the sky and landed in Lady She's hand, which read, "You've killed the evil, and contributed to the world. Here I make you Fenghua Green Dragon." Immediately, Lady She felt itchy on the head where a pair of horns emerged, and when she rolled on the ground, she became a green dragon.

The Green Dragon carried Jin straight down from the top of the mountain and flew back above its home. The mother exclaimed, "Lady She!" The Green Dragon looked back; "Brother Jin." It looked back again. Altogether, the mother called for 18 times, and the dragon turns around its head 18 times. The Green Dragon crossed Zhenhai and flew all the way to Fenghua City where it found a place to live in. Nowadays, there are eighteen bays in the river between the Xianren Mountain and Dapukou, which is said to be the Green Dragon's turning around.

17. 白老龙

传说,白老龙原来住在天宫里专管莲花池。莲花池里莲蓬结的莲子,每年归王母娘娘过生日用。白老龙交关贪吃,有一次把莲子统统偷吃了。王母娘娘气煞啦,把白老龙罚下来,就住在岑港的龙潭里。

白老龙罚下来时,吭没带龙珠来。龙珠是由蟾变的。俗话说:"做官容易上朝难,做龙容易收蟾难。"蟾专蹲在邋遢的地方。白老龙为了得到一颗龙珠,各处寻找能变成龙珠的蟾。后来晓得了福建有只蟾躲在一个寡妇屋里的夜桶下。白老龙就想到寡妇屋里收蟾。

寡妇的屋里厢还有一个三岁的小囡。这年鱼汛开始,寡妇屋里伙计有啦,可拘鱼老大吭没,寡妇急得坐在海边哭。白老龙化作一个老头,走过去问:"阿嫂侬哭啥啦?"寡妇讲:"别人屋里渔船统出海拘鱼去了,往年老大自家男人做,如今男人吭没,吭没老大,鱼拘勿来啦。"白老龙说:"我帮侬去拘好啦。"寡妇看这老头年纪介大,不放心,但又吭没别的办法,就说:"好咯。"带白老龙回屋里去啦。

第二天,寡妇请白老龙和伙计吃"出洋饭"。别人又吃又喝,可白老龙一点也勿吃,只说:"阿嫂侬只给我准备些糯米块就好啦。"吃了饭,白老龙带着糯米块上了船。船走出勿远,白老龙说:"好出网啦。"伙计出了网,白老龙就"呼噜呼噜"困起

White Old Dragon

According to legend, the white old dragon lived in the Temple of Heaven and was in charge of a lotus pond. The lotus seeds of the lotus seedpod in the lotus pond are used for the birthday of the Queen Mother every year. Once, the white old dragon was so greedy that he ate all the lotus seeds. The Queen Mother was so angry that she drove the white old dragon out of Heaven and sent him to live in the Dragon's Pond in Cengang.

The white old dragon left Heaven without his dragon ball. The dragon ball is transformed from a toad. As the old saying goes, "Being an official is easy but managing affairs is more difficult; being a dragon is easy but collecting toads for dragon balls is more difficult." Toads usually stay in slovenly places. To get a dragon ball, the white old dragon kept looking around for the toad that could become a dragon ball. Later he learned that a toad was hiding under a chamber pot in a widow's house in Fujian Province. The white old dragon wanted to catch the toad in the widow's house.

The woman's husband died, leaving a three-year-old girl at home. This year the fishing season began, and the widow had some helpers to work with, but no one to command the fishing. She was so anxious that she sat by the sea and cried. The white old dragon turned into an old man and asked the widow, "Why are you crying?" The widow said, "The fishing boats of other people's have gone to sea to catch fish. In the past, my husband was the one who commanded the fishing. But now there is no one to command since my husband died. We can't catch any fish this year."

二、舟山龙神话

觉来,只见其全身黄汗如雨,伙计看其介热,就给其扇了几扇,扇子一扇,白老龙汗马上收回去,睁开眼说:"起网。"大家把网拔拢来,鱼多猛,可统是梅童鱼。十几个伙计掏了三天三夜,才装满舱。渔船回洋靠了码头,打开舱,原来的梅童鱼统变成了三四斤重的大黄鱼。这样,寡妇一次就发了大财,真是笑煞啦。白老龙蟾呒没收到,就又留下给寡妇做长工。

有一次,寡妇十多亩田水干啦,就让白老龙去车水。其水呒没车,倒在田头打瞌睡。邻居看见告诉寡妇,寡妇正好做了些老头喜欢吃的糯米块,就担去,顺便看看田头。可其到田头一看,田里水白花花一片,奇怪的是最低的一个角,一点水也呒没,寡妇问:"大伯,整块田水已经满啦,为啥最低一个角呒没水?"白老龙说:"阿嫂,侬给我吃的糯米块,为啥少了一个角?"原来,寡妇糯米块烧熟时,被其三岁小囡挖个角吃啦。这一年,寡妇庄稼长得好不过,收下的谷,谷满仓、缸缸满,寡妇又发了大财,真是笑煞啦。

有一日,寡妇走出倒夜桶去了,白老龙乘机会走进其内室,捉到了蟾。白老龙为得到蟾,已在寡妇屋里整整做了三年长工啦。白老龙得到了蟾,要回去,寡妇要付给工钿,其不肯收。寡妇一定要给。最后,白老龙说:"侬介客气,我就面皮老老,肚皮饱饱了,侬明年七月半挑一担糯米块送给我吃吃就好啦。"寡妇问:"侬住在啥地方?叫啥名字?"白老龙说:"我姓白,住在舟山岑港小舻,门前挂着三丈六尺白布,走进白布,就是我屋里。"

从白老龙走后,寡妇日夜不忘老头恩情。第二年七月半,寡妇不怕路远,担着三斗半的糯米块,从福建来到岑港。东问西问,问来问去,呒没人晓得有姓白的人家。最后问到一个胡

The white old dragon said, "I'll help you command it." Seeing that the old man was quite old, the widow was worried but had no better method and agreed to let the white old dragon command the fishing.

The next day, the widow treated the white old dragon and helpers to have a meal before fishing. Others ate and drank, but the white old dragon didn't eat at all. He told the widow, "Please just prepare some glutinous rice pieces for me." After the meal, the white old dragon took the glutinous rice onto the boat. The boat did not go far and he said, "Cast the net." He fell asleep after the helpers cast the net. The white old dragon was sweating all over so his man fanned him. His sweat dried up at once and he opened his eyes, said, "Pull in the net." The crew pulled in the net with numerous fish, but all of them were baby croakers. It took a dozen men three days and nights to fill the boat's hold with fish. The fishing boat went back to the dock. When the crew opened the hold, the original baby fish all turned into large yellow croakers with three or four kilograms. The widow was quite happy because she made a fortune this time. As the white old dragon had not yet caught the toad, he decided to stay for the long-term hired hand in the widow's house.

Once, the widow's more than ten acres of field dried up, and she asked the white old dragon to water the field. Instead of watering, the white old dragon lay down in the field and dozed off. Neighbors saw this and told the widow. She just made some glutinous rice pieces for the old man and took them to have a look in the field. When the widow reached the field, she found the field was full of water except for the lowest corner of the field. The widow asked, "Uncle, the whole field is full of water, but why there is no water in the lowest corner?" The white old dragon said, "Why the glutinous rice you gave me missed one piece?" It turned out that when the widow was making the glutinous rice, her three-year-old daughter dug a piece and ate it. This year, the widow's crops grew

二、舟山龙神话

须雪白的老头,老头说:"阿拉岑港姓白的,只有岑港小舀的老龙。"寡妇回想起老头做长工的情景,觉得其很像龙,就挑着担子到小舀,抬头一看,龙潭上三丈六尺宽的瀑布,从上而下,好像挂着的白布。

寡妇把挑来的糯米块一块一块往龙潭里扔,说:"侬到底是不是龙,今天显显灵,现现龙身让我看看。"话音刚落,只见水里露出个龙头。龙看寡妇呒没害怕,又露出龙背,最后露出龙尾。白老龙忖:我在她屋里做长工时,待我好猛,今朝还把糯米块挑来给我吃,良心蛮好,就收其做龙吧。白老龙尾巴一甩,把寡妇卷进龙潭。

传说寡妇进了龙潭,变成了条青龙。从此以后,岑港龙潭有了两条龙,年年雨水猛足。岑港人为了感激白老龙和青龙,修了龙宫,成立了白龙会社和青龙会社,每年农历三月一出会,抬着纸扎的白老龙和青龙,敲锣打鼓,串街游行。

so well that the barn and jars were full, and the widow was glad of her big fortune.

One day when the widow went out to empty the chamber pot, the white old dragon entered the widow's bedroom and caught the toad. To get the toad, the old man worked as a laborer in the widow's house for three years. Now he got the toad and decided to go back home. The widow wanted to pay him but the old man refused. The widow insisted on giving him, so he said, "Don't mention it. I am an old man now. It is enough to fill my stomach. You can pick a load of glutinous rice for me in the middle of July next year. That's enough." "Where is your home, and what is your name?" asked the widow. The old man said, "My family name is Bai, and I live in Xiaoao, Cengang, Zhoushan. There is a white cloth hanging in front of the door. When you walk through the white cloth, there is my home."

The widow threw the glutinous rice into the dragon's pond piece by piece and said, "Are you a dragon? If you are a dragon, you should show up your real appearance for me to see." Just after she finished the words, a dragon head came out of the water. Seeing the widow was not afraid, the white old dragon bared the dragon keel and finally the tail. He thought, "When I was a laborer in her home, she treated me very kindly, and now she brings glutinous rice for me to eat. She has a good conscience, so why not let her become a dragon?" The white old dragon tailed a toss and rolled the widow into the dragon's pond.

Legend has it that the widow entered the dragon's pond and became a green dragon. Since then, there have been two dragons in Cengang Dragon Pond with abundant rain every year. To appreciate the white old dragon and the green dragon, people in Cengang constructed the dragon temples and set up the white dragon and green dragon organizations. Every year in March, people will carry the papermaking white old dragon and green dragon, beating gongs and drums and holding a street parade to memorize them.

18. 巧妹绣龙

　　从前,有个小娘,从小喜欢绣花,见啥绣啥,绣啥像啥。她绣出红虾蹦蹦跳;绣出青蟹横横爬;绣出的鱼,头会翘,尾巴摇,放到水里还会游三游! 所以大家都叫她巧妹。

　　有一年海岛发旱灾。五月勿落雨,六月勿刮风,七月太阳更猛,晒得田地豁裂,石头冒烟,老百姓叫苦连天。巧妹心里交关担忧,心忖:我去绣条龙,要是绣活了,让龙喷水化雨,那就好了。可惜从娘肚皮里出来,还呒没见过龙,咋绣绣?

　　这辰光,巧妹听到阿爹阿姆叹苦:老天勿落雨,凡人活受罪。这个月来,到白龙溪去求求雨,没料到越求天越旱,咋结煞! 这一句话提醒了巧妹,她忖:大家都到白龙溪去求雨,恐怕那里还真有条白老龙哩! 到白龙溪寻龙去,只要寻到龙,我就可照样绣龙化雨了。

　　第二天,巧妹奔进山岙,果然看到有条长长的山溪坑。这辰光,溪坑里的水老早干了,她沿着溪坑往上爬,一直爬到山顶,在一块岩石上坐落歇歇力。突然,听到有人问她:"小娘,天介热,侬到深山冷岙来做啥?"巧妹抬头一看,是个白头发、白胡须的老头,便上去叫一声:"阿公,我来寻白老龙。"

　　白胡须老头摇摇头说:"小娘,溪坑水都断了,到啥地方去寻白老龙? 侬回去算了!"叹口气,顾自走了。

　　巧妹东找西寻,寻了三天,寻勿到白老龙,走得两腿发酸,

Qiaomei[1] Embroidered Dragon

Once upon a time, there was a girl who loved to embroider. She embroidered what she saw and what she embroidered looked exactly like what she saw. The red shrimps she embroidered were bouncing, the green crab she embroidered was crawling sideways, the head of the fish she embroidered could tilt, its tail could shake, and it could even swim in the water. So people called her Qiaomei.

One year, a drought happened on the island. There was no drop of rain in May, no blow of wind in June, and the sun was hot and blazing in July. The fields were parched, the stones smoked under the sun, and people all grumbled about the devastating weather. Seeing this, Qiaomei worried so much that she thought, "If I can embroider a dragon alive, the dragon can spray water into rain which will be great." Unfortunately, Qiaomei had never seen a dragon since she was born. How could she embroider it? At this time, Qiaomei heard her father and mother sighed and said, "It doesn't rain, and the mortal people are suffering. We went to the White Dragon Creek to pray for rain this month, but the more we prayed, the more drought it became. What could we do?" Father's words reminded Qiaomei that since people went to the White Dragon Creek to pray for rain, maybe there was a real white old dragon. "Then why don't I go to the White Dragon Creek to find the dragon? As long as I can see it, then I can embroider it and let

---

[1] Qiaomei, or Sister Qiao, Qiao means smart and high skilled.

二、舟山龙神话

全身呒力，又回到老地方，在岩石上坐落歇力。刚刚坐落，白胡须老头又来了："小娘，白老龙来无影，去无踪，侬咋寻寻，还是回去吧！"巧妹还是勿肯走，她说："今朝寻勿着，明朝再寻，明朝寻勿着，还有后日，总有一日会寻到白老龙！"老头呒法，叹口气，又走了。

这样又过了三天，巧妹把山山湾湾都寻遍了，还是寻勿着白老龙。巧妹走得满头大汗，上气勿接下气，又饿又累，真吃力煞了，勿觉眼睛一花，昏倒在岩石旁边。白胡须老头又来了。这个老头是啥人？就是白老龙。他见巧妹这副模样，交关同情，用手指摸摸巧妹的眉心，巧妹才慢慢苏醒过来，一看见老头，就像看到自己的亲人一样，"哇"地哭了起来。白老龙赶紧劝说："莫哭！莫哭！勿是白老龙心肠狠，勿肯见侬，是玉帝的旨意，龙王的法令管得严，白老龙咋会出来！听话，我送侬回去！"

巧妹嘴巴石硬："勿去，寻勿着白老龙，我死也勿回去！"

白老龙听了感到一阵心酸，连他自己也勿晓得会落下两滴眼泪来。一滴眼泪一阵雨，白老龙落下两滴眼泪，

it spray the rain."

The next day, Qiaomei went to the mountain, as expected to see a long mountain stream. The water had dried up in the creek, and she climbed the mountain until she reached the top of it. When she sat down on a rock to rest, she heard someone asked, "Young girl, it's so hot. What are you doing here in the mountain?" Qiaomei looked up and saw an old man with white hair and beard. She said, "Grandpa, I come here to find the white old dragon."

The old man shook his head and said, "Young girl, where are you going to find the white old dragon when the water in the creek have dried up? You'd better go back." He sighed and left.

Qiaomei looked for the white old dragon everywhere for three days without result. She felt tired and exhausted and went back to the rock to take a rest. No sooner had she sat down than the old man showed up again and said, "Young girl, the white old dragon comes and goes without a trace. How can you find him? You'd better go back home." Qiaomei replied, "If I can't find him today, I'll continue to find him tomorrow. If I can't find him tomorrow, I will do it the day after tomorrow. I believe one day I can find him at last." The old man sighed and left without a word.

Another three days later, Qiaomei looked for the white old dragon all over the mountain and creeks but did not find him. She walked sweatily, felt hungry and tired, and suddenly felt dizzy and fell beside the rock. The old man with a white beard showed up again. Who was this old man? He was exactly the white old dragon. The old man felt sympathy for her when he saw her like this. He touched Qiaomei between her eyebrows with his fingers and the young girl slowly regained her consciousness. As soon as Qiaomei saw the old man, she began to cry as if she saw her relatives. "Don't cry. Please don't cry. It's not because of the white old dragon's cruel heart that he doesn't want to meet you. It's according to the

二、舟山龙神话

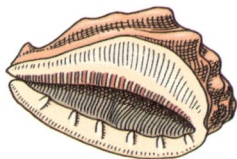

等于落了两阵雨,他一看,晓得勿对了,慌慌张张地对巧妹讲:"侬快回去,我要走了!"眼睛一眨,勿见了。

　　巧妹一看落雨了,心里蛮高兴,便"噔噔"奔到屋里,啥人料到,她前脚刚进门,白胡须老头后脚也赶到了。巧妹见他介急,勿晓得出了啥事体。老头一进屋,就说:"巧妹,我就是白老龙,只怪自己勿小心,掉了两滴眼泪,落了两阵雨,犯了天规,龙王要拿我去治罪了!"巧妹一听,吓呆了。白老龙说:"莫慌,还有办法好救,侬勿是要绣龙吗?绣一条白老龙,和我一模一样,要是龙王来抓我,侬就放出绣龙,我就有救了。"

　　巧妹一听又惊又喜,便满口答应。白老龙见巧妹答应了,便轻轻打了个滚,现了龙形。巧妹围着白老龙,看看龙鳞,摸摸龙角,从头到尾,看了三遍。白老龙开口说话了:"巧妹,侬快点绣,绣好了,就来寻我!"说完他"骨碌"一声,又变成白胡子老头,匆匆走了。

　　巧妹回到房里,头勿抬,手勿停,吭日吭夜绣,先绣出龙头,后绣出龙身,再绣出四只龙爪。三日三夜,巧妹未合眼,眼睛熬红了,手指头磨起了血泡,终于绣成了。第四天一早,她拿着绣龙去寻白老龙。可是寻遍了白龙溪,还是寻勿到白老

Jade Emperor's will. The law of the dragon king is strict, and how can the white old dragon come out against the law? Please be obedient. I will send you back home."

Qiaomei was very determined, saying, "I won't go back until I find the white old dragon."

Hearing this, the white old dragon felt a little sad, and even he did not know that he shed two drops of tears. A drop of tears gave a spatter of rain. The white old dragon fell two drops of tears equal to two spatters of rain. He knew something bad happened, and told Qiaomei, "You should go back home quickly, and I have to leave now." The old man disappeared suddenly.

Qiaomei saw the rain and went back home happily. Unexpectedly, as soon as she stepped into the door, the old man with a white beard arrived. Qiaomei found him very anxious, not knowing what happened. The old man said, "Qiaomei, I am the white old dragon. It is my carelessness to shed two drops of tears which turned into two spatters of rain. I have violated the rules of Heaven. The dragon king will punish me for my mistake." Qiaomei listened to the old man with shock. "Don't panic," said the old man, "There are ways to save me. You want to embroider a dragon, don't you? You can embroider a white old dragon exactly like me. If the dragon king comes to catch me, you can release the dragon you have embroidered, and I will be saved."

Qiaomei accepted the old man's advice pleasantly. The white old dragon then hit a roll and turned into a dragon. Qiaomei looked around the white old dragon, watched his dragon scales, and touched his dragon horn, observed every inch of his body three times. The white old dragon said to Qiaomei, "Please hurry to embroider, and come to me after you have finished it." Then the old man turned into the old man with a white beard and left hurriedly.

Qiaomei returned home, started to embroider day and night.

二、舟山龙神话

龙！喊喊，呒没回音。

白老龙到哪里去了？原来，当天夜里，海龙王就把白老龙抓到灵霄殿，告他私降泪雨，触犯天规，玉帝勿分青红皂白，将白老龙定了个斩刑。这辰光，白老龙已被绑到南天门外处斩去了。

巧妹咋会晓得，她手里拿着绣龙还是满山满野地寻。突然，"轰隆隆"一声响，白老龙处斩了，龙头落到白龙溪的山坑里——从此，这里就叫龙头坑了。接着天上落起一阵血雨，这是白老龙喷出的龙血，正巧洒在巧妹的绣龙上面。绣龙猛地一抖，活啦，"呼啦啦"腾空飞起，在巧妹头顶盘旋了一圈，一头钻进白龙溪。一转眼，白龙溪里流出一股清水。直到现在，这条山溪坑勿管天旱，水源勿会断。

She embroidered a dragon head first, then a dragon body, and at last the four dragon claws. For three days and nights, Qiaomei did not sleep, her eyes were red, and her fingers were full of blood blisters. Finally, it was completed. Early in the morning on the fourth day, Qiaomei took the embroidered dragon to meet the white old dragon. She looked around the white dragon creek but did not find the old man. There was no answer to her calling.

Where was the white old dragon? It turned out that on the very night of the rain, the dragon king arrested the white old dragon to Lingxiao Temple and accused him of breaking the rules of Heaven by shedding tears without permission. The Jade Emperor sentenced the white old dragon to be beheaded without any investigation. At this time, the white old dragon was tied to the South Gate for the death penalty.

Qiaomei did not know about the white old dragon's death. She took the embroidered dragon with her and went all over the mountains and fields to find the white old dragon. Suddenly, there was a loud rumble and the white old dragon was beheaded. The dragon head fell into a hole in the White Dragon Creek. From then on, the creek was named the Dragon Head Pit. Then the sky sprayed a spatter of blood rain which was the white old dragon's blood that just sprinkled on Qiaomei's embroidered dragon. The embroidered dragon gave a fierce shake, then alive. It lifted high in the air and began to circle above Qiaomei's head. At last, it dived into the White Dragon Creek. At once, a stream of clear water flowed out of the White Dragon Creek. Up to now, this mountain creek has maintained its water supply regardless of drought.

二、舟山龙神话

19. 锦线女龙

　　很久以前,定海紫微狭门住着一户姓郑的人家,家中只有母女两人。姑娘心地善良,人交关聪明勤劳,从小学得一手好针线,能描龙绣凤,母女俩靠帮人刺绣为生。

　　有一年,舟山大旱,庄稼统干煞,井水也干啦。姑娘着急不过,心里忖,人人统说龙能降雨,我何不绣条龙,求龙王降雨!

　　姑娘找出一块白绸,一针针、一线线,饭勿吃、觉勿困,整整绣了七七四十九天,用锦线绣成了一条龙。姑娘从山沟里找来一碗清水,把绣龙放入碗中,摆到自家房里窗台上,每日每夜守着绣龙,还像念佛老太婆样祷告着:"龙呀,快点长大,降雨救救阿拉百姓吧。"说也奇怪,装绣龙的碗里,水一天天少了,太阳落山后,绣龙还会动几下,好像每天要长一点。后来,绣龙真的慢慢大了起来。姑娘给绣龙换上脸盆,脸盆大,水多啦,绣龙好像动得更快啦,就像真的龙一样在盆里游。

　　一天,正巧是中秋节,天突然暗下来,勿一会下起大雨来了。其阿姆走进房间,看囡伏在窗台上困着啦,想叫囡上床休息,走近窗台一看,盆里一条龙翻上翻下,吓得阿姆"啊"的一声叫了起来,端起脸盆就要往外倒。囡被惊醒了,忙伸手来抢脸盆,一个抢,一个夺,两人一失手,只听"哐当"一声,脸盆摔到地上,接着"轰隆"一声响,摔下脸盆的地方,变成一个水潭,

Kam Line Female Dragon

A long time ago, a family named Zheng lived in Ziwei, Xiamen of Dinghai District. There were only a mother and a daughter in this family. The girl was kind-hearted, clever, and hard-working. She did beautiful needlework and could draw dragons and embroider phoenixes. They made a living by helping other people with embroideries.

One year, there was a drought in Zhoushan. The crops dried up and the well water dried up, too. The girl was very worried and thought, "People say the dragon can bring the rain. Why don't I embroider the dragon and pray the dragon king for rain?"

The girl took out a piece of white silk and stitched it with a thread. She did not eat or sleep for forty-nine days. She embroidered it with brocade thread into a dragon. The girl got a bowl of clear water from the gully and put the dragon into the bowl. She placed the bowl on the window of her room guarding the dragon day and night. She also prayed as the old woman do, "Dragon, please grow up quickly, and then you can bring rain to save the people." Strangely, the water in the bowl became less and less day by day. Every day after the sunset, the dragon would move a few times as if it grew a little bigger. Later, the embroidered dragon grew up slowly. The girl changed the bowl to the washbasin for the embroidered dragon. The basin was big with more water, and thus the embroidered dragon seemed to move faster in the basin and swam just like a real dragon.

One day, it happened to be the Mid-Autumn Festival on lunar August 15. The sky suddenly darkened and it started to rain heavily. The mother came into the room and saw the girl asleep on the

二、舟山龙神话

这就是现在紫微的"洞底府龙潭"。

囡一看脸盆摔破了,绣龙呒没啦,就一下跳进水潭去,头上突然长出两只角来,顿时水潭里飞出一条七色锦龙。阿姆一看着了慌,拼命抓住龙爪不放,阿姆一用力,跌落一只绣花鞋,正好跌落在一株大槐树下。阿姆正想去拾,只听"哗啦啦"一声,槐树下涌出一口泉水井,这就是现在紫微詹家的槐树井。

锦龙向紫微墩头方向飞去,一直飞到大海边。快到海边的辰光,锦龙地上一滚,滚出一道河道来,河水"哗哗"流到田地。阿姆舍勿得囡,连哭带跑向海边追,一边追一边喊:"囡回来呀!囡回来呀!"阿姆一声喊,锦龙一回头,河道就弯一弯。阿姆喊囡十三声,锦龙回头十三次;锦龙回头十三次,河道弯了十三弯,这就是如今紫微墩头大浦十三湾。阿姆喊到十四声,只见锦龙已经奔进了大海,母亲还想看看囡,一直爬上山岭。这岭,就是如今紫微的望海岭。

从此以后,紫微这个地方,有潭有井,有泉有河,再也勿担心干旱啦。人们感谢这姓郑的姑娘,就叫那龙为锦线女龙。

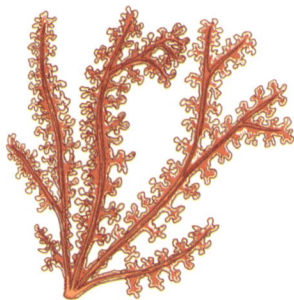

windowsill. She wanted to ask her daughter to go to the bed, but when she walked near the windowsill, she caught a look of the dragon in the basin, swaying up and down. The mother shouted with shock and picked up the basin to pour it out. The girl was awakened by her mom. Seeing this, she tried to grab the basin from her mom. They grabbed the basin from each other back and forth. Suddenly, the basin fell to the ground with a sound of clang. Then with a sound of bang, the place where the basin fell turned into a water pond, which is now called the "Dragon Pond in the Bottom of Hole" at Ziwei.

The girl saw the basin was broken and the embroidered dragon disappeared, and she jumped into the pool all at once. Suddenly, two horns grew out from her head and a seven-color brocade dragon flew out of the pool. Seeing this, the mother panicked and clung to the dragon's claws desperately. She dropped one of her embroidered shoes under a big pagoda tree. When she was going to pick it up, a spring well gushed out under the pagoda tree, which is now called the Pagoda Tree Well at Ziwei.

The Kam Line Dragon flew in the direction of quay until it reached the sea. It rolled out a river channel on the ground when it almost reached the seaside. The water from the river flew into the fields. The mother could not bear to lose the girl and ran to the beach shouting, "My girl, come back quickly, come back quickly." Every time the mother shouted, the girl looked back, and the river pathway became bent. The mother called her daughter thirteen times, the dragon turned back thirteen times, and the river had thirteen bends. This is the Dapu Thirteen Bends. When the mother shouted for the fourteen times, the Kam Line Dragon had run into the sea. The mother still wanted to see her daughter, so she continued climbing the mountain, which is named Wanghailing at Ziwei now.

From then on, there was a pool, a well, a spring and a river in Ziwei. People no longer needed to worry about drought. People showed their great gratitude toward the young girl and named the dragon as Kam Line Female Dragon.

二、舟山龙神话

20. 桃花女龙

　　传说老早,在定海洞岙新砌头的陈王潭,有门人家,屋里有两个儿子、两个囡。其小囡有个怪脾气,就是每日下午,总要拿两个脚桶,装满水,在屋里汰浴。日子一多,其阿嫂奇怪煞了,心里忖,阿拉小姑咋要每日汰浴,时间又会介长,水又要介多。

　　一日,阿嫂偷偷从门洞眼里张进去,看见屋里呒没小姑,只有一条蛇,在第一个脚桶里汰好,又到另一个脚桶里去净一净。阿嫂吓得大声喊叫:"阿娘,勿对啦,小姑被蛇吃啦!"阿娘听到媳妇一喊,急忙奔过来。这时蛇听到阿嫂的喊声,"嚓"从窗门穿了出去,变成了一条龙,沿着窗前的一条河,朝西南方向飞了去。

　　阿娘见龙向西南飞去,在后面追着喊:"囡呀,回来嘛!"龙听到喊声回头看了阿娘一眼,河就弯了一弯;阿娘又喊:"囡呀,回来嘛!"龙忖忖阿娘哭得十分伤心,又一回头,河又弯了一弯。这样龙从洞岙新砌头,一直窜到田螺峙入了海,阿娘喊了十八声,龙回了十八次头,河弯了十八个弯。人们叫这十八个弯为望娘十八弯。

　　这桃花女龙住在桃花山龙潭,一直呒没忘记自己屋里的人。

　　有一年洞岙大旱,百姓东请龙、西请龙,雨就是勿肯落。

Peach Blossom Female Dragon

Legend has it that long long ago, there was a family with two sons and two daughters in Chenwangtan, Xinqitou of Dong'ao in Dinghai District. The youngest girl had a strange habit that she would fill two buckets with water and bathed in the room every afternoon. Observing this for a long time, her sister-in-law felt very curious and wondered, "Why does my sister-in-law take a bath for such a long time every day and use so much water?"

One day, the youngest girl's sister-in-law peeped through the door and saw that the youngest girl did not stay in the room, but only a snake. The snake washed in the first bucket and then rewashed in the second. Her sister-in-law was shocked and shouted, "Mother, it's terrible. My sister-in-law was eaten by a snake!" Mother heard the shouting and came over hurriedly. At the same time, the snake sneaked out from the window and turned into a dragon. It flew southwest along the river beside the window.

The mother saw the dragon flying to the southwest and chased after her, exclaiming, "Daughter, come back!" Hearing the calling, the dragon looked back at her mother, and the river channel increased a bend. The mother called again, "Daughter, come back!" Seeing her mother crying sadly, the dragon looked back again and there appeared another bend in the river channel. In this way, the dragon flew from Xinqitou of Dong'ao to Tianluoshi and finally into the sea. During this journey, her mother shouted 18 times and the dragon looked back 18 times, and the river had altogether 18

人们就到桃花山请龙去了。这门人家的侄子也跟去了,在请龙的百姓中敲铜锣。到了桃花山,其东张张、西张张,勿小心"扑通"一声跌落到井头里。他跌到井底,睁开眼睛仔细一看,自家阿姑坐在一间亮亮的房子里梳头。

侄子说:"阿姑,侬咋会到这来了,屋里统要哭煞了。"阿姑说:"侬先回去吧,阿姑马上来。要出后门,就是侬跌落的井头方向。"侄子讲:"阿姑,好咯。"

侄子从后门往上爬。爬呀爬,爬出一看,竟是洞岙陈王潭自家门口的井头口,侄子回到屋里,就把自家遇到阿姑的事讲给屋里人听了。

呒没几日,有一朵云从桃花山方向飘过来,慢慢向洞岙移,停在洞岙陈王潭上空,下了一场大雨,干旱解除了,百姓得了救。

bends. Therefore, people call these 18 bends Wangniang Eighteen Bends.

The Peach Blossom Female Dragon lived in the Taohua Dragon Pond and never forgot her family.

One year when there was a severe drought in Dong'ao, people prayed to dragon kings for rain, but it did not rain a drop at all. People went to the Taohua Mountain to pray to the dragon. The nephew of the Peach Blossom Female Dragon also came with other people, playing the gong in the group.

When her nephew arrived at the Taohua Mountain and was looking around, he fell into a well carelessly. He opened his eyes at the bottom of the well and saw his aunt sitting and combing her hair in a bright room. He asked, "Aunt, why are you here? We are all worried about you." "You should go back home," said his aunt, "I'll be right back. You can go out through the back door which is the direction of the well." The nephew agreed.

The nephew climbed up the back door step by step. When he reached the exit, he found it was the mouth of the well at his own home. He went back home and told his family that he ran into his aunt.

A few days later, a cloud floated from the direction of the Taohua Mountain and moved slowly towards Dong'ao. It stopped moving and stayed over Chenwangtan. It rained heavily and then the drought was over and people were rescued.

二、舟山龙神话

21. 黄莽龙

金塘洋面有座小岛,叫黄莽山。山上有一条黄蟒蛇,正在修道。这一年,附近各海岛闹干旱,百姓苦不过,黄蟒蛇恨勿得立刻能成龙能化雨。做龙谈何容易,呒没五百年到一千年道行,是勿能成龙的。黄蟒蛇的道行只有三百六十年。

有一日,神仙吕纯阳要收一个徒弟,扮成老人到人间卖汤团。有一个小孩买了两个,吃落后立刻感到交关饱,一整日勿吃饭。小孩是金塘人,要乘船回屋里,当船驶到黄莽山时,由于风大浪高,小孩呕吐,将那两个汤团吐了出来,掉进海里。黄蟒蛇看到那两个汤团,立刻吞吃了。这两个汤团是仙果,一吃落肚,就顶上了二百年的修炼,黄蟒蛇立刻成了龙。龙是修上了,但还勿能行水化雨。要行水化雨,还要收到两只蟾。

俗话说:"做龙容易收蟾难。"黄蟒蛇四处寻找,发现金塘西佛岭下,有一寡妇人家的屙缸底下有一对蟾。但是这对蟾还未成熟,要与龙搭档化水还得再过三年。黄蟒蛇为了收蟾,变成种田人,到寡妇屋里做长工。

寡妇屋里有十亩水田,黄莽龙勿管是寒冬腊月,还是火热的夏天,从勿休息。耕田、插秧、收割样样统会做。别人种五亩要叫短工帮忙,他种十亩还交关空,每日下午还能躺在大树下乘凉,很快活。黄莽龙做了三年长工,为寡妇种的稻谷有一万箩。人们就把这十亩田称为"万箩丘"。三年期满,黄莽龙

Yellow Mang[1] Dragon

On the Jintang Ocean, there was a small island named the Yellow Mang Mountain. There is a yellow boa practicing on this mountain. This year a severe drought occurred in the nearby islands and people suffered a lot. The yellow boa wanted to turn into a dragon and bring rain to the people. However, it was not easy to become a dragon without 500 to 1,000 years of practice. The boa had only practiced for 360 years.

One day, the immortal Lv Chunyang wanted to recruit a disciple and he disguised himself as an old man selling rice balls in the mortal world. A child bought two rice balls and felt full after eating them. He did not have an appetite for the rest of the day. The child was from Jintang and was going home by boat. When the boat reached the Yellow Mang Mountain, the child began to vomit due to the strong wind and high waves. He spitted out the two rice balls which fell into the sea. The yellow boa saw the two rice balls and devoured them immediately. These two rice balls were fairy fruit that equalled 200 years of practice; the yellow boa ate them and turned into a dragon at once. Although it had become a dragon, it was not capable of turning water into the rain. If it wanted to bear this capability, it must collect two toads.

As the old saying goes, "It is easy to be a dragon, but it is difficult to collect a toad." The yellow boa tried hard to search for

---

❶ Mang here means serpent.

就把蟾收了去。

黄莽龙将雄蟾放进自己的左腮,雌蟾放进右腮,从此就能化水行雨了。金塘一带也就风调雨顺,年年丰收了,人们就把这地方叫作大丰。

the toads and finally learned that there was a pair of toads staying under the latrine of a widow's house at Xifoling, Jintang. However, the toads were not grown up yet, and it needed three years before they could work with the dragon to turn water into the rain. To collect the toads, the Yellow Boa changed into a farmer and worked as a long-term laborer for the widow.

The widow had ten mu[1] of paddy field. Whether it was chilly winter or hot summer, the Yellow Mang Dragon never took rests. He was capable of plowing, planting, and harvesting. While others needed temporary laborers to help to plant five mu of land, the Yellow Mang Dragon could do it all by himself and had the time to lie under the tree to enjoy the cool happily every afternoon. He worked as a long-term farmer for three years and planted ten thousand baskets of rice for the widow. People named the ten mu of land "Wanluo Hillock", which meant a land of ten thousand baskets of rice. At the end of the third year, the dragon collected the toads successfully.

The Yellow Mang Dragon put the male toad into his left gill and the female toad into his right gill, which enabled him to transform the water into the rain. From then on, the Jintang area had good weather and good harvests every year. People called this place Dafeng.

---

[1] mu, Chinese unit of land measurement, is commonly 666.7 square meters.

二、角山龙神话

22. 长白小龙

　　从前,长白岛上出过一条小龙,这小龙原是二仙山麻姑洞黄龙真人的侍童,因为失手打碎了一只玉杯,罚下凡来,投胎到一对没儿没女的老夫妻家里。

　　这家的老太婆在梦里吃了一只大红桃,怀孕了。三年后,生下了一个带尾巴的小孩。村里人统讲这小孩是妖怪,叫两老头快斩煞。两老头不忍心,就把小孩放在一只篮子里,拿到山里扔掉了。带尾巴小孩在山里修行了三年,成了一条金黄色小龙。

　　当时,长白岛已经整整三年呒没落一点雨了,太阳炙辣辣,烂泥地都晒开豁了。百姓粮食一点也呒没收,只好到海里扪鱼糊口。可人一下海,十有八九不能回来。有几个回来的人讲:"船到海里,本来是风平浪静,突然会出现一条黑蛇,张开大口把船和人统吃掉。"

　　小龙知道后,决定救救长白百姓。有一日夜里,小龙变作人形来到家,跪在两老头床边讲:"阿爹,阿姆,我是你们三年前生的骨肉,东海龙王决定八年不给长白化雨,要把你们统旱煞。你们如果要雨,每年六月廿三这天,在扔我的山上烧香泼水,我就会降雨。"说完话后,就勿见了。

　　第二天一早,两老头把这事讲给村里人听。到了六月廿三日,村里所有的人统到山上烧香泼水。正泼着,天上就出现

Small Dragon of Changbai

Once upon a time, there lived a small dragon on Changbai Island. The little dragon was originally the page of Immortal Huanglong of the Magu Cave in the Erxian Mountain. It was sent down to the mortal world because of his mistakenly breaking a jade cup and reincarnated to be the son of an old couple.

One day, the wife dreamed of eating a big red peach and then got pregnant. Three years later, she gave birth to a child with a tail. The villagers said that the child was a monster and asked the old couple to kill it. The old couple could not bear to kill the child and put him into a basket leaving it in the mountain. The child with the tail became a golden dragon after three years of practice in the mountain.

At that time, there was no drop of rain on Changbai Island for three years. The land was scorched by the sun. People collected no rice at all and had to go to the sea to catch fish to support a family. However, most of the people who went to the sea did not return. Some of the people who came back said, "When the boat went into the sea, it was calm, but suddenly a black snake appeared and devoured the boat and people."

The small dragon knew this and decided to save the people in Changbai. One night, he changed into a human and came to the old couple's house. He knelt by the bed and said, "I'm the child that were born three years ago. The Dragon King of the East China Sea was determined not to rain in Changbai for eight years. If you want

二、舟山龙神话

了一朵乌云,马上落起雨来了。大河小河统统落满了,这年粮食丰收了。

长白的老百姓有了小龙降雨之后,就不再到海里去捆鱼了。海里的黑蛇精气煞了,就想除掉小龙。

一日夜里,黑蛇精变成了一个黑黑矮矮的老头也来到小龙的阿爹、阿娘面前说:"我是侬儿子的师兄,你们要其永远为长白化雨,就得在你家门口大沙地里造一根石桥,在六月廿三那日用一把狗血犁头插在桥下面,这样师弟就能永远为长白百姓造福了。"两老头信以为真,第二日就叫村里的人动手造石桥。到了六月廿三,在桥下插了一把狗血犁头,结果桥下流出了血,当日呒没落雨,村里人真奇怪煞。

当日夜里,两老头看见儿子走到床边,他头上还有一条又长又深的口子呢,鲜血还在汩汩地流,儿子流着眼泪讲:"你们中了黑蛇精的计了,狗血犁头能铡龙,其想把我害煞,再来吃你们,你们要把桥下的血留一盆,每当六月廿三就到龙王庙去祭,雨就好落了。"

小龙讲好以后,驾起云头找到黑蛇精,大喝一声:"大胆孽虫,侬每日贪吃百姓,今日又害我小龙,犯了清规,侬性命难保。"讲好就吐出一颗碗口大的宝珠,朝黑蛇精打去……小龙血流不止,难以下海,就不顾性命危险,把一颗保命珠吐到海里去镇妖。自己呢,拖着身子爬呀,爬呀,想爬回家,再看一眼阿爹、阿娘。小龙没了保命珠,难活呀,爬了不到两百步,就慢慢地断气了。小龙头朝东,两只眼睛还定定地盯着黑蛇精住过的那座山呢。

黑蛇精知道小龙已死,就想上岛来。可是,刚游到海边,就有颗宝珠射着强强的光,挡住上岛的路,黑蛇精没法,只得

to pray for rain, just burn incense sticks and splash water on the mountain where you deserted me on June 23 every year. Then it will rain." Then the small dragon disappeared.

The next morning, the old couple told this to the villagers. On June 23, people in the village all went to the mountain to make an offering and splash water. Just then, a dark cloud appeared in the sky and it soon began to rain. Rivers were full of water now and there was a good harvest this year.

People in Changbai Island no longer needed to go to the sea to catch fish, and the black snake was angry and wanted to kill the small dragon.

One night, the black snake turned into a short black man and came to the old couple's house. He told them, "I'm your son's disciple brother. If you want him to bring rain to Changbai forever, you need to build a stone bridge in the sand area outside your house. On June 23, you need to stick a plowshare with dog's blood under the bridge so that he could serve and benefit Changbai people forever." On the 23rd day of June, they put a plowshare with a dog's blood under the bridge. However, there was blood flowing from under the bridge and no rain on that day. People felt strange about what happened.

That night, the old couple saw their son came to their bed with a long, deep gash on his head. The blood was still flowing from the gash. The small dragon said with tears, "You have been tricked by the black snake. A plowshare with dog's blood can kill dragons. He wants to kill me and then eat all of you. Now you need to save a pot of blood under the bridge. Remember to go to the Dragon King Temple to offer sacrifice on June 23 every year, adn then it will rain."

After the small dragon met his parents, he drove the cloud to find the black snake. He gave a loud shout, "You eat common

重回海底。这样，黑蛇精就被永远镇在海里啦。

那颗宝珠变成了一座山，人们叫它珠子山。小龙住过的山叫小龙山，黑蛇精住过的山叫妖岛山。为了纪念小龙，人们还在小龙山上造了座龙王庙呢。

people everyday, and now you tried to kill me. You have violated the rules of Heaven, and your life should be finished." Then he spat out a bowl-sized orb and hit the black snake. There was blood keeping going out from the small dragon's head and he could not go to the sea to catch the black snake. Regardless of his life safety, the small dragon spat the orb which guaranteed his life into the sea to drive away the evil forces of the black snake. He crawled trying to reach home to take a last look at his parents. However, he did not have the orb to protect his life and died after almost two or three hundred steps. After his death, his head was still facing east and his eyes were fixed on the mountain where the black snake lived.

The black snake knew that the small dragon was dead and wanted to come to the island. But no sooner had he reached the shore than a bright light from an orb blocked his way to the island. He had no choice but to return to the bottom of the sea. In this way, he was restricted under the sea forever.

The orb became a mountain and people called it the Bead Mountain. The mountain that the small dragon lived in is called the Small Dragon Mountain, and the mountain that the black snake lived in is called the Monster Island Mountain. In memory of the small dragon, a Dragon King Temple was built on the Small Dragon Mountain.

23. 小青龙

　　交关早的辰光，盐仓谢家岙住着一户人家。老夫妻收养着呒没父母的外甥谢海龙。海龙人小，但交关听话，舅舅、舅姆待其如亲生儿子。

　　日子过得交关快，转眼海龙也有十二岁了。这年，天大旱，三个月一滴雨也呒没落，眼看秋苗黄垄，种田人真急煞了。舅姆看近日海龙胃口勿好，人瘦落了，交关勿舍得，特意用猪油炒了几碗下饭，却忘了海龙是忌荤的。海龙吃了后肚皮交关难熬，其对舅舅讲："舅舅，我有点勿爽快，想到邱家井边去汰汰面。"舅舅说："好，侬可能吃热了，到井头边休息晌，顺便也给我带点水来。"

　　海龙挈着竹管筒，来到邱家井边，想吐，一用力，吐出一根根肠子来。海龙把肠子在井里清爽，挂到井边的杨梅树上。人呢，困在树下，想等肠子晾干了再装回肚子里去。

　　这时，有一个快嘴三叔婆路过井头，见海龙困在杨梅树下，一串肠子挂在杨梅树上，吓得狠性命叫了起来："海龙！海龙！侬勿要做人了，咋把肠子拿出来了呢。"海龙被惊醒，晓得事情勿好，大喊一声："痛死了！"就闭上眼睛，昏倒在地。

　　海龙舅父姆和左邻右舍晓得后，连忙把海龙背到家里，海龙慢慢地睁开眼睛，对舅舅讲："舅舅，侬把我带了十来年，我交关感激，我死后请你把我葬在村后的溪坑边，有朝一日再来

Small Green Dragon

A long time ago, there lived a family in Xiejia'ao, Yancang. The old couple adopted the nephew Xie Hailong whose parents died. Hailong was young but very obedient and his uncle and aunt treated him like their own son.

Time passed quickly and Hailong was twelve years old. That year, there was a severe drought without a drop of rain for three months. The crop seedlings were turning yellow and the farmers were very worried. Seeing that Hailong did not have a good appetite and lost some weight, the aunt cooked a few bowls of dishes with lard oil, forgetting that Hailong could not eat meat. After eating, Hailong felt sick in his stomach and said to his uncle, "I feel a little sick and want to wash my face by the well of Qiu's house." The uncle said, "OK, you were hot because of dinner. Go and take some rest by the well and bring me some water as well."

Hailong carried the bamboo tube and came to the well at Qiu's house. He felt sick and then began to vomit and spat out his intestines one by one. He washed the intestines in the well and hung them in the waxberry tree beside the well. He wanted to sleep for a while under the tree until his intestines dried and then put them back in his stomach. At this time, a quick-mouthed old woman passed by the well. When she saw a string of intestines hanging in the tree, she shouted at Hailong, "Hailong, Hailong, aren't you a human? How can you take the intestines out?" Hailong was awakened knowing that things were terrible, and said, "It hurts like

二、舟山龙神话

报答舅父姆的养育之恩。"说完就断了气。海龙的舅父姆哭得死去活来，含着眼泪把海龙埋在村后的溪坑边。

一日夜里，海龙的舅舅看到一条小青龙来到床边，亲亲热热地说："舅舅，我本是东海龙宫的一条青龙，爱打抱不平，被罚到凡间受苦，全靠舅父姆和乡亲们待我好，我吭没啥好报答，现在天大旱，我就想法落点雨吧。请侬老人家用邱家井边的杨梅树做一块灵牌，放到日头下暴晒三日，我就会来落雨了。"

舅舅一觉醒来，感到非常奇怪，当即讲给邻居隔壁听，又用邱家井边的杨梅树做了一块灵牌，在日头下暴晒。到第三日夜里，谢家岙的山顶上真的起了乌云，紧跟着就落起了大雨。从此以后，这一带年年风调雨顺。

勿晓得过了多少年，有一日，来了一个兑糖的奉化人，看到这里田稻碧绿，井里水满满的，感到交关稀奇：沿路别处土地统干裂了，草木都像火烧过一样。这里为啥还雨水调匀呢？其一边兑糖，一边打听，后来从那个快嘴三叔婆嘴里打听到海龙显灵的事。当日半夜，他就把灵牌偷回奉化去了。

第二天一早，海龙舅父姆发现海龙的灵牌吭没了，急得勿得了。村里的人晓得后，也到处打听，统打听勿到。

夜里，舅舅又见到了海龙来到床边，讲："舅舅，我的牌位已经被偷到了奉化，奉化人又做了同样的六块，所以侬也甬去拿了。奉化人待我也好，我就住那了，以后每年杨梅红的辰光，我会来看侬的。"说完，磕了一个头就走了。

从此，每逢杨梅红的辰光，那一带总会有一场雨，来得突然，去得也突然。每逢这辰光，乡亲们就都到龙王宫去烧香，说是接海龙回来吃杨梅。

hell!" With these words, he closed his eyes and fell to the ground.

Knowing this, his uncle and neighbors took Hailong back home quickly. Then Hailong opened his eyes and said to his uncle, "Uncle, you have raised me for more than ten years, for which I feel very grateful. After I die, please bury me by the creek behind the village. And one day I will repay your upbringing." With these words, he died. After Hailong's death, his uncle and aunt cried desperately and buried him by the creek.

One night, Hailong's uncle saw a little green dragon came to his bedside and said affectionately, "Uncle, I was originally a green dragon of the Dragon Palace in the East Sea. I was sent to the mortal world to be punished because of my habit of fighting against injustice. I owe you and the villagers for the kindness to me. Now I have nothing to repay you. Since there is a severe drought, I will try to drop the rain. Please make a soul plaque with the waxberry tree beside the well of Qiu's house and put it under the sun for three days, and then I will rain."

His uncle woke up and felt very strange. He told this to the neighbors and made a piece of soul plaque with the waxberry tree beside the well of Qiu's house, leaving it under the sun. On the third night, dark clouds were appearing on the top of the hill of Xiejia'ao, followed by heavy rain. Since then, this region enjoyed good weather and a good harvest every year.

Many years passed. One day, a sugar customer from Fenghua came here. He was very curious to see the green farmlands and abundant water sources here. Along his way, the land was all parched and the vegetation was dry as if it had been burned. Why was there so much rain here? Inquisitively, he learned about Hailong's apparition from the quick-mouthed old woman. In the middle of the night, the sugar customer stole the soul plaque and ran away.

二、舟山龙神话

Early in the morning the next day, Hailong's uncle and aunt found that the soul plaque disappeared and they were very anxious. People in the village also tried to find information about the location of the soul plaque but failed.

In the evening, his uncle saw Hailong came to the bed again. Hailong said, "Uncle, my soul plaque has been stolen and taken to Fenghua. People there made another six pieces, so you do not need to get it back. They treat me also very well, and I will live there. From now on when the waxberries were ripe, I will come to visit you every year." Then he kowtowed to his uncle and left.

From then on, when the waxberries were ripe, there would always be a rain in that region, which came and went suddenly. Every time at this time, the villagers would go to the Dragon Palace to offer sacrifices to invite Hailong to eat waxberries.

24. 青龙山小龙

东海有个黑水洋,黑水洋里有个黑魔王。黑魔王嘴巴一张,吐出一口一口的黑水;腰一伸,脚一蹬,黑水洋上就会掀起一阵阵黑水浪,卷起一团团黑旋风,渔船碰上了,船翻人遭殃。

渔民要扪鱼,硬着头皮去闯黑水洋。可是,渔船驶进黑水洋,勿是被黑旋风刮走,就是被黑水浪淹没。渔民死了交关,寡妇孤老会哭煞。

这件事被青龙山的小青龙晓得了,小青龙是条好龙,他在青龙山足足修炼了一千年。他忖:黑魔王兴风作浪,害死介多人,勿除勿太平! 于是他在地上打个滚,变成一个扪鱼后生,对扪鱼人讲:"黑魔王介坏,勿让阿拉扪鱼,阿拉要想个法子,把它除掉才会太平!"

扪鱼人听说有办法除掉黑魔王,一个个都围拢来了。小青龙讲:"阿拉去造条百年老树船,再去织顶千人头发网,阿拉一起到黑水洋去斗黑魔王!"扪鱼人听呆了,百年老树到哪里去寻? 千人头发网,咋织织? 小青龙告诉大家,老树,青龙山上有,百年老树船他去造;千人头发网咋织织? 那辰光,男男女女都养长头发,只要把头发剪落来就好织网了。大家听这个后生口气蛮大,总归有来头,便答应了。

过了一个月,小青龙果然驶来一条崭新的老树船,船头翘得老高,船身阔阔蛮大,驶起来"哗哗"响,扪鱼人从未见过,感

Small Dragon on the Qinglong Mountain

The Black Sea was in the East Sea, and in the Black Sea, there was a Dark Demon. The Dark Demon spewed black water out of his mouth. When he stretched his waist and feet, the Black Sea would set off black water waves, and rolled up a round of black whirlwind which would collide with and capsize the fishing boat and people on the boat.

The fishermen who wanted to catch fish had to venture to the Black Sea. However, the boats were either swept away by black whirlwinds or submerged by black water. Many of the fishermen died, leaving widows, orphans, and old people in families crying.

The small green dragon living on the Qinglong Mountain was good-hearted. He had been practiced on the Qinlong Mountain for 1,000 years. When he knew about the Dark Demon, he thought to himself, "The demon killed so many people. He must be killed." Then he rolled on the ground and turned into a young fisherman, and he told other fishermen that, "The demon is so evil. We need to try to kill it to guarantee our safety to catch the fish."

When the fishermen heard that there was a way to kill the Dark Demon, they all came together around the young fisherman. The small dragon said, "We need to build a boat out of a century-old tree and weave a net with the hair of a thousand people. Then we will fight against the Dark Demon together!" People were stunned. Where could they find a century-old tree? How could they weave a net with the hair of a thousand people? The small dragon said that there were old trees on the Qinglong Mountain and he would build the boat. As to how to weave the net, both men and

二、舟山龙神话

到蛮新鲜。小青龙挑选了六七个结结棍棍的后生,乘上百年老树船,带着千人头发网,找黑魔王去了。

这日,黑魔王正在洞里困懒觉。突然听到"伊哩哇啦"摇橹声,它瞪起眼睛一看,原来是条抲鱼船。它忖:我肚皮饿得"咕咕"响,正好饱餐一顿。于是它钻出洞来,腰一伸,脚一蹬,立时三刻,黑水洋上刮起一阵阵黑旋风,掀起一个个黑水浪,直向老树船扑过来。啥人晓得,风到船边,"呼啦"一声,滑走了;浪到船头,"哗啦"一声,撞碎了。黑魔王看看这招勿灵,连忙张开大嘴巴,"呼噜"一声,倒吸了一口气,只听见"咯啦啦"一声响,老树船上的钉子,一枚接一枚,"扑通,扑通"地掉进海里。船蜕钉,眼看就要散架崩掉了!

黑魔王见此情景,浮上海面,得意地哈哈大笑。船上的抲鱼人吓煞了,逃的逃,躲的躲。小青龙一看,大声喊着:"莫慌,莫慌!快撒网!"他边撒边喊,边往海里跳,在海上"骨碌"一滚,现了原形,用龙身团团把老树船绕牢,像海蜇桶打箍一样,箍得实紧实紧,仰起龙头,伸出龙爪,猛向黑魔王扑去。说时迟,那时快,黑魔王的一双眼乌珠被龙爪挖出来了,痛得它在海上乱窜乱钻。抲鱼人看得清清爽爽,胆子也大了,赶紧撒下发网,勿偏勿倚,正好罩牢黑魔王。黑魔王在网里乱颠乱钻,勿料发网越箍越紧,最后,让抲鱼人用斧头活活劈死了。

从那时起,渔民把渔船造得像条龙,前有龙头,后有龙尾,还有龙筋、龙骨,叫作"木龙"。船在海上,就勿怕妖魔鬼怪来兴风作浪了。

women keep long hair at that time. They could cut it to weave a net. After listening to this, people agreed because they felt that although the young man's tone was large, it was at least reasonable.

After a month, the small dragon was driving a new boat made of old trees with a high bow and spacious body. Fishermen were impressed because they had never seen one before. The small dragon chose six or seven strong young men, boarded the boat with the net made of 1,000 people's hair and went to the Black Sea to fight with the Dark Demon.

One day, the Dark Demon was sleeping in the cave. Suddenly he heard the sound of rowing. He found that it was a fishing boat. He thought, "I am starving now. It is the right time that I can eat them to fill my stomach." Then it drilled out of the cave, stretching out its waist and feet to make the black whirlwinds spring up from the Black Sea, and the black waves rushed towards the old tree boat. Unexpectedly, the whirlwinds slipped away when they reached the side of the boat, and the waves were broken when near the bow of the boat. The demon saw this didn't work and opened his mouth with a gasp of snoring. Then the nails on the boat began to fall into the sea one by one. Without nails, the boat was about to collapse.

Seeing this, the Dark Demon rose to the surface and laughed triumphantly. The fishermen on the boat were frightened and started to run and hide. The small dragon shouted, "Don't panic. Don't panic. Cast the net quickly." He shouted and cast as he jumped into the sea. He rolled on the surface and turned into a dragon, wrapping his body around the old tree boat, raised his head, and plunged at the Dark Demon with his claws. At this time, a pair of black eyes was dug out by the dragon's claws, leaving the Dark Demon fluttering on the sea. Other fishermen were emboldened when they saw this, and they cast the net just over the demon. It burrowed in the net, but the net got tighter and tighter. At last, the fishermen cut the demon to death with axes.

25. 港门老龙

过去辰光,沥港附近有一条港门老龙,它良心好猛。如若
侬坐船到镇海口,断了淡水,只要点香怀念,就能从海里打上
三桶淡水,想多打也是没有的,这淡水就是港门老龙送侬的。
如若谁不小心在沥港一带翻了船,尸体绝不会到别处去,过几
天定会在原翻船处找到,这也是港门老龙做的好事。

可是,到了清朝辰光,港门老龙却游到别处去了。

当时,沥港一带出了个海螺精,它经常平白无故地把海水
泛上泛下,在海洋上作业的人,经常会网丢船翻人死掉。港门
老龙去打了几回,都被海螺精打败了。

出了沥港有一个老头,已经有六十多岁了,背脊驼了,每
夜统要背着挈网到海滩推挈。这日,港门老龙变成个老板在

Gangmen Old Dragon

In the past, Gangmen Old Dragon lived near Ligang. It was very kind-hearted. When people drove vessels to Zhenhai Estuary and found themselves having no fresh water anymore, they could lift three barrels of fresh water as long as they lighted the incense and prayed. These three barrels of water were given by Gangmen Old Dragon, no more and no less. If someone's vessel was overturned around Ligang, the dead body would go nowhere but being found at the spot of shipwreck after several days. It was also the good deed done by Gangmen Old Dragon.

However, when it was in the Qing Dynasty, Gangmen Old Dragon swam to somewhere else.

At that time, there appeared a conch demon in Ligang. It frequently churned the sea water up and down for no reason at all. Therefore, those who made a living on the sea would always lose their nets, suffer from shipwreck and even lose their lives. Gangmen Old Dragon went to tussle with the conch demon several times, but was defeated by the latter every time.

There was an old man outside Ligang. He was more than sixty years old, hunchbacked. He would carry fishnet to the beach to gather seafood on the beach when the tide was ebbing every night. One day, Gangmen Old Dragon transformed into a boss and waited for him by the sea. When he came, Gangmen Old Dragon said to him, "When the tide rises, if you see a tream of wave become shiny, you cover it immediately with the fishnet in your hands. Drag

海边等其,对其讲:"侬推掗到涨潮时,要是看到有一股潮水发亮光了,就立时三刻用手里的掗网去罩,再往上拖,一直拖到海塘,一定勿要回头看,只要走上了塘墩,我包侬发财。"老头答应了。

港门老龙同老头讲定,又去寻海螺精打,把其引到海滩边。推掗老头一看,是有一股潮水透光,就"嚓"一记把掗网罩上往海塘拖,拖了许多时候,这海水仍旧齐腰深。原来,潮水也随着掗进的海螺精向上涨。老头吃慌了,心里忖:是这老板弄讼我,还是我走错了路?看看天,望望大塘,就把头扭转看潮水。头一扭,手一松,潮水"呼啦"一下全部退掉,海螺精逃走了。

港门老龙又动脑筋了,其到把守镇海关的宁波道台吴大人那里托梦,明天午时三刻潮水有一股清一股浑,请其一定要对准海里浑水放一炮。第二日,吴道台醒了,叫来了两个亲信,吩咐准备炮弹,时辰一到就放炮。

这日,港门老龙又同海螺精打,边打边退,到午时三刻,正好退到镇海关。镇海口潮水也一浪一浪高起来,道台的两个亲信急忙去报。这日是端

it until you reach the seawall. Never look back. As long as you reach the mound of the seawall, I can assure you of a fortune." The old man agreed.

After Gangmen Old Dragon made the deal with the old man, it again went to fight with the conch demon, drew it to the beach. The old man looked and saw there was indeed a stream of wave shiny. Thus he covered it with his fishnet at once and dragged it towards the seawall. He dragged it for a long time; the seawater was still up to his waist. It turned out the tide rose along with the conch demon netted. The old man panicked, and thought to himself, "Did boss play tricks on me, or am I going the wrong way?" He looked up into the sky, looked out at the sea dike, and then he turned his head around to look at the tide. Once he turned his head, he loosened his grip on the rope. It was followed by an abrupt ebb. The conch demon made its escape.

Gangmen Old Dragon again racked his brain. He made himself appear in the dream of Governor Wu in Ningbo, who was guarding the gate of Zhenhai. In the dream, the dragon told Governor Wu that tide would be coming at 12:45 the next day, with one stream clear, the other one muddy. He requested Governor Wu to fire a cannon at the muddy stream. The next day, when Governor Wu woke up, he summoned two closest subordinates, telling them to prepare a cannon and blast when it was due.

That day, Gangmen Old Dragon fought with the conch demon again. He kept retreating while fighting with the conch demon and reached the gate of Zhenhai at 12:45. The tide of Zhenhai Estuary went higher and higher. The two subordinates rushed to the governor to report. However, it was Dragon Boat Festival that day. Local civilians brought in lots of delicious food: steamed rice dough, *Zongzi*, wine and dishes. The governor was befuddled by drink, seeing the two subordinates coming, and they reported, "Time is

午,老百姓送进来许多东西:蒸团、粽子,还有好酒好菜。道台大人老酒吃醉了,迷迷糊糊看见两个亲信来报:"午时三刻到了,是勿是要开炮?"其讲:"开炮!"也没讲是朝清水开,还是朝浑水开。两人跑过去,旗子一挥,炮手"噔"开了一炮,刚刚打着一股清水。清水下面是港门老龙,其一只眼睛被打瞎了,自忖再也没办法同海螺精打斗了,只好逃进了东海大洋。

从此之后,海螺精就经常在沥港一带兴风作浪,海里也不再太平了。

up. Shall we fire the cannon?" He responded, "Fire." He failed to clarify at which to fire, the clear stream or muddy stream. The two subordinates ran over and waved a flag. Thus the artilleryman fired the cannon and hit right on the clear stream, under which was Gangmen Old Dragon. With one of his eyes struck blind, he thought to himself that he could never fight with the conch demon, thus had to flee into the East Sea.

From then on, the conch demon frequently stired up waves around Ligang, thus the sea was no longer safe again.

26. 郑家山老龙

管家老龙

　　舟山岛有个大展庄,大展庄里有个翁家岙,翁家岙后面有座郑家山,山上有个小小龙潭,潭里住着郑家山老龙。

　　郑家山老龙深居简出,日子过得倒也清静。有日夜里,老龙突然觉得神思不宁,坐卧不安。他步出龙潭,在郑家山上朝远处一看:只见北边天际,杀气弥漫,星月无光,原来是金兵把枣阳城团团围住了。城内宋营里,兵断水,马断草,眼看就有全军覆没的危险。老龙不忍城破民亡,国土沦陷,便驾起一朵祥云,直朝枣阳城奔去。跨过东海大洋,越过高山峻岭,到了枣阳城上空。他按下云头,摇身一变,变成一个白发苍苍的老头,挑着一担东西,匆匆忙忙向宋营走去。到了枣阳城下,他被一个守城的宋兵拦住了:"呔!老头,不准过来!"老头喘口气,抹把汗,说:"我是给侬拉送东西来的,快让我进城!"

　　宋兵把那担东西仔细看了一番,前头是一小桶清水,后头是一小捆稻草,再也呒没啥东西了。那个宋兵看了只摇头,哭笑勿得,老头是一片好心,可是这点水,勿够十个人喝,这捆草,勿够喂一匹马,有啥用场好派?

　　老头摸摸白胡须,讲道:"军情紧急,先用着再说。"他边说边挑担进了城。

Old Dragon on the Zhengjia Mountain

Old Housekeeper Dragon

Zhoushan Island had a place named Dazhanzhuang. There was a mountain called Zhengjia Mountain behind Wengjia'ao, which was located in Dazhanzhuang. On the mountain, there was a small dragon pool in which an old dragon lived.

The old dragon lived a quiet and smooth life in the mountain. One night, he felt disturbed and became restless suddenly. He went out of the dragon pool, stood on the Zhengjia Mountain to look in the distance. He saw that the northern sky was covered with murderous aura and the stars and moon were not shining. It seemed that the troops of the Jin surrounded the city of Zaoyang. The Song camp inside the city was cut off from water, the horses had no grass, and the whole army was in danger of being wiped out. The old dragon could not bear to see the city broken down and the people fall, so he rode an auspicious cloud and ran straight to Zaoyang City. He went across the East Sea and over the mountains and peaks to the city of Zaoyang. He changed into a gray-haired old man, carrying a load of things, and hurriedly went to the Song camp. When he reached Zaoyang City, he was stopped by a soldier who was guarding the city. "Old man, don't come over," the soldier said. The old dragon took a breath, wiped his sweat, and said, "I am here to deliver something to you. Let me enter the city."

The soldier took a close look at his load. There was only a

　　　　　　　　　　　二、南山龙神话

城内军民闻讯拥来，这个舀了一勺清水，喝下去顿觉神志清醒，精神百倍；那个扯了一把稻草，战马吃了立即迎风嘶吼，威风凛凛。于是，大家抬水的抬水，挑草的挑草。人欢马叫，热闹非凡。几万人马吃了三天三夜，勿见小桶里的水浅了一滴，那捆稻草也吭没少了一根。

枣阳城里有了水，有了草，真是兵强马壮斗志昂扬，守城官兵交关感谢，都奔来问白发老头："老人家姓啥叫啥？屋里住啥地方？"

"我姓郑，住在舟山府大展庄翁家岙。"

第二天，宋营开城决战，把金兵打得落花流水。宋兵绝处逢生，反败为胜，就更加感激那个白发老头了，可是满城寻人，连个影子也吭没寻着。带兵的将军只好如实奏明宋皇，为白发老头请功。宋皇听了，感慨不已，当即降旨派钦差到舟山查访此人，当面封赏。

钦差奉旨出京，过关穿城，弃马登舟，来到舟山。在茅洋埠头上岸，乘八抬大轿，鸣锣开道，来到翁家岙村口，看见三个女人在晒谷，便上前问话："哎！妇人家，村里可有一位姓郑的老公公？"

"翁家岙统姓翁，吭没外姓人，阿拉勿晓得姓郑的公公是啥人！"

那个钦差大臣，本来就不满这份苦差事，现在听说翁家岙吭没姓郑的老头，便带着原队人马返回茅洋，开船走了。官船到了观门港，突然风浪大作，乌云遮天，官船只得落篷抛锚。可是，锚一抛落，海面就平风息浪了。官船再起锚拔篷，风浪又来了。这样反反复复，吓得大小官员骨骨抖抖，钦差大臣毕竟比别人高出一头，一看这光景，感到事有蹊跷，赶紧合掌祈

small bucket of water in the front, and a small bundle of straw in the back. He shook his head, embarrassed, and said, "You came here with a good intention, but this amount of water is not enough for a single person to drink, and this bundle of straw is not enough to feed a horse. How could it be useful?" The old man stroked his white beard and said, "The situation is urgent. Let's use it first." He carried the load into the city.

People in the city heard about this news and came to the old man. Some people scooped a spoonful of water and immediately felt sober and full of energy after drinking it. Some people pulled a handful of straw to feed the warhorse, and the horse became majestic and lively right away. Tens of thousands of people drank the water and horses ate straw for three days and nights. The water and the straw did not become less at all.

With the water and straw, the army in the Zaoyang City became stronger and the spirit of fighting was high. The officers and soldiers were very grateful to the old man and asked, "What is your name, and where do you live?"

"My family name is Zheng, and I live at Wengjia'ao in Dazhanzhuang, Zhoushan."

The next day, they opened the city, had a duel and beat the Jin soldiers to death. They turned defeat into victory and felt more grateful to the white-haired old man. They searched for him all over the city but even a shadow of him was not found. The general who led the army reported this to the emperor to claim credit for the old man. The emperor was so impressed that he sent an imperial envoy to Zhoushan to find the old man in person to give him credit and reward.

The imperial envoy was ordered to leave the capital and traveled to Zhoushan. After disembarking at the port of Maoyang, he sat in a palanquin and reached Wengjia'ao with gong-sounding.

二、舟山龙神话

祷:"要是枣阳城解围的老翁是此地神灵,请即刻平风息浪!"他话音刚落,风浪就平息了,钦差当即宣读了皇上诏封,官船果然平平稳稳地开走了。

原来,兴风作浪的是观门老龙。当他得知皇帝要封赏郑家山老龙,眼睛红了,现在晓得郑家山老龙呒没封到,他在这里兴风作浪,来个拦路讨封。

郑家山老龙看得一清二楚,心里忖忖好笑,他本来就勿想讨封,也勿想离开郑家山。没料到糊涂钦差会碰到争功的观门老龙,竟会糊里糊涂地封了下去。不过,也怪那几个晒谷女人,明明我在翁家岙,咋会讲呒没这种人?他灵机一动,要和晒谷女人去抬城隍了。等到割稻晒谷辰光,翁家岙女人把谷晒出,老龙就来施法术,猛猛太阳落阵雨,晒谷女人"噔噔"奔到晒场,把谷簟收拢,雨又停了,太阳也出来了;等她们再把谷簟摊开晒谷,阵雨又来了。翁家岙的晒谷女人,奔进奔出,脚骨奔断,小苦吃煞!

不过,老龙依旧住在郑家山的龙潭里,经常出来察看天象,为大展庄行雨赐福,所以大家都称他为"管家老龙"。

老龙扛鱼

一次,郑家山老龙看见有个女人,手里抱着个未满足岁的小囝,在滩横头眼泪流流,哭得交关伤心。老龙心肠软,便变成一个五十岁的老头,去问女人为啥介伤心。这女人讲,她老公原本也是个扛鱼人,这次出海,遇到风暴,落海死了,留下孤儿寡妇,今后的日脚就难过了!

老龙听了孤孀老妮的话,便满口答应到她屋里去做年。还说:"侬莫担心,我困困船里,吃吃船里,每日给我做三斗三

Seeing three women drying grain, he asked, "Is there an old man surnamed Zheng in the village?"

"People in the Wengjia'ao are all surnamed Weng. We do not know anyone who is surnamed Zheng."

The imperial envoy felt dissatisfied with this hard work to find the old man, and now knowing that there was no old man surnamed Zheng, he led his team back to the Maoyang Port right away and left. When the official boat arrived at the Guanmen Port, there appeared the strong wind and waves and dark clouds were all over the sky suddenly, and they had to anchor the boat. However, the sea became calm after they anchored. When they lifted the anchor, the wind and waves came again. This strange repeated phenomenon frightened the officer and soldiers. The imperial envoy felt that something was strange and prayed, "If you are the old man who helped Zaoyang City, please calm down the storm." As soon as he finished speaking, the wind and waves subsided. After the imperial envoy immediately read out the emperor's edict, the official boat sailed away smoothly.

It turned out that it was the Guanmen Old Dragon who made the wind and waves on the sea. When he learned that the emperor wanted to reward the old dragon on the Zhengjia Mountain, he was green with envy. Later, knowing that the old dragon had not been awarded, he made waves on the sea to ask for a reward.

Seeing the whole happening, the old dragon laughed secretly, did not want to ask for a reward and leave the Zhengjia Mountain. And he did not expect the confused imperial envoy would meet the Guanmen Old Dragon who wanted the reward and rewarded him disorientedly. But, he wondered why the three women who dried the grain said he was not living in Wenjia'ao? The old dragon had an idea and wanted to tease the women. When the time came to cut the rice and dry the grain, the women put the grain out. And

升糯米块送来,别的样样勿要其,来的鱼,统归侬!"

老龙把船修好,网补好,雇了几个后生,等孤孀老妮把三斗三升糯米块挑到船里,就开船抲鱼去了。船驶到洋地里,老龙在舵舱里坐坐,糯米块吃吃,等他糯米块吃饱了,才叫伙计张网抲鱼。网一张出,他又躺在舱背墩"呼呼"困晏觉,困得满头大汗,连衣服都湿透了,等他一觉困醒,就催伙计起网,抲上来一网梅子鱼。一网梅子鱼有多少东西,十箩只光十箩,廿箩只光廿箩。统统叫伙计倒进舱里。他对伙计说:"有了,阿拉好拢洋了。"伙计心里忖:"一日只抲一网,一网抲眼梅子鱼,回去咋交代?"

船到埠头,伙计把舱盖打开一看,啊唷,满满一船黄鱼!这是咋回事?原来,老龙的人身在舱背墩困晏觉,龙身到海底下赶鱼去了;抲上来看看是梅子鱼,实际上统是大黄鱼!

这份人家让老龙走进后,每日会抲进一船黄鱼,一个洋生抲落,发财了。

有一日,老龙对孤孀老妮讲:"好了,我好走了!"孤孀老妮听说他要走,眼泪"滴扑碌"流落来了。老龙见她心里难熬,劝她莫哭,现在有了,只要把小人养养大,日脚好过去了!

孤孀老妮晓得留勿牢,问:"阿伯,侬要到哪里去?"

"我要回去!"

"侬是啥地方人,日后小人大了,也好叫他来寻侬!"

"好咯,叫他到大展翁家岙来寻我!"

翁家岙哪里有介相貌的老头,勿是郑家山老龙,还会是啥人?

the old dragon cast a spell to rain on a sunny day. So the women had to run to the sunbed field to put the grain away. Then the old dragon stopped the rain. When the women spread out the grain, the rain came again. Repeatedly like this, the women ran around and suffered a lot.

However, the old dragon still lived in the dragon pool in the Zhengjia Mountain, and he often observed the sky. He brought rain and blessing to the people in Dazhanzhuang, so people called him "Old Housekeeper Dragon".

Old Dragon Caught Fish

Once upon a time, the old dragon on the Zhengjia Mountain saw a woman holding a child less than one year old crying very sadly at Tanhengtou. The old dragon was soft-hearted and turned into a fifty-year-old man who asked the woman the reason. The woman said that her husband was a fisherman and died in a storm at sea, leaving them orphaned and widowed for the rest of their lives.

The old dragon listened to the woman and promised to work in her house as a long-time worker. He said, "Don't worry. I eat and sleep on the boat, and please bring me three buckets and three liters of glutinous rice every day and don't take anything else. You can have all the fish I catch."

The old dragon repaired the boat, mended the net, hired a few young people, and then went to catch fish when the woman picked the glutinous rice to the boat. The boat sailed to the sea, and the old dragon sat in the cabin to eat glutinous rice. When he was full, he asked the men to cast the net to catch fish. Then he lay down in the cabin to sleep, sweaty, and even the clothes were soaked. When he woke up, he asked the men to put away the net and caught a net of baby fish. He said to the men, "Well, we can go

老龙割稻

有年六月秋场，满畈稻谷金黄，十有八九熟了，种田人看看年成蛮好，满心欢喜，家家户户忙着准备开镰割稻。勿料，天勿作美，长沙港里那条老龙"哄哄"叫叫，要做风水了。眼看到手的稻谷，啥人舍得让风水刮走？田畈里的人们割的割，挑的挑，忙得勿可开交。

有个孤孀老妮，她在刘家潭种了一丘稻，自家呒劳力，平日靠雇人种田，眼下风水要来了，啥人有空帮她割稻？她急得"哐哐"奔到田头，"噔噔"奔进屋里，勿晓得做啥好！事有凑巧，正好碰上郑家山老龙，他"骨碌"变成个老头，去问孤孀老妮："阿嫂，侬为啥介急？"

孤孀老妮讲："老阿伯，勿满侬讲，眼看风水要来了，呒人帮我割稻，咋会勿急？稻割勿进，屋里吃啥？"老龙看她眼泪汪汪，介伤心，便劝她莫急，答应帮她割。孤孀老妮看看介瘦一个老头，走路脚骨打跄，大风吹得倒，咋会割稻，便说："唉，侬介大年纪，我咋交代得过！"

"我来割，能割多少算多少，比呒人割总好嘛！"孤孀老妮忖忖也勿会错。"割好，到我屋里吃昼饭。"

老龙要孤孀老妮先带他到田里去看看，再回来吃饭，他还讲："小菜勿论好坏，老酒勿要吃，侬做三斗三升糯米块给我当点心。"

吃好昼饭，老龙又讲了："我腰骨酸痛，想去躺一躺！"孤孀老妮让他上床躺着，自己去做糯米块，等她把糯米块蒸熟，太阳已经偏西，可老龙还未困醒。她忖，让侬困吧，譬喻未雇到人！勿料，老龙一直困到天黑，困得满脸绯红，浑身淌汗，衣服

back now." The men thought strangely, "How can we explain that we only caught one net of fish a day, and only caught baby fish?"

The boat arrived at the port, and the guys opened the cabin to see a boat full of yellow croakers. What happened? It turned out that the old dragon's human body was sleeping, but his dragon body went to the bottom of the sea to catch the fish. And they were baby fish when he caught them, but in fact, they were all big yellow croakers.

The old dragon caught a boatload of yellow croakers for the widow every day, and the widow became rich.

One day, the old dragon said to the woman, "Well, I should go." When the widow heard that he was leaving, tears flowed down her face. The old dragon saw her sadness and persuaded her not to cry, saying that now that she had money, she could live well and she only needed to raise her child.

The widow knew she couldn't keep the old man, so she asked, "Where are you going?"

"I'm going back."

"Where do you live? I'll let the child find you when he grows up."

"Okay, let him come to me at Wengjia'ao, Dazhan."

At Wengjia'ao, except for the Old Dragon on the Zhengjia Moutain, who else had the appearance of the old man?

Old Dragon Cut Rice

One year in lunar June during the autumn harvest period, the rice in the field was golden and almost ripe. The farmers were so happy to see a good harvest that every family was busy preparing to cut the rice. Unexpectedly, the old dragon in Changsha Harbor started to blow the wind. People did not want to let the wind blow away the rice they had in their hands. They were busy cutting and

也湿透了。孤孀老妮看他困得呼呼响,勿好意思把他叫醒。

到了吃夜饭辰光,孤孀老妮听到后屋有响动,她忖,隔壁人家稻割好,谷进仓,老阿伯还在困晏觉,一株稻也吭没割过,还是把他叫醒,吃好夜饭,早点让人走。她刚进屋还未开口,老龙自己醒了:"阿嫂,稻统割进了,侬屋里吃吃有了!"孤孀老妮讲:"老阿伯,莫见笑,侬困了一昼过,咋去割稻?""我叫别人帮忙割的,全割好了,统统收进谷仓里,稻草堆在晒场上,侬自己去看,我走了!"

孤孀老妮连忙挽留说:"吃过夜饭再走,糯米块做好了,侬也带去。"她话音刚落,老龙勿见了。她忖忖蛮稀奇,奔到晒场一看,稻草堆着,回到后屋一看,谷仓里稻谷堆得满满的,她用箩量了量,足足有一万箩。

picking rice in the fields.

A widow planted a mound of rice in Liujiatan. Her family had no laborers, so she usually hired someone to plant the field. When the wind and rain were about to come, how could anyone have the time to help her cut the rice? She ran between the field and her home anxiously, not knowing what to do. She ran into the Old Dragon of the Zhengjia Mountain, who turned into an old man. The old man asked the widow, "Why are you so anxious?"

The widow said, "Uncle, the wind and rain are coming, but there is no one to help me cut the rice, so how can I not be anxious? If I can't harvest the rice, what will the family eat?" Seeing that she was in tears and very sad, the old dragon told the widow not to be anxious and promised to help her cut the rice. When the widow saw that the old man was so thin and stumbled that he could fall over in a gale, she thought how he could cut the rice, so she said, "Oh, you are in such an age. How can I make you work?"

"I'll cut as much as I can. It's always good to have someone to cut." The widow thought about it and said, "Well, let's eat at home."

The old dragon asked the widow to take him to the field first and then come back for lunch. The old dragon said, "It's okay whether the food is good or bad, and I don't drink wine. You can make three buckets and three liters of glutinous rice for me to eat as snacks."

After eating, the old dragon said, "I have a sore back and want to lie down for a while." The widow told him to go lie down on the bed, and she went to make glutinous rice. By the time she had steamed the glutinous rice, the sun had set, but the old dragon was still asleep. The widow thought to herself, "Just go to sleep as if I haven't hired anyone to work." Nobody would have thought that

the old dragon slept until almost night. His face was red, he was sweaty, and his clothes were soaked. The widow saw him sleeping well and felt embarrassed to wake him up.

When it was time for dinner, the widow heard a noise in the back room, and she thought the neighbor had cut the rice and the grain had been put into the barn while the old man was still sleeping and didn't cut a single piece of rice, so she wanted to wake him up and let him have dinner and leave. The widow just entered the house and before she could say anything, the old man himself woke up and said, "The rice is all cut, and your family has food to eat." The widow couldn't believe what the old man had said. The old man said, "I asked someone else to help me cut it. It's all cut and put into the barn, and the straw is piled up on the sunbed. You can see for yourself. I'm leaving."

The widow quickly asked the old dragon to stay and said, "Please have dinner before you leave. The glutinous rice is ready; you can take it with you." As soon as she said that, the old dragon disappeared. The widow thought it was strange and ran to the sunbed to see the straw piled up on the sunbed. She went back to the back room and saw that the barn was full of rice. She measured it with a bamboo basket, and it was 10,000 bamboo baskets.

二、舟山龙神话

27. 韭菜龙

舟山小沙乡有个寺怀村,村西山岭下有个坑,叫龙头坑,水深深的,终年不干。人们到附近山上斫柴,总要到那里坐坐;天热时,小孩好坏都要到那里玩耍,抲小鱼小虾、翻石蟹、汰浴。

相传,在很久以前,这里吭没几门人家,人们靠种田来吃,生活都苦猛了。有一天,两个小孩来到这里,在石缝下抲着一条小鳗,这条小鳗交关白,亮锃锃的。

这条小鳗是咋来的呢?原来这龙头坑和东海相通。一日东海龙王的三太子,在龙宫里住着没趣煞了,偷偷从龙头坑走了出来。当时正是春天,山花统开了,红的、黄的、白的交关好看,他只顾玩,忽然看见来了两个小孩,来不及从坑里逃回,就变成一条小鳗,在石岩缝里幽着,两个小孩东翻西翻,结果小鳗被抲住了。

这两个小孩,平时抲着小鱼、小蟹、泥鳅,都要带回屋里,烧熟当下饭。这两个小孩看抲着一条小鳗,交关高兴地带回屋里,阿娘把小鳗放进锅里,摘把韭菜,盖了锅盖,烧起来。不一会,只见满屋雾气腾腾,啥都看不清,锅盖像被气顶着一样,"嘭嘭"作响,阿娘以为烧熟了。等到中午吃饭辰光,把锅盖掀开一看,奇怪煞了,小鳗连影子都不见了,只剩下一个空碗。

第二天,两个小孩又到龙头坑去玩,看见那条小鳗仍旧

Garlic Chive Dragon

There is a village named Sihuai in Xiaosha, Zhoushan. In the western Sihuai, there is a pit at the foot of the mountain, which is called Dragon's Head Pit. The water is deep there, never being dry all year round. People who cut firewood in the mountain nearby will sit around there. When it is hot, children will play around there anyhow, catching fish and shrimp, turning over rocks to search for crabs, and swimming.

According to legend, long long ago, there were few households there. People made a living by farming, and life was extremely hard. One day, two children came here and caught an elver between the stones. The elver was white and glistening.

How did the elver come here? It turned out that the Dragon's Head Pit was connected to the East Sea. One day, the third son of Dragon King felt bored in the palace, so he sneaked out of Dragon's Head Pit. It was spring at that time. Wild flowers were blossoming on the hills, with different colors like red, yellow, white, etc. Surrounded by this beautiful scenery, he was immersed in playing around. All of a sudden, he caught sight of two little kids walking towards him. It was too late for him to escape from the pit. Thus he turned into an elver and hid himself between rocks. The kids rummaged around and caught the elver.

Usually, whenever the two kids caught small fish, crablets or loaches, they would bring them home, heat them up and eat as dishes. This time, they brought the elver home cheerfully. Their

二、舟山龙神话

在，因用韭菜烧过，原来雪白的身上添了许多韭菜一样的花纹，变成花花的了。小孩急忙奔回去告诉阿爹阿娘，大家跑来一看，果然是原来那条。这样，人们都说这小鳗有来历，拜了又拜，称之为"韭菜龙"。

韭菜龙虽然借着雾气从小孩家逃出回到龙头坑，只因被烧熟了，就再也回不到东海了。

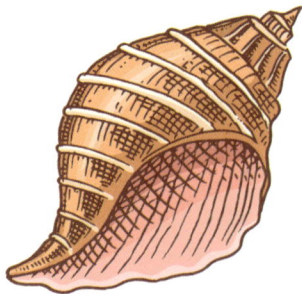

mother put the elver in a pot, picked a bundle of garlic chives and put them in, lidded the pot, and heated it up. After a while, the room became cloudy with a heavy haze of steam. Everything became invisible. The lid looked as if it was being lifted up by steam, keeping banging on the pot. The mother thought the elver was cooked enough. It was not until lunchtime did they surprisingly find the elver had disappeared from the pot when they opened the lid.

The next day, when the two kids hanged out around Dragon's Head Pit, they spotted the elver was still there. However, because it was cooked with garlic chives, its body turned from snow-white into stripes like garlic chives. The kids rushed back home to tell their parents. When they came back to Dragon's Head Pit, they found it was the elver indeed. From then on, everyone began to say this elver had its story. They kowtowed to the elver again and again, and called it Garlic Chive Dragon.

Although the Garlic Chive Dragon fled from the kids' home to Dragon's Head Pit by means of the haze of steam, it could never go back to the East Sea because it was cooked.

28. 北宿老龙

据说,北宿老龙原是人间一个孤老头,家在沥港龙王堂。龙王堂旁边有一个齐脚踝深的龙潭和三间茅屋,北宿老头独自住在那里。其插了千把株番薯,种了十几株杨梅和一片毛竹,空闲辰光到海涂里抲蟹、拾黄蛤,遇到刮风下雨就在家里编竹箩,一日到夜呒没空。

北宿没小人,看见别人家的小人,交关欢喜。杨梅熟时,其拿平日编的小箩装杨梅一箩一箩送给小人吃。

有一年,海龙王的孩子也来吃杨梅了,北宿老头看到这个白白胖胖的十一二岁的小孩,心里蛮喜欢,就拣最大最圆的紫红色的杨梅给其吃。临走时,又让其带上一茶箩。以后,海龙王的孩子每年都要来。许多年后,北宿老头生病了,困在眠床上爬勿起来,要死了。海龙王的孩子看见交关伤心,就跑到龙宫,向阿爹求救。海龙王想想北宿老头心地善良,自己的孩子又受过其恩惠,就拿出一颗龙珠,叫孩子带给北宿老头吃。

北宿老头吃了龙珠,变成了一条老龙,专管金塘岛的雨水。北宿老龙对自己管辖的地方交关负责,勿漫大水,呒没旱灾,岛上年年丰收,百姓安居乐业,因此,多次受到海龙王的赏赐。北宿老龙在海岛多年,还呒没娶老婆,海龙王就想将自己的外甥女许配给其。

海龙王的外甥女介好看又聪明,大大小小的龙都要娶她。

Beixiu Old Dragon

It is said that Beixiu Old Dragon was once a single and childless old man in the mortal world. He lived in the Longwangtang in Ligang. There was an ankle-deep dragon pool and three thatched cottages, where the old man Beixiu lived. He planted a thousand sweet potato shoots and dozens of waxberries and a patch of bamboos. In his spare time, he would go catching crabs and collecting yellow clams on the shoal. Whenever it was stormy, he would stay at home weaving bamboo baskets. Anyway, he kept busy all day long.

Beixiu had no children and always rejoiced to see others' children. Whenever waxberries were ripe, he would fill bamboo baskets, which were woven by himself on ordinary days, with waxberries, and send them to children.

One year, the child of the Dragon King also came to Beixiu to ask for waxberries. Beixiu heartily liked the plump kid, who was twelve years or so. He picked up the biggest and roundest purple-red waxberries to the kid. When the kid was leaving, Beixiu let him take a basket of waxberries. From then on, the child of the Dragon King would come every year. After many years, Beixiu fell seriously ill. He was confined to his bed, dying. It grieved the Dragon King's kid, who rushed to the Dragon Palace and cried for help from his father. The Dragon King thought of Beixiu's kind-heartedness as well as the favor his child had been given. Thus he took out a dragon pearl, and told his child to take it to Beixiu to eat.

Beixiu ate the dragon pearl and transformed into an old dragon,

二、舟山龙神话

镇海招宝山有条青龙,早相中了,得知海龙王要将其许配给北宿老龙,交关气不过。

一天早晨,天还呒没亮,青龙偷偷带了一把青龙剑,向北宿老龙住的地方游去。其为了使北宿老龙认勿出,就变成了一只像脚桶样大的海螺精,浑身生刺,眼睛像铜铃。

海螺精经过的地方,海水发出"哗啦哗啦"声,声音大猛。北宿老龙听声音勿对,走出龙潭,看到海螺精,大声道:"大胆孽畜,竟敢闯入我的海域兴风作浪!"海螺精哈哈大笑,说:"少啰唆! 今天老子要教训教训侬!"北宿老龙和海螺精都有法术,就打斗起来,打了一日一夜,打得海螺精支持勿住了,偷偷取出青龙剑,朝北宿老龙刺去,北宿老龙来勿及躲避,被刺中了左眼,昏倒在海中。海螺精趁机逃了回去。

北宿老龙醒来后,眼睛痛得要命,就变成一个小姑娘,来到了人间,到名医屋里治眼睛。名医把脉息一搭,对其说:"小姑娘,侬要现原形,我才能医治。"北宿老龙说:"我现了原形,侬要吓煞的。"名医说:"我勿怕。"北宿老龙现了龙身。名医从来呒没看到过龙,怕猛,但仔细看看,其生得交关和善。名医叫其缠在屋柱上,头朝下,好动手术。

名医因在楼上看到龙,觉得交关好奇,拿来剪刀纸头,把龙剪了出来。后来人们描龙和在屋里柱上雕刻龙,统是照这剪纸的样子。名医为龙动完手术,对龙说:"侬的眼睛需要调养,每年吃点杨梅。"北宿老龙点点头,谢过名医,回到龙潭养。

北宿老龙眼睛被伤的事,被东海龙王晓得了,其一气之下,把青龙压在山下。这座山就是现在金塘西丰村的青龙山。

北宿老龙眼睛治好后,就与龙王的外甥女成了亲。每当

in charge of rainfall in Jintang Island. Beixiu Old Dragon was particularly responsible for his jurisdiction. Neither flood nor drought affected the island. Local populace lived in peace and contentment. Thus, Beixiu was granted rewards by the Dragon King many times. Beixiu lived in the island for many years, unmarried. Having heard of Beixiu's condition, the Dragon King wanted to marry his niece to him.

The Dragon King's niece was pretty and smart, and all kinds of dragons wanted to marry her. There was a green dragon in Mount Zhaobao in Zhenhai. He had taken a fancy to her for a long time. When he learnt of the Dragon King's intention, he became furious.

One morning before dawn, the green dragon sneaked a falchion and went to where Beixiu lived. In order not to be recognized by Beixiu, he transformed into a conch demon as big as a bucket, with spines all over the body and eyes staring like bells.

Wherever the conch demon passed through, the sea splashed violently and loudly. Beixiu perceived the abnormity from the noise. He came out of the Dragon Pit, caught sight of the conch demon and shouted, "You evil beast, how dare you intrude my waters to make trouble!" The conch demon roared with laughter, "Just shut up! Today I will teach you a lesson!" Both Beixiu and the conch demon had magical power, so they tussled with each other. After a full day and night, the conch demon couldn't hold out any more. He took out the falchion on the sly and stabbed at Beixiu. The sheer unexpectedness frustrated Beixiu. The falchion was stabbed into his left eye, and he fell in a faint in the sea. The conch demon seized the chance and fled.

When Beixiu recovered consciousness, his eye hurt like hell. Thus he transformed into a young girl to get treatment at a clinic of a famous doctor. The doctor tried to feel her pulse on her wrist, and said to her, "Young lady, only if you transform yourself into

153◀ 　　　　　　　　　　　　　　　　二、舟山龙神话

杨梅成熟的辰光,就带着海龙王的孩子来吃杨梅。这时,海上会突然刮起西北风,海浪大猛,树上的杨梅也会落下许多,人们统说:"这是北宿老龙来吃杨梅了。"

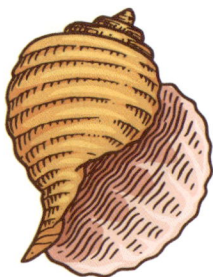

your true form can I treat you." Beixiu responded, "I'm afraid to scare you if I show my true form." The doctor said, "I will not." Thus Beixiu transformed back to the form of dragon. The doctor had never seen dragon before. However, when he took a close look at the dragon, he found the dragon looked quite genial. Thus he asked it to twine around the pillar in the clinic, with head downward, in order to do surgery.

The daughter of the doctor saw the dragon from upstairs. Out of curiosity, she got scissors and paper and cut out a paper dragon. From then on, when people draw dragons or engrave dragons on the pillars in the house, they would follow the look of this paper dragon. After the doctor completed the operation, he said to the dragon, "Your eye needs time to recuperate. You should eat some waxberries every year." Beixiu nodded, thanked the doctor and went back to the Dragon Pit to heal his wounds.

Then the incident of Beixiu's eye injury was learnt by the Dragon King in the East Sea. In a rage, the Dragon King trapped the green dragon under a mountain, which is exactly the Green Dragon Mountain in Xifeng Village of Jintang.

When Beixiu's eye was healed, he married the niece of the Dragon King. Whenever waxberries were ripe, Beixiu would bring the sons and daughters of the Dragon King to eat waxberries. When they came, the northwest wind would blow suddenly on the sea, the waves would roll, and the waxberries all over the mountain would fall down from the trees. People would say, "It is because Beixiu come to eat waxberries."

29. 棕绳龙

　　过去,有一条船沉到海底,烂掉了,抛锚用的棕绳呒没烂。天长日久,棕绳变成了一条龙。这条棕绳龙是一条好龙,镇守着镇海关,一直到伏龙山,不让大风大浪侵犯。

　　这一年,镇海口外有一只龙虾也修炼成龙了,就想夺取镇海关,和棕绳龙打了起来,棕绳龙五爪伸出去,把龙虾的头罩牢了。龙虾伸出虾须,把棕绳龙一只眼睛刺伤了。棕绳龙疯狂起来,爪牙一用劲,把龙虾捏死了。

　　棕绳龙忖起镇海有位名医叶天士,就变成一个秀才去求医。

　　叶天士一看这秀才,心中有数,讲:"侬来求医,医眼睛我是会医,但侬一定要讲出侬的来历。"

　　棕绳龙讲:"我是本地人。"

　　叶天士讲:"勿是人,我看得出,讲出真话来,我给侬医,勿讲出真话,我医也医勿好。"

　　棕绳龙呒没办法,只好讲出自家来历。叶天士一听,把其带到一间小屋去看。叶医生有一个囡,已经有十八九岁,人蛮聪明,叶天士先对其讲好:"侬走到窗头去看看,等晌一个秀才现真身,侬用笔把其描落来。"囡答应了。

　　叶天士对棕绳龙讲:"侬现出真身来,我好给侬医眼睛。"

　　棕绳龙现出一只龙头,头里有角,两只眼睛凸出,一只

Palm Rope Dragon

Long ago, a vessel sank to the bottom of the sea. The vessel rotted away while the palm rope did not. As time went by, the palm rope turned into a dragon. It was a benign dragon, guarding the gate of Zhenhai, and all the way stretching to Mount Fulong. It protected the region from violent storms and waves.

One year, outside Zhenhai Estuary dwelt a lobster who had been practicing and transformed into a dragon. It tried to usurp the gate of Zhenhai. Thus it scuffled with the Palm Rope Dragon. Sticking out five claws, the Palm Rope Dragon caged the head of the lobster, which stuck out palpus to wound one eye of the Palm Rope Dragon. Becoming violent, the Palm Rope Dragon crushed the lobster to death with its claws.

The Palm Rope Dragon thought of a famous doctor named Ye Tianshi in Zhenhai. Thus it transformed into a scholar to see him.

Doctor Ye got some idea of the scholar at the first glance. He said, "You came to me to seek treatment. I can heal your eye injury, but you must let me know your past history. "

The Palm Rope Dragon replied, "I'm a local."

In disbelief, Doctor Ye said, "I can tell you are not a human being. Tell me the truth, and I can heal you. Otherwise, it's beyond my ability."

The Palm Rope Dragon had no choice but to tell the doctor about its background. After getting to know everything, Doctor Ye took the scholar to a closet. Doctor Ye had a daughter, in her

二、舟山龙神话

伤了。

只现出一个龙头，身体还是秀才身体。

这辰光，叶天士的囡囡在窗头外面偷偷把龙头描下来了，等其描好，叶天士已把棕绳龙的一只眼睛医好了。

以后，各地方行会，抬出龙来，龙头统是一式一样，因为统是照叶天士的囡囡描的样子做的。就是尾巴没一定，有的弯上，有的弯落，有的三叉，有的二叉，七奇八怪，各式各样的都有，因为呒没人亲眼看见过龙身龙尾巴。

highteen. She was a very smart girl. To her Doctor Ye said, "Go stand outside the window and look in. A scholar will transform into its true form. Sketch it with your brush." She agreed.

Doctor Ye said to the scholar, "Show your true form, and then I can treat your eye."

The scholar showed a head of a dragon, with two horns and two eyes bulging, one of which was wounded.

With the head of a dragon being revealed, the scholar maintained his human body.

The daughter of Doctor Ye secretly sketched the head of the dragon outside of the window. When she completed the sketch, Doctor Ye had already healed the eye of the dragon.

From then on, when dragons are carried out in festival fairs in different regions, we can see the looks of the heads of dragons are the same. It is because they all follow the sketch drawn by the daughter of Doctor Ye. However, there is no fixed shape for the dragons' tails: some sticking upwards, some sticking downwards, some three prongs, some two prongs, with all sorts of strange shapes. It is simply because no one has seen a dragon's tail with his own eyes.

二、舟山龙神话

30. 泾河老龙

　　泾河老龙原来是分管人间旱涝的龙,有一年,玉帝对其说:"今年勿准落雨,让老百姓吃点苦头。"泾河老龙看老百姓苦勿过,又不敢违抗玉帝命令,只好每夜落露水,落下的露水像小雨一样。老百姓夜里把衣裳外面放着,露水落下来,第二天天亮绞点吃吃,这样统吭没渴煞,地里种的东西也都吭没晒煞。

　　有一天,鬼谷仙师在城里的河底种茄,正巧泾河老龙从河边路过,看见他在河底种茄,故意问:"老伯,河底种茄,要淹死咯。"鬼谷仙师讲:"勿会淹死咯,雨还有六个月好停。六个月旱过,啥东西勿好收上。等我茄吃好,茄秆拔掉,其再落雨。"泾河老龙听其这么一讲,交关不服气,心忖:侬讲淹勿死,我偏要淹侬煞,跟侬比个高低。

Old Dragon of Jinghe River

The old dragon of Jinghe River was originally a dragon in charge of drought and flood in the world. One year, the Jade Emperor said to him, "Don't make rain this year, and let the people suffer." The old dragon of Jinghe River saw that the common people were suffering and did not dare to disobey the orders of the Jade Emperor, so he had to drop dew every night. The falling dew was like a light rain. People left their clothes outside at night when the dew fell down, and they twisted some water out of the soaked clothes at dawn the next day, so that there was no thirst, and the things planted in the fields were not dried.

One day, Priest Guigu was planting eggplants at the bottom of the river in the city when the old dragon happened to pass by. The old dragon saw him planting eggplants at the bottom of the river and deliberately asked, "Pop, these eggplants planted at the bottom of the river are going to be drown." Priest Guigu said, "That's unlikely. It won't rain for another six months. After six months of drought, everything will be harvested. After my eggplants are eaten, the eggplant stalks are pulled out and it will rain again." The old dragon was unconvinced when he heard what Priest Guigu said. He thought, "You said the eggplants were not to die after flooding. I must let you have a taste of flood to see who is right."

The common people would barely survive as there was no rain for a long time. One day, the Jade Emperor said to the old dragon, "It has been dry for many days. Give them some rain." The old

二、舟山龙神话

长期勿落雨,老百姓快熬不过啦。有一天,玉帝对泾河老龙讲:"已经旱介多日子啦,侬去落点雨吧。"泾河老龙问:"这雨咋落落?"玉帝讲:"少许落点,只落十分,城里落三分,城外落七分;初一落小雨,初二落大雨。"

这时,鬼谷仙师的茄已经快收啦,其也晓得玉帝让落点雨,城里三分,城外七分;初一小雨,初二大雨,共落十分,落介点点雨,茄淹勿死,其交关放心。泾河老龙只顾跟鬼谷仙师比高低,特意掉个头,城里落七分,城外落三分;初一落大雨,初二落小雨。玉帝让其落十分,其听成百分。雨水太多啦。城里有城门,水流得慢,城里淹没,鬼谷仙师的茄子统余去了。鬼谷仙师到玉帝面前奏一本,玉帝下令让鬼谷仙师去斩泾河老龙。

泾河老龙后悔猛,为了几株茄子,闯下大祸。其跑到唐皇李世民地方求情,唐皇说:"鬼谷仙师那里我会想办法咯,侬现在还是快逃吧。"泾河老龙听唐皇这么一说,就逃跑啦。

唐皇送出泾河老龙,把鬼谷仙师请来,故意请其吃老酒,使其打瞌睡。过去斩人都有时辰,时辰一过就斩勿

dragon asked, "How?" The Jade Emperor said, "Don't give them too much. Give them a total of ten portions, assigning three of them to the city, the other seven to the areas outside the city. Let light rain fall on the first day of lunar month and let heavy rain fall on the second day."

At this time, the eggplants of Guigu were almost ripe enough to be harvested, and he also knew that the Jade Emperor allowed the rainfall, with three portions in the city and seven portions outside the city, and there was light rain on the first day of the month and heavy rain on the second day of the month, a total of ten; with so little rain, Guigu assured that the eggplants would not be flooded. The Old Dragon of Jinghe River, only obsessed about competing with Guigu, deliberatly changed his plan, giving seven portions in the city and the other three outside the city. It rained heavily on the first day of lunar month and drizzled on the second day. The Jade Emperor let him give ten portions in total but he mistook it as one hundred. There was too much rain. There was a gate in the city, in which the water flowed slowly, so the city was flooded. And the eggplants of Guigu had gone. Guigu reported the issue to the Jade Emperor, who ordered him to behead the old dragon.

The Old Dragon of Jinghe River was greatly regretful about the fact that he ran into such great trouble just because of a few eggplants. He came to the Tang Emperor Li Shimin in order to ask him to intercede for him. The emperor said, "I will deal with Priest Guigu. You'd better run away now." The old dragon ran away after he heard what the emperor said.

The Tang Emperor sent out the old dragon before inviting Priest Guigu, and deliberately treated him to wine so that he would doze off. In the past, beheading should be executed at a predetermined moment, past which the action would not be carried out. Guigu

二、舟山龙神话

来的。鬼谷仙师老酒吃饱，伏在桌上困着啦。可唐皇不晓得，其人困了，其灵魂已走出，在赶泾河老龙，一个逃，一个赶。唐皇只见鬼谷仙师伏在桌上，挥汗如雨，就用扇扇其三扇。三扇扇过，鬼谷仙师困得更熟啦，正好赶上泾河老龙，在梦里把老龙头斩落。鬼谷仙师醒后对唐皇说："侬真友好，多亏侬助我三扇，使我赶到，泾河老龙头被我斩落，在午朝门外吊着呢。"

唐皇一听，马上到午朝门外去看，泾河老龙头虽脱落，嘴巴还含着口血，等唐皇一靠近，其"吃"一记，一口鲜血统统喷到唐皇脸上。泾河老龙狠猛，大骂："侬有介刻薄，向侬求情，侬反助其三扇。"唐皇吓煞啦，好几天不还魂。

唐皇醒过后，感到交关对不住泾河老龙。为了纪念其，在屋檐、庙宇、宫殿的屋脊头上，统描上泾河老龙的头，这风俗一直传到现在。

drank the wine till he was full and fell asleep at the table. But the emperor did not know that his soul left the body to run after the old dragon despite the fact that he was asleep. One was fleeing and the other chasing. The Tang Emperor saw Guigu lying on the table, sweating. So he fanned him to cool him down. After that, Guigu fell into deeper sleep. Just at this moment Guigu caught up with the old dragon and cut off his head in the dream. After waking up, Guigu said to the emperor, "You are really nice. Thanks for cooling me down so that I can make it. I arrived. I cut off the old dragon's head and hung it over the city gate."

Hearing this, the Tang Emperor immediately went to the gate to have a look. Although the old dragon was beheaded, his mouth still contained blood. As soon as the Tang Emperor approached, all blood was sprayed on the emperor's face. The old dragon was fierce and cursed, "You were so mean that you made him cool down despite the fact that previously I asked you for help." The Tang Emperor was so scared that he did not recover for several days.

After the Tang Emperor recovered, he felt extremely sorry for the old dragon. In memory of it, the head of the Old Dragon of Jinghe River was painted on the ridge of eaves, temples and palaces. This custom has been passed down to the present.

31. 水底眼

现在捕鱼有鱼探机,能测到海底的鱼群,其实,鱼探机就是渔人常讲的"水底眼"。过去抲鱼希望有个"水底眼",所以才有这样一个故事。

从前,燕窝岛有个小囝,屋里穷,日脚难过,十五岁就到长元船上去当了"二浆"。

有一日,这只船抲到一条鱼,交关好看,它全身鱼鳞金黄铮亮,背脊墩有条鲜红鲜红的花纹,头顶红彤彤,嘴唇黄澄澄,唇边有两条又细又长的胡须,黄鱼勿像黄鱼,鲤鱼勿像鲤鱼,有七八斤重。船上的伙计从未见过这种鱼,长元老大说这是黄神鱼,叫二浆囝把鱼杀掉烧鱼羹,让大家尝尝鲜,补补神,夜里好抲大网头。

到了夜里,网张落抲鱼,船上的伙计趁空都钻进舱里歇歇力,打个盹,只有二浆囝看着黄神鱼发呆,心忖,介好看的一条鱼杀掉烧鱼羹多可惜! 他心里勿舍得,手里拿起鲞刀,"嚓嚓"磨了两下,就要动手剖鱼,吓得黄神鱼乱蹦乱跳。二浆囝抲来抲去抲勿着,仔细一看,这条鱼流出眼泪,眼泪"唰唰"地流。二浆囝奇怪煞了,别的鱼抲上来,勿管侬杀也好,勿杀也好,勿会出眼泪,难道这条鱼通灵性! 这囝心软了,放下鲞刀,用手去揩黄神鱼的眼泪,自说自话:"莫哭,莫哭,我放侬回去!"他双手捧起黄神鱼,轻轻地放回海里,还拿起鲞刀,用力在舱板

Underwater Eyes

Now there are fish detectors that can detect fish on the bottom. The fish detector is what fishermen often call the underwater eye. In the past, fishermen wanted to have underwater eyes, so there is a story.

Once upon a time, there was a boy on Yanwo Island who was poor and lived a hard life, so he went to work as a second oarsman on a boat at the age of 15.

One day, they caught a fish, which was very beautiful. The scales of the fish were golden and shiny, there was a bright red pattern on the back, the top of the head was red, the lips were yellow, and there were two long and thin whiskers around the lips. Not like a yellow croaker and not like a carp, full of seven or eight pounds. The crew had never seen this kind of fish before. The boss said this was the yellow god fish, and told the second oarsman to kill the fish to make fish soup for everyone to taste so that they could feel energetic to catch fish at night.

At night, after casting the nets in the sea, the crew took the time to go into the cabin to rest. Only the second oarsman looked at the yellow god fish, dumbfounded, thinking, "It is such a pity to kill such a beautiful fish to make fish soup." Although he did not want to, he picked up the knife sharpened twice to kill the fish, and the fish thrashed around hearing the sound. The second oarsman grabbed the fish, took a closer look, and saw the fish's tears flowing. He felt very strange because other fish whether to be killed or not to be killed would not shed tears. Was this fish spiritual? He was

　　　　　　　　　　　　　二、舟山龙神话

墩上"笃笃笃"斩了三刀。这是故意斩给长元老大听的。

黄神鱼放回海里,"骨碌"一转,又浮上来,对着二浆团,把头点了三点,开口讲话了:"侬救我一命,我也呒啥好报答侬,我哭出来的眼泪水,侬眼睛去揩揩,对侬会有用处!"

真稀奇,这条鱼咋会开口讲话呢?原来这条黄神鱼是东海龙王的三公主,今朝她偷偷摸摸逃出龙宫,东看看,西望望,一时贪玩,勿小心撞进网里了。二浆团回到前舱一看,果真舱板墩上还有眼泪水,他用手揩来一把眼泪水,放在自家眼睛里一擦,这一擦,只觉得眼前一片锃亮,黑夜变成了白天,黑暗中看东西煞清爽。再朝海里看看,海底里是鱼是礁,也看得清清爽爽,明明白白,二浆团的眼睛变成"水底眼"了。他越发稀奇煞了,伏在船边,望着海水出神。突然看到一群大黄鱼朝这边游来。

他大声喊了起来:"老大,有黄鱼,快放网!"

老大勿相信:"侬这个小团,晓得啥东西?"

"勿会错,我看见是群大黄鱼,侬放网好了。"

老大半信半疑,张一网就张一网试试,果然,抲上来满满一网大黄鱼。从此,二浆团指到那里,老大就抲到那里,网网勿落空,上来的鱼要比别人多得多,生意特别好。

这样一来,"水底眼"出名了,燕窝岛的渔民统跟他出海抲鱼,日脚越过越兴旺,大家统感激二浆团。这可把东海龙王吓煞了,赶紧把乌龟丞相找来,商量对策。乌龟丞相说:"这事难办,二浆团救过三公主的命,三公主赠他一对神眼珠,成了'水底眼'。"他把三公主咋出宫,咋落网遇救的事向龙王讲了一遍。

龙王想了想说:"救命之恩要报,但神眼珠一定要收回!"

soft-hearted and put down the knife, wiped the tears of the yellow fish with his hand, and said, "Do not cry. Do not cry. I will set you free." He picked up the yellow fish with both hands and gently put it back into the sea. Then he picked up the knife on the cabin board and cut three times, which was deliberately let the boss listen.

The yellow gold fish returned to the sea, and came up to the second oarsman, nodded three times and said, "You have saved my life. I have nothing to repay you. You can use my tears to wipe your eyes. It will be useful to you."

Strangely, how could this fish speak? It turned out that this fish was the East Sea Dragon King's third daughter. That day she secretly escaped from the Dragon Palace to see around, and accidentally fell into the net. The second oarsman returned to the cabin to take a look and found tears on the cabin board. He grabbed a handful of tears and wiped his eyes. After wiping, he felt a bright in front of the eyes, the night changed into daytime, and he could see things clearly in the dark. And when he then looked at the bottom of the sea, the bottom of the fish and reefs could be seen clearly. His eyes became underwater eyes. He felt stranger and stranger lying on the side of the boat, staring at the sea. Suddenly he saw a school of big yellow croakers swimming towards him.

He shouted out, "Boss, there are yellow croakers. Cast the net."

The boss didn't believe him and said, "What do you know?"

"It's true. I see a school of yellow croakers. You just cast the net."

The boss was half-convinced, and then he cast the net in and caught a net full of yellow croakers. From then on, he would cast the net wherever the second oarsman pointed. He caught more fish than anyone else, and his business was good.

In this way, the underwater eye became famous. All the fishermen of Yanwo Island went fishing with him. Life was getting better and better, and everyone was grateful to the second oarsman. The Dragon King of the East Sea was frightened, and he

二、舟山龙神话

乌龟丞相讲："收回神眼珠，二浆团就会双目失明，恐怕三公主勿肯！"

龙王急得团团转，勿晓得咋弄弄好！还是乌龟丞相歪点子多，他对龙王如此这般讲了一番，龙王点点头说："事到如今，只好如此了。"

一日，二浆团出海抲鱼，突然刮来一阵大风，一个浪头把他卷到海里去了。二浆团只觉得昏天黑地，随浪漂去，勿晓得漂到啥地方。他睁开眼睛一看，只见面前有幢富丽堂皇的宫殿，乌龟丞相站在门前，把他接进宫殿里。宫殿里老早摆好一桌酒筵。乌龟丞相客客气气请二浆团入席，端起酒杯向二浆团道喜，说龙王要招他当驸马，二浆团听得朓头朓绪，眼睛瞪得老大，呆煞了。龟相眯眯笑笑说："煞通灵性的黄神鱼，就是龙王的三公主，侬救过她的命，龙王才答应招你当驸马！"

二浆团起先忖忖蛮高兴，后来一忖，勿对，龙公主咋会嫁给一个穷渔民："公主是金枝玉叶，到人间去吃勿起苦！"他讲好就要往外走。龟相赶紧上前拦住："已经来了，甭再走了！"二浆团勿肯，一定要去。龟相一急，态度变了，起面孔喝道："龙王有旨，勿愿留在龙宫，只好收回神眼珠！"他一招手，出来一群乌贼，围住二浆团直喷乌墨，二浆团只觉得眼乌珠火辣辣地痛，痛得他昏倒在地。

勿晓得过了多少辰光，二浆团才缓过气来，发觉自己躺在海滩上，两只眼睛已经瞎了。

龙公主得知了，急匆匆赶来一看，只见二浆团躺在海滩上双目失明，神色难看，心里交关难熬，她上去扶起二浆团说："走，阿拉到屋里去！"

二浆团听声音是三公主来了，心里又感激又难熬，说自己

called the Turtle Prime Minister to discuss countermeasures. The Turtle Prime Minister said, "This is difficult. The second oarsman had saved the life of the third princess, so the third princess gave him a pair of divine eyes which became the underwater eyes." He told the Dragon King how the third princess went out of the palace and how she was saved by the second oarsman.

The Dragon King thought about it and said, "We have to repay the kindness of saving our lives, but we have to take back the divine eyes."

The Turtle Prime Minister said, "If we take back the eyes, the second oarsman will lose his eyesight, which the third princess will not agree with."

The Dragon King was so anxious that he didn't know what to do. The Turtle Prime Minister told the Dragon King an idea. The dragon king nodded his head and said, "We have no choice but to do so."

One day, when the second oarsman was out fishing, a big wind came and swept him into the sea. He felt dizzy and didn't know where he had been drifted. When he opened his eyes, he saw a magnificent palace in front of him, and the Turtle Prime Minister was standing in front of the door, taking him into the palace. In the palace, there was a banquet set up a long time ago. The Turtle Prime Minister invited the second oarsman to the banquet and told him that the Dragon King wanted him to be his son-in-law. The second oarsman was stunned after hearing this. The Turtle Prime Minister smiled and said, "The yellow gold fish is the third princess of the Dragon King, and you saved her life, so the Dragon King promised to make you his son-in-law."

At first, the second oarsman was happy, but then he thought, "No, why would a dragon princess marry a poor fisherman?" He said, "The princess is a descendant of royal family, and she will suffer if she goes to the mortal world!" He was going to go out after saying so. The Turtle Prime Minister rushed to stop him, "As

　　　　　　　　　　　　　　　二、舟山龙神话

眼睛瞎了，勿愿连累三公主，催她快回龙宫去，别管他。三公主听他口气交关坚决，忖了忖说："好，侬一定要我回去，先让我看看侬的眼睛！"

二浆团只好答应，便躺在海滩上。三公主把嘴巴一张，"噗"一声，吐出一颗龙珠，落在二浆团的眼睛上，一转眼工夫，二浆团眼睛里的毒汁都让龙珠吸去了，眼睛又亮了，可是，龙珠变黑了。三公主失去龙珠，浑身发软，"扑通"一声，跌坐在沙滩上，眼泪汪汪地说："龙珠失明，我只好回龙宫养身，侬我再也难见面了！"二浆团也交关难熬，扶住三公主，勿晓得咋弄弄好！三公主脸色煞白，微微一笑说："侬双目复明，我也放心了，待我回到龙宫，恳求父王，每日奉献海产万担，算是报答侬的救命之恩！"讲好，"哗"一声，现出龙形，游到海里去了。

据说，后来海龙王只好答应每日奉献海产万担，算是报答二浆团的救命之恩。

long as you've come, don't go anymore!" But the second oarsman insisted on going. The Turtle Prime Minister changed his attitude and shouted, "The Dragon King has decreed that if you don't want to stay in the Dragon Palace, then you have to give back the divine eyes!" At his beck and call, a group of squids came out and surrounded the second oarsman, spraying ink toward his eyes. The second oarsman felt great pain in his eyes and fainted on the ground.

It took him a long time to recover from the pain. He found himself lying on the beach, blind in both eyes.

The third princess came, and saw him lying on the beach with his eyes blinded. She was so upset that she picked him up and said, "Come on. Let's go to the house!"

When he heard the voice of the third princess, he was grateful and sad. He said he was blind and didn't want to get her into trouble, so he urged her to go back to the Dragon Palace and leave him alone. The princess found his tone very determined, thought for a while, and said, "Well, since you insist on letting me go back, let me see your eyes first!" The second oarsman agreed and lay on the beach. The third princess spit out a dragon pearl that fell on the second oarsman's eyes. In a flash, the dragon pearl sucked all the poison out of his eyes and they became bright again. The third princess without the pearl fell on the beach with tears in her eyes, saying, "The pearl is gone, so I'll have to go back to the Dragon Palace to recuperate, and we'll never see each other again." The second oarsman was also very sad. He held the third princess and didn't know what to do. The third princess looked pale, but smiled faintly and said, "When I return to the Dragon Palace, I will ask my father to sacrifice 10,000 quintals of seafood every day to repay you for saving my life!" After saying that, she turned into the dragon shape, and swam back to the sea.

It is said that the Dragon King promised to give 10,000 quintals of seafood every day to repay the kindness of the second oarsman.

　　　　　　　　二、舟山龙神话

32. 龙外孙的故事

　　东海渔民喜欢打扮自己的渔船。船舷两侧画着漂亮的图案，船屁股常画着一条海泥鳅。俗话说："屁小小泥鳅，掀不起大浪。"渔民为啥画条海泥鳅呢？

　　从前，东海龙宫有条敲更鱼，生得黑不溜秋，经年累月在龙宫里敲更报时。眼看龙子龙孙成双配对，他年过三十，还是光棍一条。一年到头，抱着个冷锣，为龙宫里敲更锣，走呀，走呀……想起自己的身世，他不禁眼泪嗒嗒滴，唱着悲凉的五更调。

　　有一天晚上，明亮的月光，照着白玉铺地的水晶路。悲凉的五更调从远处传来，惊动了深居珠楼的彩珠龙女。这位龙女年纪已到婚配之期，还未受聘。平常，她又寸步不离珠楼，从不与外界接触。每当她听到冷冰冰的更声和凄惨的曲调，心里就有一种说不出来的滋味，有时，竟伤心地哭了起来。似乎敲更鱼叹咏的正是自己心头想要倒出来的苦水。一个月亮夜，彩珠龙女在珠楼的楼台上赏月，正好同敲更鱼打了个照面。龙女羞答答地看了敲更鱼一眼，就进了珠楼，敲更鱼像抛了锚，傻乎乎地呆在那里。

　　敲更鱼简直不相信自己的眼睛，难道一阵风把月亮里的嫦娥吹下海来？还是天上的仙女到龙宫里来采珠？虽然，他也偷看过一些美丽的龙女公主，却没有一个比她更美。他想，

The Legend of the Dragon's Grandson

Fishermen in the East China Sea like to decorate their fishing boats. Beautiful patterns are painted on both sides of the boat, and a sea loach is often painted on the bottom of the boat. As the saying goes, "A little loach can't lift big waves." Why do fishermen draw a loach?

Once upon a time, there was a totally black fish in the Dragon Palace in the East China Sea, whose job was to strike a gong to tell the hour. Seeing that the children and the grandchildren of the dragon were all married, he was over 30 years old and still single, all the year round, holding a cold gong, walking around the Dragon Palace, knocking the gong for them. When thinking of his life experience, he couldn't help crying and singing the sad tune of *Wu Geng*.

One night, the bright moonlight shone on the crystal road paved with white jade. The sad tune came from a distance, disturbing the dragon princess of Caizhu who lived in the Pearl Building. The princess had reached the age of marriage but was still single. Usually she never left the Pearl Building and never exposed herself to the outside world. Whenever she heard cold gong sounds and sad tunes, there was an indescribable feeling in her heart. Sometimes, she was so sad that she burst into tears. It seemed what the fish sang completely matched her bitter feeling. One moon night, the princess was enjoying the moon on the balcony of her building, just in time to meet the fish. She looked at

the fish shyly and went into the building. The fish seemed to be anchored to where he was and stayed there foolishly.

The fish could hardly believe his eyes. Did a gust of wind blow Chang'e in the moon into the sea? Or did the fairy in the sky come to the Dragon Palace to collect pearls? Although he also peeked at some beautiful dragon princesses, none of them were more beautiful than her. He thought that the princess might come out again, so he just raised his head and looked up, looking, looking. After two hours passed, she still didn't come out. Was it true that she was Chang'e in the sky and had returned to the Moon Palace? Seeing that the fifth watch was approaching, he had to leave the Pearl Building with a gong in his arms and go to the Grand Marshal's Office to report the tide.

From then on, it seemed that the fish was bewitched. Every night, he would pass by the Pearl Building, thinking that she would appear eventually. However, three months passed and the princess had not yet shown up. Why? The fish thought over and over. Tantu Fish was well informed and came to tell him that the princess was put under house arrest by the Dragon King because she was caught enjoying the moon, which was not allowed. The fish had no more illusions about the matter. However, he was so lovesick that he became skinny. Soon he died of depression. On his deathbed, he said to his good friend Tantu Fish, "Although I can't see the princess again when I am still alive, I want to accompany her when I am dead." So he asked his friend to bury its body under the Pearl Building. Tantu Fish did what he wanted to do.

Soon after, the place where the fish was buried grew a rare sea tree. This tree was like a cycas and also like a bamboo. It grew very fast. In less than half a month, the branches climbed to the window of the Pearl Building. One night, the sea tree suddenly blossomed. The one at the top of the tree was very big and beautiful.

二、舟山龙神话

这龙女也许还会在珠楼上出现,就一直呆呆地抬着头,朝上面望着,望呀,望呀,一更过去了,龙女还是没有出来。难道真的是天上嫦娥回到月宫里去了?眼看五更将近,他只得抱着更锣,离开珠楼,到大元帅府去报潮。

从此,敲更鱼像中了邪。天天晚上到珠楼下面来探望。他想,总有一天龙女会露面。三个月过去了,龙女还没有露面。这是什么缘故呢?敲更鱼想得神思昏昏。还是弹涂鱼消息灵通,跑来告诉他,说是龙女赏月,被人知道,报告龙王,龙王已把公主关起来了。敲更鱼这才死了心。然而,他已相思成疾,瘦得皮包骨头像根灯芯草,不久就郁郁闷闷地死了。临死前,他向好朋友弹涂鱼说:"生不能再见公主一面,死了也得陪伴在她身旁。"他要求弹涂鱼把他的尸体埋葬在彩珠龙女的珠楼下。弹涂鱼依照他的心愿做了。

过了不久,珠楼下埋鱼的地方,居然长出一株千年罕见的大海树来。这株树又像铁树又像翠竹,一个劲往上长,长得特别快,不到半个月,枝头攀上了珠楼窗口。有一天晚上,海树突然开花了。树顶的那一朵特别大,特别好看。黑油油的好像郁金香,十里外闻得到香气。彩珠公主闻到这阵阵香气,像是喝醉了酒,她伸手在窗口采下此花,用嘴细细地嚼着,花汁像仙露般甜蜜。嚼着,嚼着,不知不觉,龙女把整个花朵吃到肚子里去了。想不到,过了不久,彩珠龙女怀了孕,肚皮一日比一日大起来。这件事被当作一桩龙宫秘闻,很快传开来,不久,龙王也得知了。龙王是个暴君,当然不能容忍这种丑事。他气势汹汹地提着鱼肠剑赶到珠楼来杀公主。公主深感委屈,她纵有千张嘴也说不清楚,吓得嘴唇雪白,战战兢兢,像虾漭直不起腰来。正当龙王举剑要杀的辰光,彩珠龙女肚皮内

Shing black, it looked like a tulip, and you could smell the fragrance ten miles away. The princess smelled the fragrance, as if she was drunk. She stretched out her hand to pick the flower at the window and chewed it carefully. The flower juice was as sweet as fairy dew. Chewing, chewing, unconsciously, she ate the whole flower into the stomach. Unexpectedly, the princess became pregnant and her belly grew bigger and bigger day by day. As a secret story of the Dragon Palace, it soon spread, and soon the Dragon King also learned about it. The king was a tyrant. Of course, he couldn't tolerate this scandal. He rushed to the Pearl Building with Fish Intestine Sword to kill the princess. The princess felt deepy wronged. Even if she had a thousand mouths, she couldn't tell clearly. She was so scared that her lips were white and trembling, and she couldn't stand up like a shrimp. Just as the Dragon King was about to raise his sword to kill her, the baby suddenly shouted in the belly of the princess, "Don't kill me! Don't kill me! I'll come out myself." At this point, a black smoke came out of the princess's mouth and slowly turned into a green cloud. A monster like a dragon but not a dragon and a fish but not a fish flew in the green cloud. This was a sea loach.

The sea loach, with black skin and smooth body, opened his mouth and spewed out a mouthful of mud, making a mess of the building. The Dragon King became angry and ordered all the soldiers to come and arrest it. But because he was as smooth as oil, no one could capture him. He jumped into the Dragon King's ear, and got into the dragon belly and lung all the way, biting and tearing at random. The Dragon King was the king of the sea. How could he stand this ordeal? He had to beg him for mercy, asking him to come out and promising to raise him to Fish Emperor, who would govern all kinds of fish and grass in the East China Sea. All kinds of fish would respect him. The loach just emerged from the

忽然传出婴儿的喊声："别杀！别杀！我自己出来。"说着公主嘴里冒出一股黑烟，慢慢地变成一朵青云，青云里飞腾着一条似龙非龙、似鱼非鱼的怪物。这就是海泥鳅。

　　海泥鳅，肤黑似漆，全身光滑，一张嘴，喷出满嘴污泥，把个好端端的珠楼弄得一塌糊涂，龙王发怒了，命令各路将兵前来捉拿。但因他光滑似油，谁也擒他不住。只见他七跳八跳跳进了龙王的耳朵里，一直钻进了龙肚龙肺，乱咬乱扯一通。龙王乃是九五之尊，怎经得起这折腾，只得向他求饶，请他出来，封他做鱼皇帝，管辖东海各类鱼草，不论穿鳞袍的有鳞鱼，还是穿油袍的无鳞鱼，都要让他三分。海泥鳅这才从龙王耳孔里钻出来。至于龙王毁约，偷偷把他赶到海泥涂，那是后来的事了。但它钻到龙王肚里去捣心捣肺的事也着实使众水族有点心惊肉跳，所以，海里不管多么凶恶的大鱼，见到海泥鳅都急忙躲避，不敢扰乱。捕鱼人出于安全第一的考虑，就在船屁股上画条海泥鳅以求大吉大利。

dragon's ear. As for the Dragon King's breaking his promise and secretly driving him to a muddy place, it was part of a story to be recounted later. However, the fact that it went into the Dragon King's belly to pound its heart and lungs really made all the submarine creatures a little scared. Therefore, no matter how ferocious the big fish in the sea were, they hurried to escape when they saw the loach, and did not dare to disturb him. The fisherman who took safety into consideration would draw a loach on the bottom of the boat for good luck.

33. 龙王嫁女

　　泗礁岛在古代叫"马迹山"，样子像匹马，马屁股在马关岙。勿晓得哪一个朝代，马关岙出了个小后生，名叫马郎。有一天，马郎到海边赶潮，看见一条生得七棱八角浑身披金鳞的怪鱼，搁在浅滩里。有一只老虎从山顶窜落来，要吃那条搁滩的怪鱼。马郎看见怪鱼眼泪汪汪好像在求情，他就飞射出一把雪亮的渔叉，把大老虎赶跑了。

　　怪鱼得救了，马郎意想不到得到了一份厚报。原来，这条怪鱼是误了潮搁滩的老龙王。龙王为了感谢马郎的救命之恩，就把最心爱的小囡嫁给他做老婆。

　　龙王要嫁女了，龙宫里很热闹。嫁妆摆满了十里海街。

　　珍珠、玛瑙、珊瑚自不必讲，就说那顶大花轿，用了三千六百九十九颗猫儿眼宝珠串成，远远看去像一块碧玉，临近看看又像花轿，真是海中宝贝。龙王还叫大鱼在前面鸣锣开道，金鸡在旁边引颈高叫，并派出黄龙和五龙两位龙太子为龙公主保驾护轿。四只海老鼠抬着大花轿，吹吹打打，离开龙宫朝马关岙方向走来。

　　轿到基湖大海湾，突然从高山上窜下来一只大老虎，把四只海老鼠吓昏脱了。原来，在基湖四角凉亭旁有个老虎潭，里面住着一只大老虎。那一天，怪鱼快成为老虎口中之食，被马郎救走，老虎交关仇恨。今末夜头，听说马郎要抬新娘子，故

The Dragon King Getting His Daughter Married

In ancient times, Sijiao Island was called Majishan. It shaped like a horse, whose rump was located in Maguan Gully. Nobody knows in which dynasty, there was a young man named Ma Lang born in Maguan Gully. One day, while Ma Lang was gathering seafood on the beach, he caught sight of a grotesque and golden-scaled fish, getting stranded. At that time, a tiger rushed from the top of the mountain and was about to eat the stranded fish. Ma Lang saw the fish look like begging for his mercy, with its eyes wet with tears. He hurled a shiny harpoon and the tiger was driven away.

The grotesque fish was saved, and Ma Lang got a generous reward unexpectantly. It turned out that the fish was the Old Dragon King who was stranded because he missed the tide. In order to express his gratitude to the young man for saving his life, he wanted to marry his beloved daughter to him.

The Dragon King was going to marry his daughter off, and an atmosphere of jollification hanged over his palace. The dowry spread all over the street in the sea.

Not to mention pearls, agates, corals, the bridal sedan chair was indeed a treasure in the sea; it was strung together with three thousand six hundred ninety nine opals. It looked like a jade afar, and a sedan chair closely. The Dragon King ordered Biggie Fish to pave the way ahead, and Golden Pheasant to crane its neck to crow. Meanwhile, two dragon princes Huanglong and Wulong were dispatched to escort the princess. Four sea mice carried the sedan

　　　　　　　　　　　　　　　二、舟山龙神话

意出来捣蛋。俗话讲,老鼠怕猫。老虎样子像猫,威势更比猫凶恶。这老虎嗷叫,把四只海老鼠镇吓住了。老鼠身子往下一沉,只露出了一个头,在海面东张西望,观看动静。龙女的轿子停下来,不动了!

龙女出嫁,半路上是不能停下来的。这样一停,停了几千年,再也没有往前挪动半步。马郎在马关岙,头朝浪岗,一直望着新娘的花轿到来。望呀,望呀,日子一长,成了个石人像。现在,马关岙还有这个石人像,叫马郎礁。

前来送小姊出嫁的五龙和黄龙勿晓得半途中会发生介大变故。为使龙女勿受损害,他们就在泗礁岛附近一些小岛定居落来。

至于大鱼和金鸡,一直跑在轿子前头,勿晓得后头发生啥事体。他们见花轿迟迟未来,就跑到金平岛上去歇脚。听老一辈人讲,每当太阳升起辰光,泗礁海湾里,有大鱼蹦出海面,金鸡高叫山头,龙女探头观景,花轿闪闪发光的奇景。

chair and set off from the palace to Maguan Gully, with drums beating and trumpets blowing.

When the bridal sedan chair arrived at Jihu Grand Gulf, a giant tiger rushed down from the mountain suddenly. The four mice were terrorized. It turned out that a tiger lived in a tiger den in Four-feet Pavilion in Jihu. The other day, the tiger was about to make the grotesque fish delicious food. It became revengeful because the fish was saved by Ma Lang at last. This night, it heard that Malang was going to marry, so he came to make trouble deliberately. Common saying goes that rats fear cats. Tigers look like cats, but more ferocious than cats. The roar of the tiger petrified the mice, who sank their bodies, with heads above the sea, looking around to observe the surroundings. Thus the sedan chair of the princess stopped moving ahead but kept still.

It is said that dragon princesses can't stop on their way of being married. So when the princess stopped, she remained there for thousands of years, without moving forward a step anymore. Malang was expecting the arrival of sedan chair all the time by gazing into the distance to the direction of Wave Hillock in Maguan Gully. Even now, there is a stone statue in Maguan Gully, known as Ma Lang Reef.

The princes Wulong and Huanglong, who came to escort their sister, didn't expect such an accident on the way. In order to protect the princess, they settled down in some small islands near Sijiao Island.

As to Biggie Fish and Golden Pheasant, they were far ahead of the sedan chair, thus didn't know what happened behind them. After waiting for the sedan chair for a long time, they went to Jinping Island to take a rest. According to older generations, whenever the sun rises at dawn, in Sijiao Gulf, there would be an extraordinary sight that a giant fish would jump above the sea, a golden pheasant would crow on the top of a mountain, and the dragon princess would lean out of her shiny sedan chair to enjoy the view.

二、舟山龙神话

34. 渔翁斗龙王

　　老早辰光，沈家门还是个荒秃秃的茅草岗，只有一个姓沈的枸鱼老头在这里收篷落脚，靠出海枸鱼度日。

　　这日，枸鱼老头在海上枸鱼，枸来枸去一条鱼也呒没枸着，看看天色快暗了，风浪也大了，刚要歇手拢洋，看见有几只江㓜在不远的海面盘来盘去，心里忖，有江㓜准定有鱼枸，随手把船摇过去枸了一网。勿料又是空网。枸鱼老头忖忖呒趣相，只好网整整打算回去，一整两整，"骨碌"一声，网袋里跌落一颗闪亮的印章。这颗印章是玉石刻的，印章周围盘着一条金龙，龙头翘搭起，嘴巴里含着一粒珍珠。珍珠光头雪雪亮，照在洋面上，当即平风息浪。老头晓得今日宝贝得着了，随手贴身藏好，欢欢喜喜回转屋里去。第二日天亮，老头在茅草岗墩搭了一间草凉棚，把印章挂在棚当中。茅草岗周围的海面上，变得呒风也呒浪，船驶得稳稳当当。枸鱼人看见这块地方好，停下来勿肯走了。呒没几日，茅草岗就住了交关多枸鱼人。

　　这颗玉石印章，原来是玉皇大帝给东海龙王的镇海宝印，龙嘴里含着的是颗定风珠。那日，青龙三太子私自带着宝印到外头游玩，勿小心失落了。龙王丢了宝印，急也急煞，吓也吓煞，生怕玉皇大帝得知，问罪下来，这可咋弄，现在祸已经闯了，只好把三太子绑起来拷打一顿，派虾兵蟹将到各处去寻。

　　虾兵蟹将东寻西寻，角角落落寻遍，总算在茅草岗把其寻

Fisherman Fighting the Dragon King

A long time ago, Shenjiamen was still a barren thatched hillock, only an old man surnamed Shen living here to catch fish for a living.

One day, the old man was fishing in the sea, but he didn't catch a single fish. Seeing that the sky was almost dark, the wind was strong and the waves were big, he prepared to call it a day. Then he saw a few river valves circled in the nearby sea, thinking that there must be fish. He rowed toward it to cast a net. Again there was no fish in the net. The old man felt bored and planned to put away the net to go back. Suddenly, a shiny seal fell from the net with a sound of a bang. This seal was carved with jade, on which a golden dragon was around the seal. The dragon's head was cocked, and the mouth contained a pearl. When the pearl shone brightly on the surface of the sea, the wind and waves calmed down immediately. The old man knew that he had gotten a treasure today, hid it inside his coat, and went home happily. The next day, at dawn, the old man built a grass pergola at the thatched hillock and hung the seal in the middle of it. The sea around the thatched hillock became windless, and the boat sailed steadily. When the fishermen saw that the place was good, they stopped and decided to stay. In a few days, there were a lot of fishermen living in the thatched hillock.

This jade seal was the sea-sealed pearl that was given to the East Sea Dragon King by the Jade Emperor. There was a wind pearl in the dragon's mouth. That day, the third prince of the Dragon

二、舟山龙神话

着了。龙王一听，当即带了青龙三太子和虾兵蟹将急吼吼朝茅草岗奔来，只见海面上刮起乌风狂暴，潮水"哗哗"漫上来。鱼老头晓得风头勿对，赶紧喊拢鱼人爬上岗墩，把挂着宝印的草棚团团围牢。茅草岗墩挂着镇海宝印，潮水漫勿上来，龙王气煞，大声叫喊起来："啥人介大胆子，敢来拿我龙宫宝物，还勿快快还来?!"鱼老头一点勿怕，对龙王讲："侬平日兴风作浪，欺侮阿拉㧎鱼人，今日宝印到了阿拉手里，咋好随便还侬?"龙王气得胡须笔笃翘，嘴巴一开，朝着岗墩"哗哗"喷水。

㧎鱼老头举起宝印讲："侬再凶，我就把宝印砸糊!"这下龙王吓煞了，连连讨饶："莫砸! 莫砸! 只要侬还我宝印，水晶宫里金银珠宝随侬拣。"

㧎鱼老头讲："阿拉金银珠宝勿稀奇，要还侬宝印，依我三事体。"龙王讲："是啥三桩? 快讲!"

"第一，今后勿可兴风作浪欺侮阿拉㧎鱼人。"

龙王头点点答应了。

"第二桩，潮水涨落要有时辰，勿好随侬高兴。"

龙王忖忖好办，讲："依侬依侬。"

"第三桩，每日送一万担海货给㧎鱼人。"

介许多海货要送出去，龙王肉痛煞啦! 咕咕忖忖，要讨还镇海宝印，只好咧着嘴巴答应了。㧎鱼老头从龙嘴里摘落定风珠，把镇海宝印掼给龙王，讲："免得侬日后反悔，我留定风珠做凭据!"龙王肚里恶煞，又勿好发作，只怪自己儿子闯祸作孽，就气狠狠瞪了三太子一眼。这辰光，青龙三太子看看㧎鱼老头介犟头倔脑，肚里早就气鼓鼓了，现在又让龙王眼乌珠一瞪，更是火上加油，便"呼"一声蹿到半天里，叫来结拜兄弟白虎。青龙和白虎牙齿咧咧，脚爪伸伸，扑下来要夺回定风珠。

King took the seal to play outside secretly, and accidentally lost it. The Dragon King felt anxious and scared, and was afraid that the Jade Emperor knew this. What could be done? Since the mistake had been made, the third prince was tied up and beaten, and the Dragon King sent shrimp and crab soldiers to look for it everywhere.

Soldiers searched everywhere and finally found it in the thatched hillock. The Dragon King knew this, and immediately took the third prince and soldiers towards the thatched hillock. The sea blew the windstorm, the tide "clatter" overflowing. The old man knew that things were not good, and hurriedly shouted to the fishermen to climb on the pier, and surrounded the grass pergola in which the precious seal hanging. Because the thatched hillock hung with the seal of the sea, the seawater could not overflow, the Dragon King was furious and shouted, "How can you be so bold and dare to take my Dragon Palace treasures? Return it quickly." The old man was not afraid, and said to the Dragon King, "You usually make waves, bullying us fishermen. Now the treasure seal is in our hands. How can we just return it to you casually?" The Dragon King was angry, his beard sticking up, and he opened his mouth, spraying water towards the hillock.

The old man held up the seal and said, "If you are aggressive again, I will smash the seal!" The Dragon King was afraid, and begged for mercy, "Do not smash! Do not smash! As long as you return the treasure seal to me, the gold, silver and jewelry in the crystal palace are at your disposal."

The old man said, "We do not care about gold, silver and jewelry. If you want me to return your seal, you promise me three things." The Dragon King said, "Which three? Tell me!"

"First, you can not make waves to bully us fishermen in the future."

The Dragon King nodded his head and agreed.

二、舟山龙神话

柯鱼老头看得清爽，拿起定风珠一记打过去。只听得"扑通"一声，青龙被打落在茅草岗的东边，化作一座青龙山；白虎被打落在茅草岗西边，化作一座白虎山，定风珠跌落在南边海里，变作一个小岛，就是现在的鲁家峙。

　　从此，茅草岗脚下潮水退落三丈，左有青龙，右有白虎，前面有鲁家峙挡住风浪，变成了顶好的避风港。这就是现在的沈家门渔港。

"Second, the tide should have time to rise and fall, not as you like."

The dragon king thought it and said, "Okay, okay."

"Third, send 10,000 quintals of seafood to the fishermen every day."

So much seafood was asked to send out, and the Dragon King was heartbroken! But thinking about getting back the seal, he had to agree. The old man took off the wind pearl from the dragon's mouth, and gave the seal back to the Dragon King, and said, "To avoid you later backtracking, I will keep the wind pearl for proof!" The Dragon King was angry but could not show out, only blame his son's trouble with a glare at the third prince. At this time, seeing that the old man was so stubborn, the third prince had long been angry. What was worse was that the Dragon King glared at him for his mistake. He scurried to the sky, and called his sworn brother White Tiger. The Green Dragon and White Tiger grinned teeth and claws pounced down to retrieve the wind pearl.

The old man saw it clearly, and he picked up the sea-sealed pearl to hit the third prince. With a splash, the Green Dragon was beaten down in the east of the thatched hillock, and changed into the Green Dragon Mountain; and the White Tiger was beaten down in the west of the thatched hillock, and changed into the White Tiger Mountain. The wind pearl fell in the south of the sea, and became a small island, which is now called the Lujia Island.

Since then, the tide at the foot of the thatched hillock receded three feet. The Green Dragon Mountain stands on the left, and the White Tiger Mountain stands on the right. And the Lujia Island blocks the wind and waves and turns the place into a very good shelter, which is now named the Shenjiamen Fishing Port.

三、舟山观音神话

　　观音菩萨是佛教诸多菩萨中，中国老百姓最熟悉、最亲切、最受欢迎的菩萨。观音菩萨源于印度佛教。在印度关于观音的传说中，观音菩萨是一位男菩萨，从小侍奉阿弥陀佛，具有"大慈与一切众生乐，大悲与一切众生苦"的德能，能三十二中化身，救十二种大难，是"西方三圣"之一。传到中国后与中国文化相融合，尤其是隋唐时期观音的兴盛，使观音逐步被改造成女儿身，散发出女性的慈善光辉。观世音这个称法是梵文的意译，又有观自在、光世音和观世自在等称法。在唐朝时期将观世音略称为观音，原因是避唐太宗李世民的名讳。

　　观音传说是民间的口头创作，又是民间观音神话信仰的承载方式。观音菩萨是佛教众多菩萨中最为突出的，其信仰范围之广、程度之高都是无与伦比的。可以说，观音传说对中国观音菩萨的形象塑造起了至关重要的作用。舟山的观音传说，增强了普陀山观音道场的魅力，提高了普陀山的知名度，给普陀山佛教文化增添了浓厚的色彩。

普陀山自古就有观音显灵说法的传说，普陀山也成为中国佛教四大名山之一，成为著名的佛教道场。普陀山的观音节主要有观音菩萨生日、成道日和涅槃日，即观音菩萨诞生、出家和得道的日子，称为三大香会，分别是在农历的二月十九、六月十九和九月十九。

三、舟山观音神话

35. 不肯去观音院

　　早先，有个叫慧锷的日本和尚，来中国游历名山古刹。这日，他来到五台山，见这里风景蛮好，交关幽静，就在五台山住了下来，和老方丈交上了朋友。有一日，慧锷在大殿后院，看到有尊用檀香木雕的观音佛像。他交关欢喜，站在佛像前左看右看，看得连饭也忘记吃。老方丈见他看得介入迷，便笑眯眯地说："如果法师喜欢，就给你供奉吧！"

　　慧锷一听，高兴煞了，连忙合十顶礼，拜了再拜，他接过观音佛像，打算回到日本造座寺院，让日本众生都来朝拜。

　　慧锷离开五台山，转道宁波，乘船回国。没料到，船到普陀山洋面，突然刮起风暴，又是风，又是雨，把帆船刮得东倒西歪。慧锷吭法，只好把船驶进普陀山的一个岙里避风。

　　第二天，风息了，慧锷扬帆开船。

Refusing-to-Go Guanyin Temple

Early on, a Japanese monk named Hui'e came to China to visit the famous mountains and temples. One day, he came to Mount Wutai. Seeing the beautiful and secluded scenery, he stayed there and made friends with the old Buddhist abbot. One day, Hui'e saw a statue of the Guanyin Buddha carved from sandalwood in the back yard of the main hall. He adored it so much, therefore he was so absorbed in watching it that he forgot to eat. Seeing that he was so fascinated, the old abbot smiled and said, "If you like it, I can offer you the opportunity to enshrine it."

Hui'e was elated to hear that, and he quickly clasped his hands and bowed. He took over the Guanyin Buddha statue, intended to build a temple after he returned to Japan, making all Japanese sentient beings to worship it.

Hui'e left Mount Wutai, via Ningbo and went back to his country by boat. Unexpectedly, when the boat reached the surface of Mount Putuo, a sudden storm blew up, causing heavy wind and rain to make the sailboat stagger. Hui'e had no way out but to sail into a sea bay in Mount Putuo to take shelter from the wind.

The next day, the wind died down and Hui'e set sail. Unexpectedly, as soon as the boat left the mouth of the sea bay, a cloud of gray smoke rose over the sea, like a tent, just in front of the boat, blocking the way. Hui'e stood in the bow and looked at the blue sky above his head and the shining sea on either side. He then turned the boat round, trying to steer forward through the smoke.

勿料,船刚驶出岙口,洋面上又升起一团灰蒙蒙的烟雾,像顶帐篷,正好挂在船头前面,挡住去路。慧锷站在船头看看,头顶是一片蓝天,左右两边是锃亮的大海。慧锷调转船头,想绕过烟雾朝前驶。可是绕了一圈,还是回到普陀山洋面。慧锷只好把船驶进山岙里。

　　第三天一早,慧锷走出船舱一看,太阳刚露了头,满天霞光。突然他看到在彩云中间,有幢彩色牌楼,罗汉、仙女来来往往。他忖,一定是观音菩萨显灵,他连忙跪倒,朝天拜了三拜,赶紧扬帆开船。啥人会料到,船一驶出岙口,天上的景色没了,海上又刮起风浪。慧锷发急了,老是这样下去,啥辰光才能回到日本,他双手合十,口念佛经,求观音菩萨保佑。果然,风浪慢慢平静下来了,可是,船没驶出多远,突然像抛了锚一样,勿会动了。他朝海上一看,只见海上飘来一朵朵铁莲,把帆船团团围在中间。慧锷大吃一惊,一次一次开船,都有风浪阻挡,今日又有铁莲锁舟,难道是观音菩萨不肯去日本?他走进船舱,跪在观音佛像跟前,祷告:如若日本众生无缘见佛,

But after a circle, he came back to the surface of Mount Putuo and had to sail the boat into sea bay.

The third day early in the morning, Hui'e went out of the cabin and looked out, the sun just exposing the head, the sky glowing, brimming with rosy clouds. Suddenly he saw a colorful memorial archway in the middle of the colorful clouds, where arhats and fairies came and went. Considering that it must be the Goddess of Mercy (Guanyin), he knelt down and bowed to the sky three times. He set sail quickly. No one could have predicted that as soon as the boat left the sea bay, the scene in the sky disappeared and the wind and waves appeared again. Hui'e was very worried. If it kept going on like this, when could he return to Japan? He clasped his hands and chanted the Buddha Sutra, praying to Guanyin to bless him. Sure enough, the wind and waves gradually subsided. But before the boat sailed far, it suddenly seemed to be anchored and would not move. He took a look at the sea, and saw the boat surrounded by iron lotus. Hui'e was shocked, because every time the boat set out, there was wind and waves to obstruct, and that day the iron lotus locked boat. Did the Guanyin Buddha refuse to go to Japan? He went into the cabin and knelt down in front of the Guanyin Buddha statue. He prayed, "If sentient beings in Japan have no priviliage to see the Buddha, I will follow your instructions and build another temple to worship the Buddha."

After he finished speaking, he suddenly heard a "roar" and an iron ox came out from the bottom of the sea. It opened its mouth and took a big bite of the iron lotus. Soon a channel appeared on the surface of the sea. The boat then followed the iron ox. Suddenly, there was another "roar", the iron ox sank to the bottom of the sea, and the lotus was gone. Hui'e looked intently. It turned out that the boat sailed into the sea bay in the mountain again.

At this time, a fisherman surnamed Zhang came down from

　　　　　　　　三、舟山观音神话

我定遵照大士所指,另建寺院,供奉我佛。"

话音未落,忽听到"轰隆"一声,从海底钻出一头铁牛,张开嘴巴,大口大口吞嚼着铁莲,一歇功夫,洋面上就现出一条航道。帆船跟在铁牛后面驶去。突然,又是"轰隆"一声,铁牛沉入海底,满洋铁莲也无踪无影了。慧锷定神一看,原来帆船又驶进普陀山的这个山岙里来了。

这辰光,有个姓张的渔民从山上走下来,对慧锷说:"这几天的事,我看得煞清爽,你走不成了,还是请法师到我屋里住几天再走吧!"

慧锷见他介热情,便捧着观音佛像,跟渔民爬上了普陀山。他看普陀山有山有海,地方蛮好,心忖,观音菩萨不肯去日本,就在这里造座寺院,让观音菩萨定居在普陀山吧!

没过多少日脚,普陀山就造起了一座小庵堂,慧锷把观音佛像留在普陀山,自己回日本去了。所以,这座小庵堂叫作"不肯去观音院"。

the mountain and said to Hui'e, "I see clearly what's happened these days. You can't go away. Please come to my house and stay for a few days before you leave."

Seeing how enthusiastic the fisherman was, Hui'e followed the fisherman to climb up Mount Putuo, holding the statue of the Guanyin Buddha. Along the way, he saw mountains and sea in Mount Putuo. "It is a very nice place." He thought, "The Guanyin Buddha refused to go to Japan, so I would build a temple here and make her settle down in Mount Putuo."

A few months later, a small temple was constructed in Mount Putuo. Hui'e left the statue of the Guanyin Buddha in Mount Putuo and went back to Japan. Hence, this small temple is called "Refusing-to-Go Guanyin Temple".

36. 观音借普陀

　　很早以前,观音不是在普陀,而是在岱山的大巨。大巨有座山,观音就在这里登佛殿,受民香火。人们说从这山顶望去,周围有一百个山头。可观音数来数去,只有九十九个山头,屁股下坐的一个山头忘记数了。数不到一百个山头,做勿来佛殿,观音就离开了大巨。

　　观音离开了大巨,来到了洛迦山,在洛迦山山头上,又数开了,心忖这回可别把屁股下坐的这山头忘记了。就先从洛迦山数起,她是慧眼,舟山的一半山头都被她数去了,数到九十九个,屁股下坐的一个又被她数进了,洛迦山被数了两遍,这样正好是一百个山头,观音就在洛迦山住下了。

　　观音住在洛迦山的潮音洞,住下后感觉太拥挤,就想到普陀山去住。普陀山当时被一条红蛇精占领着。普陀山和洛迦山面对面,只隔一条港。

　　一天,观音站在洛迦山山头,对红蛇精讲:"侬这地方可以借给我住住吗?"红蛇精当然不肯。一个要借,一个不肯,结果就打起来了。一个是佛,一个是怪,怪咋能打胜佛。蛇精打不过,只好讲:"我打侬打不过,只有把普陀山借给侬,但要讲好条件,一是侬几时把普陀山还给我,二是侬叫我住到啥地方去?"观音说:"侬打不过我,就老老实实到东福山去住吧。普陀山啥时间还给侬呢? 等到普陀山千步沙浪头呒没了就还

Guanyin Borrowed Mount Putuo

A long time ago, Guanyin was not in Mount Putuo, but in Daju, Daishan. There was a large mountain, where Guanyin built the temple to accept the people's incense offerings. Reportedly, there were a hundred mountains around it when seeing from the top of the mountain. But as she counted, there were only ninety-nine mountains, and she had forgotten to count the one she sat on. Without a hundred mountains, the temple could not be built, so Guanyin left Daju.

Guanyin came to Mount Luojia, where she began to count again. Did not forget the mountain on which she sat this time, she thought. On account of her wisdom eyes, she counted half the mountain tops of Zhoushan. Up to ninety-nine, the one she was sitting on was counted by her again. The consequence was that Mount Luojia was counted twice, so there were just one hundred mountains, and Guanyin lived there ever since.

Guanyin lived in the Chaoyin Cave at Mount Luojia. It was too crowded to live in, so she decided to move to Mount Putuo, which was occupied by a red basilisk. Mount Putuo and Mount Luojia were adjacent, separated only by a harbor.

One day, Guanyin stood at the top of Mount Luojia and asked the basilisk, "Would you please lend me this place to live in?" Of course, the basilisk refused. One wanted to borrow it, the other refused, and a fight broke out. One was a Buddha, and the other was a monster. How could a monster beat a Buddha? The basilisk

三、舟山观音神话

侬。"事情就这样定了。

红蛇精被迫住到东福山,但心不服气,总要走出来,看看千步沙。所以现在不管咋好的天气,东福山山头,总有一团雾,那就是红蛇精出来了,看千步沙浪头吭没了没。千步沙的浪头呢,几千年过去了,一直高猛呢。

could not beat Guanyin, so he had to say, "I can't beat you, so I can only lend you Mount Putuo, but we have to agree on conditions. First, when will you return Mount Putuo to me, and second, where do you want me to live?" Guanyin said, "You can't beat me, so just go and live in Mount Dongfu. When will Mount Putuo be returned to you? It depends on when the wave of Qianbusha of Mount Putuo is gone." It was settled then.

The red basilisk was forced to live in Mount Dongfu, but it was not convinced and always wanted to go out to see Qianbusha. Hence, no matter how fine the weather was, there was always a cloud of fog on the top of Mount Dongfu. It was the red basilisk coming out to find out if the wave of Qianbusha had disappeared. Nevertheless, the wave of Qianbusha has been high and fierce for thousands of years.

三、舟山观音神话

37. 观音跳

　　早先,普陀山是个蛇岛。后来,观音菩萨修炼成佛,看中普陀山做道场,才把蛇精赶走。

　　这天,观音在西天参拜过如来,离开雷音寺,脚踩莲台,要到凡间找个山头设庙传经,她早就听讲普陀山风景优美,是个开设道场的好地方。可是,她来到莲花洋上空,低头一看,只见普陀山上毒雾阵阵,树叶枯了,百花凋谢,变成了瘴气弥漫的癞头山。她一时摸勿清底细,便先在洛迦山上住了下来。

　　原来,这个岛上,有条从云雾洞来的蛇精,自称蛇王。这蛇精浑身火红,眼睛像灯笼,嘴巴像稻桶,只要打个呵欠,便会将全岛弄得乌烟瘴气,它还时常出来东游西荡残害生灵。

　　第二天,观音去找蛇精,远远就看见梵音洞里出来一个红脸大汉,走到观音面前问:"喂,侬到蛇岛来做啥?"观音一看,晓得他是蛇精的化身,便向前施了个礼,说:"侬是蛇仙吧! 为啥要占据佛门圣地,在这里糟蹋生灵?"

　　蛇精把眼睛一瞪:"咋话? 我在这个岛上住了好几百年了,咋会是侬的佛地?"

　　观音想,这蛇精性格粗暴,讲话傲慢,勿能与他硬撞,还是略施小计,让他心服口服! 于是,观音心平气和地说:"侬原先住在东福山云雾洞,如今又来普陀山,独占两地有啥用? 侬行个方便,把普陀山借我设庙传经,好伐?"

Guanyin Jump

In the early days, Mount Putuo was a snake island. Later, Guanyin Bodhisattva became a Buddha and took a fancy to Mount Putuo to be her Buddhist field. Only then did she drive the basilisk away.

One day, after visiting Tathagata in the west, Guanyin left the Leiyin Temple, foot on the lotus, to look for a mountain and set up a temple in the mortal world to preach scriptures. She had heard that Mount Putuo had an extraordinary scenery, which was a good place to open a Buddhist field. But when she arrived at the sky above the lotus sea, she looked down, but a thick poisonous mist on Mount Putuo caught her eyes. The leaves and all the flowers had withered, turning it into a mangy hill brimming with miasma. For a moment she did not know exactly what was going on, so she settled on Mount Luojia.

It turned out that on this island, there was a basilisk from the Yunwu Cave, claiming to be the king of snakes. His body was red with fire, his eyes were like lanterns, and his mouth was like a huge barrel for threshing rice. A yawn would poison the whole island, and he often wandered about to spoil creatures.

The next day, Guanyin went to find the basilisk, and saw a red-faced man coming out of the Fanyin Cave. He walked up to Guanyin and asked, "Hey, what are you doing on the snake island?" Guanyin knew that he was the incarnation of the basilisk at a glance. Therefore, she gave a salute, and said, "You are a snake

三、舟山观音神话

蛇精一听，观音讲话和和气气，他的态度也两样了："侬要借，可以商量，勿知啥时候还我？"观音眯眯笑笑，说："等到普陀山木鱼勿响，千步沙潮水勿涨，当即还侬！"

蛇精火暴脾气又发了："这哪里是借，明明想霸占我蛇岛嘛！勿借，勿借，侬快离开洛迦山！"观音说："难道洛迦山也是侬的？"

蛇精说："普陀、洛迦本来就是一个山头，侬勿晓得？"

观音见蛇精发火，故意用话激他："侬口口声声说普陀山是侬的，有啥依据？"

蛇精说："我的真身正好绕岛一圈。"

观音说："我勿信，侬绕给我看看！"

蛇精忖，这有啥难，绕就绕，他摇身一变，变成一条大蛇。一眨眼，蛇身越伸越长，沿着山脚边，弯弯曲曲向普陀山的周围伸去，眼看头尾就要接拢了。观音抬脚轻轻一蹬，把洛迦山蹬出老远老远。从此，普陀、洛迦分开两个山头。

等蛇精将身子绕普陀山一圈，头尾相接时，观音却站在洛迦山上哈哈大笑起来："蛇仙，侬讲普陀、洛迦是一个山头，侬为啥只能绕普陀一圈，洛迦呒没绕进去？可见这个岛勿归侬所有！"

蛇精晓得上当了，连忙说："勿算，勿算，让我再绕一次！"

这辰光，观音拿出一只金钵，对蛇精说："勿用再绕了，侬如果能在这个金钵口上绕一圈，我就把普陀山让给侬！"

蛇精看看金钵，心忖，这有啥难！只见他在地上一滚，"哗啦"一声，身子越缩越小，"扑"地一跳，盘在金钵沿口上。观音趁机用手指一拨，蛇精跌进金钵里去了。观音用手捂牢钵口，闷得蛇精喘勿过气来，连声求饶："观音饶命！观音饶命！"

spirit, aren't you? Why do you occupy the holy place of the Buddha and spoil creatures here?"

The basilisk glared at Guanyin and said, "What do you mean? I have lived on this island for hundreds of years. How can it be your Buddha land?"

Guanyin thought, this basilisk was rough, conceited and outrageous, so she couldn't use force and needed to utilize some tricks to make him sincerely convinced! Hence, Guanyin said equably, "You used to live in the Yunwu Cave in Mount Dongfu, and now you come to Mount Putuo. What's the use of monopolizing the two places? Could you do me a favor to let me set up a temple to preach scriptures on Mount Putuo?"

The basilisk saw Guanyin speaking gently, he also turned his attitude to a different one, "You want to borrow it from me. That's okay, and we can discuss about it, but when can I get it back?" Guanyin smiled and said, "Wait until the wooden knocker in Mount Putuo does not ring, the tide of Qianbusha does not rise. Then I will give it back to you."

The basilisk became angry again, "It isn't borrowing. Obviously you want to occupy my snake island! I won't lend it to you. You must get out of Mount Luojia!" Guanyin doubted, "Is Mount Luojia also yours?"

The basilisk said, "Putuo and Luojia are the same mountain. Don't you know that?"

Guanyin found the basilisk lost his temper, and then deliberately enraged him with words, "You keep saying that Mount Putuo is yours. What evidence do you have?"

"My real body can just circle the island," The basilisk answered.

But Guanyin countered, "I do not believe. Come and show me!"

"It's not hard. I'm not afraid to show it." The basilisk thought. Then he transformed into a big snake. In the twinkling of an eye,

三、舟山观音神话

观音想了想说:"好,放侬一条生路,回云雾洞去吧!"

她把金钵一倒,将蛇精倒进海里。蛇精抬起头,苦苦哀求:"云雾洞呒树呒草,全是岩石,一年到头,太阳晒得全身出油,实在呒法住,求大士另指去处!"

观音顺手折朵莲花,往空中一抛,变成一朵"莲花云",对蛇精说:"只要侬能改邪归正,让这朵莲花云为侬遮阴,侬要再作恶,一定勿饶!"

蛇精磕头拜谢,随"莲花云"回到东福山,一直到今天,那朵"莲花云"还飘浮在云雾洞上空!

观音赶走了蛇精,从洛迦山上纵身一跃,跳上了普陀山。在她落脚的那块岩石上,留下了一只深深的脚印,人们都叫它"观音跳"。

the snake stretched its body longer and longer, along the foot of the mountain, to zigzag around Mount Putuo. Seeing that his tail was about to be closed, Guanyin lifted her feet and gently kicked off Mount Luojia. From then on, Putuo and Luojia separated from each other.

When the basilisk was circling Mount Putuo, head to tail, Guanyin stood on Mount Luojia and laughed, "Snake spirit, you bragged that Putuo and Luoja were the same mountain. Why can you only circle Putuo and Luoja and doesn't go in? So you don't own this island!"

The basilisk knew that he had been deceived, so he hurriedly said, "No, no, let me go around again!"

At this moment, Guanyin took out a golden bowl and said to the basilisk, "There is no need for you to circle the mountain again. If you can circle the mouth of the golden bowl once more, Mount Putuo will be possessed by you!"

The basilisk looked at the golden bowl, estimating that it was easy enough for him. He rolled on the ground, and with a crash, his body shrank smaller and smaller. With a pop, he landed on the rim of the golden bowl. Guanyin took the opportunity to push the snake into the bowl with her fingers. She also used her hand to cover the mouth of the golden bowl, stifling the basilisk gasping for breath, repeatedly begging for mercy, "Please spare my life! Please spare my life!"

Guanyin thought for a moment and said, "Well, let you be alive and go back to the Yunwu Cave!"

She emptied the golden bowl and poured the basilisk into the sea. The basilisk raised his head and begged piteously, "There are no trees or grass in the Yunwu Cave, and it's all rocks. The sun shines all year round so that I really can't live there. I beg you to show me another place to live in!"

三、舟山观音神话

Guanyin plucked a lotus at will and threw it into the air, turning it into a "lotus cloud". She told the basilisk, "As long as you can forsake evil and return to the righteousness, this lotus cloud would shade for you. If you do evil again, I won't forgive you!"

The basilisk kowtowed for appreciation and followed the "lotus cloud" back to Mount Dongfu. Until today, the "lotus cloud" is still floating above the Yunwu Cave!

Guanyin drove away the basilisk and leaped from Mount Luojia to Mount Putuo. On the rock where she fell, a deep footprint left, and people all called it "Guanyin Jump".

38. 二龟听法

在普陀山盘陀石附近的山坡上,有两块状似海龟的石头,人称"二龟听法石"。

很早的时候,观音菩萨独自在普陀山修道,每天夜里在盘陀石上说法讲经,吸引了许许多多飞禽走兽、游鱼跳虾。消息传到东海龙宫,龙王十分眼馋,要龟丞相设法将观音念的那部经卷偷来。龟丞相手下有两只海龟,记忆力极强。龟丞相就派它们去偷经。起初,两只海龟只在莲花洋里偷听,后来越听越有味道,渐渐靠近观音洞,慢慢爬上了山坡。到了第八十一个晚上,它们偷偷爬到盘陀石附近。

坐在盘陀石上的观音菩萨,早知道龙王派了两只海龟来偷经。这天晚上,她故意延长讲法念经的时间。两只海龟听得入了迷,直到阳光照到身上,才发觉错过了时辰,急想返回大海,可是四脚已经麻木僵化,接着,身上也僵硬起来,渐渐失去了知觉。就这样,两只海龟一个伸着脖子,侧耳聆听,一个抬着头,出神地望着盘陀石,从此,再也没有动一动。

Two Turtles Listening to Sutras

On the hillside near the Pantuo Stone of Mount Putuo, there are two pieces of stone shaped like turtles, known as "Two Turtles Listening to Sutras Stone".

Long long ago, Guanyin cultivated herself alone according to Buddhism doctrine in Mount Putuo, preaching on the Pantuo Stone every night, which attracted numerous birds and beasts, fish and shrimps. The news spread to the Dragon Palace of the East China Sea. The Dragon King was so greedy that he asked the Turtle Prime Minister to try to steal the scriptures Guanyin read. The Turtle Prime Minister had two turtle subordinates with strong memory, so he sent them to steal scriptures. At first, the two turtles only eavesdropped in the lotus sea, and then they became more and more addicted, thus gradually climbed the hillside near the Guanyin Cave. On the eighty-first night, they crept up secretly near the Pantuo Stone.

The Guanyin Bodhisattva, sitting on the Pantuo Stone, knew that the Dragon King had sent two turtles to steal the Sutras. That night, she deliberately prolonged the time of preaching and chanting. The two turtles were fascinated, and did not realize that they had missed the hour until the sun shone on them. They were anxious to get back to the sea, but their legs had become numb and rigid. Then their bodies also stiffened and gradually lost consciousness. Hence, one of the two turtles stretched out his neck and listened attentively, the other raised his head and stared at the Pantuo Stone. From then on, they did not move anymore.

　　　　　　　　　　　　　　　三、舟山观音神话

四、舟山历史人物神话

　　据考古挖掘推测，舟山最早的人类活动遗迹可以追溯到新石器时代，文字记录可到春秋时期的《左传》和《国语》所提及的"会稽句章县东海中洲"，之后在旷世奇书《山海经》的《南山经》中也有提及，但都只是寥寥几笔带过，并没有可深入考证的文字资料。自唐开元二十六年（738），舟山设置翁山县，"山在县东，乃徐偃王所居之地，旧址尤存"❶，初设于定海区盐仓，后又迁至镇鳌山，以后以此为中心的定海区一直都是舟山政治、经济、文化和交通的中心。然而在大历八年（773），海寇袁晁在附近海域作乱，翁山县建立不久便因此而废，也未曾留有修志之作，书证可查不多。到北宋端拱二年（989），在县西十二里处设置晓峰盐场，今仍有地名盐仓。柳永，字耆卿，为屯田郎于晓峰盐场，并留诗句于此。至宋熙宁六年（1073），鄞邑令王安石上朝堂请命，随后设立富都、安期、蓬莱三乡，之后又于宋元丰元年（1078）增加定海县金塘乡。之后到明朝，海寇猖獗，朝廷实行海禁并且迁走部分海岛居民于内地，同时为了增强舟山的防御能力，调任何汝宾，字寅之，为舟山参将，后又将其升任副总兵，他在任期间编修《舟山志》，为后世了解舟

❶ 凌金祚：《宋元明舟山古志·点校本》，舟山市档案馆，第1页

山的这段历史立下了功劳。清康熙二十五年（1686），"从大臣请开复舟山，於是匠蛟龙之窟，府虎豹之居，辟莱抽棘之民，从仁人而归者如市"[1]。至此，舟山已逐渐发展成繁华城镇，而之后虽然历经鸦片战争等，但仍保得大致的规模至今日。在这丰富的历史中，许多历史人物也在舟山留下了他们的足迹和故事。有的故事过于久远，已经没有办法去辨其真伪，但在舟山地方文化里产生了不小的影响。

[1] 《康熙定海县志·点校本》，凌金祚点校注释，舟山市档案馆，第1页。

四、舟山历史人物神话

39. 徐偃王和玉几砚

两千多年前,西周的辰光,周穆王在位时,有个诸侯背着周穆王自封为徐偃王。

徐偃王有个传家之宝,名叫玉几砚。相传这玉几砚和后来的和氏璧生产在同一个地方。玉几砚能在黑暗中放出光来,夜里把玉几砚放在书桌上,磨墨写字就不用点灯了;玉几砚里盛的水,磨的墨,不管天多寒地多冻,都不会凝冻起来。

周穆王老早就想得到这玉几砚了。谁知道徐偃王把玉几砚看得比性命还值钱。周穆王想看看这个宝贝,徐偃王也推阻回去。

现在周穆王见徐偃称起王来,就正好寻找借口杀掉徐偃王,把玉几砚弄到手,他就下令调集各路诸侯,向徐偃王兴师问罪。

那时,徐偃王在现在的绍兴会稽山一带。周穆王带了成千上万兵马冲杀过来,徐偃王一看苗头不对,坐上大船,从海上向东退走。周穆王追到东海边,没有船,过不了海,只好退回会稽山。

徐偃王坐船来到定海。他马上叫来风水先生看风水,替他寻找安兵立足的地方。风水先生看中距定海东南三十里一个叫城隍山头的地方,说这儿可创万世基业。徐偃王就在城隍山头造起一座徐城。

King Xuyan and Yuji Inkstone

More than two thousand years ago, when King Mu of the Zhou Dynasty was in power, a nobility appointed himself as King Xuyan, but without informing King Mu of Zhou of it.

King Xuyan had a family heirloom named Yuji Inkstone, which was said to be from the same place as the Jade of the He, a priceless gem, which came into being hundreds of years later. The inkstone emitted light in the dark. Therefore, when someone put it on the desk at night and rubbed an ink stick against it in order to write, no lamp was needed. Another amazing thing was that the water or ink in the inkstone would not freeze no matter how cold it was.

King Mu of Zhou had yearned for this inkstone for a long time. But, it turned out that King Xuyan would rather die for it. He even turned down King Mu of Zhou's demand to see this treasure.

King Mu of Zhou was angered. He took King Xuyan's self-appointment as an excuse to slay him. He gathered the nobility's armies and launched a punitive war on King Xuyan.

At that time, King Xuyan's palace was in the area which is now around the Kuaiji Mountain in the city of Shaoxing. When King Mu of Zhou and his tremendous army arrived, King Xuyan found himself in grave danger. Terrified, he and his followers fled to the East Sea on dozens of big boats. King Mu of Zhou chased to the coast, but no more boats were available. After glaring at the sea, he returned to the Kuaiji Mountain in disappointment.

几年以后,徐偃王兵精粮足,决心去找周穆王报仇。他带了宝贝玉几砚,坐了大船,带了几千兵马,在靠近会稽山的海边上岸。

徐偃王带兵到达会稽山,周穆王早已做好了迎战准备。双方在会稽山决一死战。徐偃王的军队虽然十分勇猛,可周穆王的军队多,时间打得长了,徐偃王只有节节败退。最后他自己也在会稽河边被周穆王的军队包围了。

周穆王派人去告诉徐偃王,只要交出玉几砚,可保他一世荣华富贵。可徐偃王不甘心,就抱着这块玉几砚投会稽河了,当时河水溅起几丈高。

徐偃王死后,周穆王派了大批人马在河里寻找徐偃王的尸体和玉几砚。奇怪的是,不管穆王派多少人去寻找,就是找不到徐偃王的尸体和玉几砚。

后来,定海的老百姓知道徐偃王死了,都很悲伤。他们筹集钱,在鼓吹峰山建了一个偃王祠。

After a long voyage, King Xuyan reached Dinghai City. Immediately, he called on a geomancer to select an auspicious place to settle down. The geomancer picked somewhere named Chenghuangshantou, 15 km southeast of Dinghai and said that the place could be a foundation for all generations. In consequence, King Xuyan and his followers built a town there and named it Xu Town.

A few years later, King Xuyan had a large army of veterans and ample supplies and the determination to revenge himself on King Mu of Zhou. With his precious Yuji Inkstone and thousands of soldiers, he landed on the sea coast near the Kuaiji Mountain.

When King Xuyan's troops marched to the Kuaiji Mountain, King Mu of Zhou had already prepared for the battle. They finally fought in the Kuaiji Mountain. Although the soldiers of King Xuyan were very brave, they were outnumbered. They had to retreat, as the battle proceeded. In the end, King Xuyan was surrounded by King Mu of Zhou's troops by the Kuaiji River.

Proudly, King Mu of Zhou sent someone to tell King Xuyan that he could keep his prosperous life if he handed out Yuji Inkstone. King Xuyan did not give in. He held Yuji Inkstone and jumped into the Kuaiji River. The splash was dozens of meters high.

Seeing this, King Mu of Zhou sent a large number of people to search for the body of King Xuyan and Yuji Inkstone in the river. Strangely enough, no matter how many people King Mu of Zhou sent to look for it, the body of King Xuyan and Yuji Inkstone could not be found.

Knowing the death of King Xuyan, the people of Dinghai were sorrowful. They raised money to build the Temple of King Xuyan to remember him on the Guchuifeng Mountain.

40.鲁王避风蓬莱岛

清顺治八年秋天,清朝皇帝派定南将军刘之源进攻舟山。

张名振想去打清军后方吴淞,就和鲁王带了主力部队离开了舟山。

农历八月廿一,天下大雾,清兵偷偷登上了舟山的螺头门。九月,清兵占领了定海,张名振和鲁王从吴淞回来,舟山早成清兵的地了,他们只好到福建去。

因为黑夜里匆匆忙忙,鲁王的战船驶错了方向,往南驶,弄成了往北驶,鲁王坐的船竟然驶到了号称蓬莱的岱山岛,在岱山剪刀头咸水浦里泊锚了。那辰光岱西还没有大海塘,海水一直通到剪刀头村的山脚下,张名振带领一些人上岸去看地形。鲁王坐在船舱里感到心中烦闷,他说要活动筋骨,就独自走上岸来了。他走着走着,越走越远,后来别人也不知道他走到哪里去了。

待张名振回来准备开船时,却不见了鲁王,他吃了一惊,立即派人四处寻找鲁王。

原来,鲁王走着走着,来到一个小山,山上种满了番薯。鲁王在船上几天,老是晕船,不大吃东西,现在一走动,肚子饿得"咕咕"叫,他一见满地番薯,连忙用手扒开泥土,扒出一个番薯来,也顾不得上面有泥,就狼吞虎咽般吃起来。

鲁王接连吃了两个番薯,一看山下有人上来,以为是番薯

King Lu Took Shelter from Wind on the Penglai Island

In the autumn of 1651, during the Qing Dynasty, the Emperor Shunzhi sent Dingnan General Liu Zhiyuan to attack Zhoushan City, which was held by King Lu, a king of the Ming Dynasty.

General Zhang Mingzhen, who was loyal to King Lu, wanted to attack Wusong City, which was in the rear of the Qing army. He and King Lu left Zhoushan with the main force.

On August 21 of the lunar calendar, it was foggy. The Qing soldiers secretly occupied the stronghold Luotoumen. In September, the Qing army conquered Dinghai. When Zhang Mingzhen and King Lu returned from Wusong, Zhoushan was under the rule of the Qing soldier. Without any other choice, they headed for Fujian Province.

In a hurry and in the evening, King Lu's warships sailed in the wrong direction, heading north instead of south. Unexpectedly, they arrived at Daishan Island, which was then called Penglai, and anchored in the shoal of Jiandaotou Village. At that time, there was no big seawall in the west of Daishan, and the sea water went all the way to the foot of the mountain in Jiandaotou Village. Once there, Zhang Mingzhen led some people to go ashore to see the terrain. Sitting in the cabin, King Lu felt bored and agitated. He said he wanted to do some exercises, so he went ashore alone. He went farther and farther until no one knew where he had gone.

When Zhang Mingzhen returned to prepare for sailing away from the island, King Lu was nowhere in sight. He was shocked

四、舟山历史人物神话

地的主人来了,连忙把吃下的番薯皮、番薯蒂头用泥盖好。谁知上来的人正是来找他的士兵。

后来,鲁王泊船的那个地方,就取名叫"寻王跟"(跟:意指这一带,这地方)。鲁王上山到地里吃番薯走过的路,就被称为"圣路"。有个石匠还在那路旁岩石上刻了"圣路"两字,那字至今还在。

and immediately sent people to look for him.

It turned out that King Lu ended up on a hill where sweet potatoes grew. The king hadn't eaten much on the boat for a few days due to seasickness. After such a long walk, his stomach began to rumble. Seeing the sweet potato vines all over the field, he rushed to dig out a sweet potato and ate it like a hungry wolf, forgetting the mud on it.

King Lu ate two sweet potatoes one after another. When he saw that someone was coming up, he thought it was the sweet potato field's owner. He quickly covered the skin and stems of the sweet potatoes eaten. But the person was in fact a soldier who was searching for him.

Many years passed. The place where King Lu moored his boat was named Xunwanggen (literally, the searching-for-king place). The path leading to the sweet potato field was later called Emperor Road. A stonemason carved the characters meaning "Emperor Road" on a rock beside the path. The characters are still there.

四、舟山历史人物神话

41. 葛总兵的宝刀

　　早先,定海城状元桥东头有家姓吴的铁匠铺,铁匠吴师傅六十六岁了,身子骨还像小后生一般活络。其打出的刀,在整个舟山都有名气。

　　有一天,铁匠铺里来了个武官模样的中年人和一个年轻的兵勇,让吴师傅替其打一对宝刀。吴师傅怕招惹是非,推说自己只会打菜刀、镰刀、杀猪杀牛羊刀,勿会打仗用的宝刀。那武官听后,叹息一声就出门走了。兵勇在后面说:"葛老爷,阿拉到别家铁匠铺去打宝刀吧。"

　　那师傅一听"葛老爷"三个字,连忙把武官追了回来。兵勇告诉其,眼前就是总兵葛老爷,吴师傅连忙说:"葛大人打宝刀是为了打红毛鬼子,我老头子就是拼了老命也要为葛大人把宝刀打出来。"

　　葛云飞听了十分高兴,忙叫兵勇付定钿,吴师傅勿肯收,说:"大人打红毛鬼性命都勿管,我打宝刀理所当然咯。"

　　从此以后,吴师傅勿做别样生活,一心一意打宝刀。过了几天,年轻兵勇送来一个条幅和两张小纸。原来,两张小纸上分别写了"昭勇""成忠",那是葛云飞为宝刀取的名字。条幅上是葛云飞写的《宝刀歌》:

　　　　快逾风,亮夺雪,

General Ge's Treasured Knife[1]

There was a blacksmith shop at the east end of the Zhuangyuan Bridge in Dinghai City. Although the shop owner Wu was sixty-six years old, he was as agile as a young man. The knives made by him were famous around Zhoushan.

One day, an official-like middle-aged man and a young soldier came to the blacksmith shop to ask Wu to forge a pair of knives for him. Wu didn't want to be involved in illegal affairs. He said that he could not make a knife for war but only sickles and knives for cutting vegetables and butching pigs, cattle and sheep. Hearing this, the official sighed and left. "Master Ge, we could try another blacksmith," said the soldier.

Hearing the words "Master Ge", Wu hurried to catch up with the official. Being confirmed that it was General Ge, Wu said, "It is the red haired ghosts (British soldiers) whom General Ge fights. Whatever it costs, I will forge a pair of satisfactory knives for General Ge."

Ge Yunfei was very happy when he heard that. He asked the soldier to pay a deposit, but Wu refused to accept it. He said, "General Ge risked his life when he fought against the red haired ghosts. How could I ask for money for a pair of knives?"

From then on, Wu devoted himself to the knives. After a few days, the young soldier brought a banner and two pieces of paper.

---

[1] Ge Yunfei (1789 - 1841) was a famous patriotic general who fell in the First Opium War.

四、舟山历史人物神话

恨斩奸臣头，

渴饮仇人血。

有时上马杀贼贼胆裂，

灭此朝食气烈烈，

吁嗟乎！男儿自处一片心肠热。

兵勇让吴师傅按照纸上笔迹刻在宝刀上。吴师傅花了七七四十九天，终于将宝刀打好献给葛总兵。葛云飞给其一百两银子，其一两也勿肯要。

后来，葛云飞用这两把宝刀杀了无数红毛人。其阵亡后，宝刀落到红毛头子手里。红毛头子见这宝刀吹毛就断，削铁如泥，真高兴煞，就把宝刀挂在自己房间里。不料两把宝刀每夜发出"铮铮嗡嗡"的声音来，弄得红毛头子困勿着觉。其十分恼火，把宝刀给别人舍勿得，自家用用又害怕，就拿到铁匠铺叫吴师傅火化掉。

吴师傅正为葛总兵遇难伤心，一看其用过的宝刀，愈加难过，就假意答应红毛头子等到明朝炉子旺了再火化宝刀，可自己连夜带了宝刀，坐上小船，逃回老家温州去了。

It turned out that on the two small pieces of paper were the words "Zhaoyong (illuminating bravery)" and "Chengzhong (realizing loyalty)", which were the names Ge Yunfei took for the two knives. On the banner was Ge Yunfei's *Knife Song*:

> "Faster than the wind, brighter than the snow,
> Hatedly beheading treacherous officials,
> Drinking the blood of the foe,
> The knives are wielded by the knights,
> bringing overwhelming terror to the evil.
> Victory is the belief they hold.
> With passion they glow."

The soldiers asked Wu to engrave the words in the knives, retaining the handwriting on the paper. Wu agreed and started to work. After forty-nine days, he presented the knives to General Ge. Ge Yunfei intended to pay him a fortune, but he would not accept a coin.

Later, Ge Yunfei killed many British soldiers with these two precious knives. After his death, the knives fell into the hands of a British official, who was amazed by the sharpness of the knives and kept them in his bedroom. Unexpectedly, the knives gave clangs and buzzes every night, waking him up time and time again. He was very angry but found himself in a dilemma. On the one hand, he was unwilling to give them away. On the other hand, he dared not keep them to himself. In consequence, he took them to Wu's shop and ordered him to cremate them.

Wu was grieving for the death of General Ge. Seeing the knives, his sorrow went deeper. He pretended to promise the official that he would cremate the knives the next morning when the stove temperature was ready, but in the evening he took the knives, got on a boat and fled back to his hometown—Wenzhou City.

42. 俞将军抗倭

相传在嘉靖三十一年,海盗头子汪直勾引倭寇到金塘一带抢妇女、抢财物、杀人放火。时间久了,这些冤屈的鬼魂聚集在沥港小山的岩石上,白天发出奇怪的声响,夜里则变成一束白光,人们说它是神灯,正盼望早日消除倭患,安居乐业呢。

有一日,人们正在烧香祈祷,忽然起了一阵大风,将纸钱吹得满天乱飞,其中一张贴在岩壁上。风息后,有个名叫侯得的壮年人,取下这张纸钱,上面显出"军民协力,倭寇必灭,倭寇复来,俞将军即到"十七个字。

不到十天,倭寇又来了。俞大猷获悉后,前来追歼。这时,侯得等几位壮士,要求见俞将军。俞大猷热情地接待了他们,并采用了他们的意见。俞大猷将军命参将汤克宽埋伏在西堠门,命张四维驻扎龙山、郭巨两地,命侯得假投倭贼,到约定时间焚火烧毁

General Yu Resisting the Japanese Invaders[1]

In 1551, in the Ming Dynasty, the pirate leader Wang Zhi seduced the Japanese pirates to rob the Jintang Island, snatching away women and properties, massacring civilians and setting fires. After a long time, the ghosts of the murdered people gathered around the hills in Ligang Town, making strange noises during the daytime and turning into a beam of white light at night. People said that it was a magic lamp, showing the ghosts' wish to eliminate the Japanese pirates and return the life in peace and contentment.

One day, people were burning incense and praying. Suddenly, a strong wind blew paper money all over the sky. One piece landed on a cliff. After the wind faded, a young man named Hou De took down the paper money, and saw the following words, "General Yu will arrive when the Japanese pirates come back. With the cooperation of the army and the people, the Japanese pirates will be eliminated."

In less than ten days, the Japanese pirates came again. Yu Dayou really came to annihilate the enemy. At this time, Hou De and several other brave men requested to see General Yu. Yu Dayou warmly received them and adopted their suggestions. General Yu Dayou ordered General Tang Kekuan to prepare an ambush at the stronghold Xihoumen, ordered Zhang Siwei to be

---

[1] General Yu Dayou (1503 - 1579) was famous for fighting in the wars against Japanese pirates in the Ming Dynasty.

四、舟山历史人物神话

敌营。俞大猷自己秘密移营到木岙等候。

　　第三天半夜，倭贼营寨大火顿起。俞大猷趁机急速出兵进剿。倭贼惊慌失措，不知兵从何来，纷纷夺船逃命，溺死的不计其数。唯有汪直率领一队精锐倭贼，突围逃生，逃往日本。

　　汪直到了日本以后，发动三十六岛浪人，自造几十艘巨舰，过了三年又来侵扰，藏在外洋小岛上等待时机。俞大猷一边命各地守军伏击，一边派遣两只大船，装扮成商船，前去诱惑。倭盗见财眼红，果然追赶而来。这夜，风声雷声连成一片，四周都黑乎乎的，分不清哪是天，哪是海。奇怪的是，俞大猷将军站立的沥港小山脚既没有风，也没有雨。一直到第二天早上，四更时分，还不见倭贼进港，俞大猷和衣枕刀，在小山脚躺了一会。他刚一入睡，眼前就出现了一幅贼军布阵图，并有神人向他指点了歼盗路线和方法。俞大猷高兴地笑醒过来，马上和诸将商议出兵退敌。

stationed in Longshan and Guoqu, and ordered Hou De to set fire to the enemy camp at the appointed time after surrendering to the Japanese pirates in pretense. As for Yu Dayou, he secretly moved to Mu'ao and waited for the fire.

In the middle of the night of the third day after the pirates' arrival, a big fire broke out in their camps. Yu Dayou took the opportunity and quickly led troops to attack the enemy. Totally unprepared, the Japanese pirates were in a panic. They swarmed to their boats and many of them were drowned. Only Wang Zhi and a team of elite Japanese pirates managed to escape. They fled to Japan.

After Wang Zhi arrived in Japan, he gathered many ronins from the thirty-six major islands in Japan and built dozens of huge ships. After three years, they headed off to invade again. At Zhoushan, they hid on offshore islands and waited for the moment. Knowing this, Yu Dayou ordered the local garrisons to prepare an ambush, and sent two large ships, which pretended to be merchant ships, to lure the pirates out. The greedy pirates took the bait and went out to chase the ships. At that night, it was windy, thundering, and pitch-black. One could not tell where the sea began and the sky ended. Strangely enough, there was neither wind nor rain at the encampment of General Yu Dayou, which was located at the foot of the hills in Ligang Town. Until four o'clock in the next morning, no Japanese pirates were in sight. Yu Dayou took a nap in his armour, with his knife as the pillow. As soon as he fell asleep, a map of military formation of the pirates appeared in front of him, and a divine man showed him the route and method to eliminate the pirates. Yu Dayou was so happy that he woke up with a smile and immediately shared the tactics with the generals.

It turned out that at that night the pirates did not have enough time to enter Ligang Town, and turned to Cengang Town for shelter.

四、舟山历史人物神话

原来,昨夜倭盗来不及进入沥港,而是转往岑港避风。天刚亮,倭盗就被岑港的守军赶了出来,只得重向金塘进犯。伏守在天打岩的卢镗,故意放其入港。倭贼以为金塘没有守军,便大胆闯入。一进港里,只听得四面炮声大作。倭贼回头急退,被伏在天打岩的卢镗,用炮火截住。倭贼便纷纷窜上大平山,被黄应微军击杀无数。残余倭贼退到港边,想夺船逃奔。贼船早已被张四维军纵火烧着了。最后,贼首汪直被擒拿,倭寇大败。

　　从此,在我国沿海各省祸害二十余年的倭患,才被消除根绝,舟山百姓为了纪念俞大猷抗倭胜利,就在他当年躺过的小山脚下立了一块石碑,叫平倭碑。

Just after dawn, they were driven out by the garrisons of Cengang Town. With no choice, they attacked Jintang again. General Lu Tang, who was stationed at Tiandayan, deliberately let the pirates into the harbor. The Japanese pirates thought that there was no garrison in Jintang, so they broke in boldly. As soon as they entered the harbor, they heard the sound of gunfire from all sides. Shocked, they turned back and retreated, but were soon intercepted by Lu Tang. The Japanese pirates rushed to the Daping Mountain but were hit hard by troops of General Huang Yingwei. The remaining Japanese pirates retreated to the harbor, trying to seize the boats and run away. But the boats had been set ablaze by General Zhang Siwei. Finally, the Japanese pirates were completely defeated. Wang Zhi was captured alive.

With this victory, the Japanese pirate invasion, which had plagued China's coastal provinces for more than 20 years, was eradicated. In order to commemorate Yu Dayou's feat, Zhoushan people set up a stone monument named Pingwobei (monument commemorating the wiping out of Japanese pirates) at the foot of the hill where he once took a nap.

43. 状元桥的传说

　　从前,定海有一户人家,屋里只有夫妻两人,男的叫祝富,以养鸭过日子。一天其妻子生下了一对双胞胎,都是男孩,长得白白胖胖,交关可爱。夫妻俩高兴得整天合不拢嘴。

　　转眼过了十个年头。一天,祝富带着两个孩子,到远处去放鸭。他们把鸭子赶下湖,不知不觉统打起了瞌睡,呒没想到,鸭子钻到财主的一块田里去了。财主叫家丁把鸭子圈起来,并把祝富父子三人拖到家中。财主老婆看见两个白白胖胖的小孩,把嘴靠近财主的耳朵讲了一通悄悄话,财主忙对家丁说:"好饭好菜招待他们,勿得怠慢。"财主怎么一下子大发慈悲,生起菩萨心肠来了呢? 原来,他的胖老婆生勿出孩子,看这两个小孩好猛,决定收作自己的孩子。吃罢饭,财主老婆替两个小孩换好衣服,冷一声热一声地叫:"心肝宝贝。"并请了读书先生教两个孩子读书,让孩子的生父在家里当佣人。

　　不知不觉过了八年,这年正好是大比之年,财主叫两个孩子去赴考,不料要走的头天夜里,两个孩子的眼睛统瞎了。四处名医统医勿好,急得财主像热锅上的蚂蚁团团转。

　　原来八年前,祝富的妻子见丈夫、孩子一去不归,整天哭,哭得死去活来。一天,走来一名风水先生,见其哭得介伤心,问明了原因后说:"你的命介苦,我看看侬的祖坟做得好勿好。"他来到其祖坟,前看三次,后看三次,突然说:"啊呀,运道

The Legend of the Zhuangyuan Bridge

Once upon a time, there was a duck-raising family in Dinghai City. The husband was named Zhu Fu. One day, his wife gave birth to a pair of chubby and healthy boy twins. The couple was happy and often smiled.

Time flied. Ten years passed. One day, Zhu Fu and his two children went somewhere distant to feed ducks. They drove the ducks down to the lake and waited besides. Being tired, they dozed off. Unexpectedly, the ducks got into a rich man's field. The rich man ordered his servants to catch all the ducks and dragged Zhu Fu and the two children to his home. The rich man's wife saw the cute twins and whispered to the rich man. Then, the rich man said to the servants, "Serve them good dishes." How come the rich man became kind and merciful? It turned out that his fat wife could not give birth to children. As a greedy woman, she wanted to take away the twins as her own children. After dinner, she changed the clothes of the two children and called them "sweetheart". She also found them a tutor. As for Zhu Fu, he was forced to be a servant.

After eight years, the imperial examination took place. The rich man asked the twins to take the exam. But the night before they left, they suddenly lost their sight and no doctor could cure them. The rich man was as anxious as ants on a hot pot.

The cause of the odd thing was traced back to eight years ago. Failing to find her husband and children, Zhu Fu's wife cried her heart out. One day, a geomancer was passing by. Seeing her crying

来哉！侬的两个儿子将来一定好做高官,侬祖坟内有一潭水,里面有两条河鲫鱼,这是侬两个儿子的化身,如今侬两个儿子在别人家读书,等十八岁时,侬择个日子,把这两条鱼的眼睛包好,侬儿子的眼睛就瞎了！那辰光,你扮作医生到那户人家医眼睛,向他要一个儿子作为报酬,侬回家后解开黑布,儿子的眼睛就会亮了,侬就能得到状元儿子了。"

祝富的妻子按照风水先生的话去做,两个儿子的眼睛果然被她医亮了,财主让他们去赶考,并答应送一个儿子给她做报酬。两个儿子都中了状元,双双回家。祝富的妻子在桥头等待儿子赶考回来,听见开锣鸣道声,就赶上前拦住轿,向两个状元儿子说明真情,两个状元连忙跪在桥头拜见生母,又去财主家救生父。一家骨肉团聚了。

后来,人们就把当时状元跪地认母的桥叫作"状元桥"。

so bitterly, he stopped and asked for the reason. Then he remarked, "Your life is so bitter. Let me see if your ancestral tomb is well built." When he came to her ancestral grave, he looked at its front three times and its back three times, and suddenly said, "Ah, what a good fortune! Your sons will be high level officials in the future. There is a pool of water in your ancestral grave, in which there are two crucian carp. These are the incarnations of your sons. Now, they are studying in another family. When they are 18 years old, choose a day and wrap up the eyes of these two fish, and your sons will be temporarily blind. Then, you should pretend to be a doctor and go to that family. Promise them that you will cure the blindness only if they can reward you a son. When you return, unwrap the fish, and your sons will see the world again, and they will win the title of Zhuangyuan[1]."

Zhu Fu's wife did what the geomancer told her. Her two sons' eyes were really bright again. The rich man asked them to take the exam and promised to send a son to her as a reward. Both sons became Number One Scholars. On their way home there was a bridge, on which Zhu Fu's wife was waiting. Hearing sound of gongs, she stopped the sedan chairs and told the truth to her sons. Her sons knelt down before their birth mother and went to the rich man's home to save their father. The family was reunited.

Later, people called the bridge where the Number One Scholars knelt down to recognize their mother as the Zhuangyuan Bridge.

---

[1] Number One Scholar, the title conferred on the one who came first in the highest imperial examination

四、舟山历史人物神话

44. 乾隆三吃闭门羹

　　有一年，乾隆下江南来到普陀山。他一上码头，就被这里的海景山色迷住了，便独自一人"噔噔"爬上佛顶，"哐哐"奔到梵音洞，再到千步沙看看海浪，又去潮音洞听听潮音。他边走边看风景，忽然迎面飘来几点雨滴，抬头一看，啊哟，日近黄昏，海雾上升，天上还稀稀弄弄落着毛毛细雨。到这辰光他才忖到应找个投宿的地方了。

　　乾隆沿着小路，急呼呼往普济寺走去。勿料地生路勿熟，东一弯，西一拐，套了一大圈，走了交关多冤枉路，等找到普济寺，天色已经全暗了。他三脚两步朝普济寺山门走去，啥人晓得，他刚刚踏上正门石阶，"哐当"一声，两扇大门关煞了。他见东边门还开着，赶紧往边门走，"哐当"一声，东边门也关上了。乾隆吃了闭门羹，心里气鼓鼓，转身回到正中山门，抡起拳头，"嘭嘭嘭"把两扇山门擂得震天响。

Three Cold-Shoulders for the Qianlong Emperor[1]

~~~~~~

One year, the Qianlong Emperor came to Mount Putuo during his southern inspection. As soon as he got on the dock, he was fascinated by the sea and mountains scenery here. Therefore, alone, he climbed up the Foding Mountain, ran to the Fanyin Cave, then went to Qianbusha for the waves, and the Chaoyin Cave for the tidal sounds. As he walked, engaged in his sightseeing, he felt some head-on raindrops. He looked up. Oops. It was nearly dusk with a light drizzle, and the fog over the sea was rising. It was only at this time that he thought it was time to find accommodation.

Qianlong rushed to the Puji Temple along the path. However, unfamiliar with the place, he turned here and there, making his route longer. It had been already dark by the time he found the Puji Temple. Quickly, he headed for the gate. But as soon as he stepped onto the stone steps of the main gate, the two doors closed with a loud "bang". Noticing the east door was still open, he rushed to the side door. Another "bang", the east door was also closed. Being rejected, Qianlong seethed with rage, and returned to the main gate. He raised and

---

[1] The Qianlong Emperor (September 25, 1711 – February 7, 1799) was the sixth emperor of the Qing Dynasty in China.

四、舟山历史人物神话

看守山门的小和尚听到有人敲门,从西边门伸出头来,喉咙胖胖喊道:"侬啥人,为啥乱敲山门?"

乾隆满肚皮气呒地方出,没料到钻出个小和尚,便没好气地说:"高老爷要进寺院,快把山门打开!"

小和尚一听,也没好气地说:"啥高老爷矮老爷,你呒没长眼睛,这里勿是开着山门?"

乾隆心忖,这个小和尚真勿知天高地厚,要我当朝天子走边门! 他把面孔一板,说:"高老爷从小呒没走过边门,你去告诉方丈,叫他大开正门相迎!"

小和尚听乾隆口气介大,心里暗暗盘算:做事体还是小心谨慎些好,要是这人真有啥来头,方丈责怪下来,吃罪勿起。他这么一忖,口气也软了勿少,说:"好,你在外面等一等!"便急匆匆跑了。

这辰光,乾隆在外面雨淋淋,风吹吹,骨骨抖,等得真急煞。小和尚去了老半天,才慢吞吞地从后院走了出来。乾隆急忙上前问道:"方丈咋话?"

小和尚说:"方丈讲,国有国法,佛有佛规,普济寺也有规矩,过了时辰,勿可乱开山门!"

乾隆有火发勿出,只好耐着性子说:"啥国法佛规,今天就破一破这个规矩,把山门开开让我进去!"

小和尚用手指指乾隆说:"你讲话勿损腰,这是历代祖师传下来的规矩,啥人敢违反? 方丈讲了,时辰一过,就是皇帝老子来了,也勿准开!"

乾隆呆了呆,这话勿是有意冲着我讲的吗? 但看看自己这身打扮,只好转弯抹角地说:"普济寺的规矩真有介森严?"

"啥人骗你!"

swung his fist. Wham! The doors were hit hard.

Hearing the noise, the little monk who guarded the mountain door, stuck his head out from the west door, shouted, "Who are you? Why knocking on the door?"

Full of anger, Qianlong did not expect a small monk, so he said, "Lord Gao (Gao literally means long) wants to enter the temple. Open the door!"

When the monk heard that, he also said in a bad mood, "I don't care whether you are Lord Gao or Lord Ai (Ai literally means short). Can't you see this door is open?"

Qianlong thought to himself, "This little monk really gets the nuts. He required the emperor to take the side door!" He said with a stern face, "I have never walked through the side door since I was a child. Go and tell the abbot to open the main gate wide to welcome me!"

The little monk noticed that Qianlong spoke boldly enough, and he thought, "It's better to be circumspect. What if he is a big man? I could not afford to be blamed by the abbot." He said in an apparently softer tone, "Well, wait outside for a while!" Whereupon, he hurried away.

Qianlong suffered from the wind and rain, shivering and waiting anxiously. The monk went for a long time before slowly coming out of the backyard. Qianlong rushed forward and asked, "What did the abbot say?"

The monk replied, "The abbot said that the country has the national law, so does the Buddhist. The Fuji Temple also has its rules. The main gate cannot be opened indiscriminately when it is the curfew!"

Qianlong said patiently, "What kind of the national law and Buddhist rules. Break this today. Open the gate and let me in!"

The monk pointed his finger at Qianlong and said, "It is easy

"勿可变通变通？"

"变通勿来格！"

"当真勿开？"

小和尚越听越勿耐烦了："勿开！勿开！"

乾隆心急了，脱口讲："勿开，勿开，以后勿准再开！"

小和尚一听，火了，气冲冲地说："谅你没介大的权！"讲完"哐当"一声，关上西边门，顾自走了。

乾隆吃了闭门羹，心里着实恼火，但又有啥办法呢？只好另找住处。第二天，他下了道口谕：普济寺的正中山门，从今后不准再开！方丈明知乾隆有意刁难，又勿敢违抗圣旨。所以，一直到现在，普济寺的正中山门老是关着，勿随便打开，平日里，只从东西边门进出。

for you to say so, but who would dare to violate the rules handed down by our ancestors. The abbot has said that once the hour has passed, even if the emperor comes, the door will not be allowed to open!"

Qianlong was dumbfounded, thinking, "Isn't that an innuendo to me?" But looking at his own outfit, he beat around the bush, saying, "The rules in the Fuji Temple are so strict?"

"Why lie to you!"

"Could you bend the rules?"

"No way."

"Serious?"

The monk became more and more impatient, "No! No!"

Qianlong was furious and blurted out, "No door! No way! Then never open the door."

Hearing this, the monk seethed and said, "Are you that capable?" Whereupon, "bang", he shut the west door, and left.

Qianlong was so livid to receive that cold shoulder. But what could he do? He had to find another accommodation. The next day, he issued a decree that the main door of the Puji Temple was forbidden to open from that moment forward.The abbot knew that Qianlong intended to be harsh, but he dared not disobey the imperial decree. Therefore, until now, the main gate of the Puji Temple has always remained closed and not opened at will. Ordinarily, the access is available only at the east and west doors.

45. 安期生泼墨成桃花

老早,桃花岛是个荒岛。

有一日,有个叫安期生的居士,乘着一只小船,来到这个岛上。跳上去一看,这个岛无人居住,四面是海,东西两头是山,两山之间是一片平地。有山有水有平地,气候暖和,风景优美,他看看蛮中意,就在这个岛上住了下来,设炉炼丹,开垦种植,空落来写写诗,画画画,日脚过得蛮舒意。

每年桃花水涌进港里来的辰光,这里乌贼就会旺发,潮水冲冲,也会把乌贼冲上海滩,勿用到海里去抲,在滩横头撮撮,也能撮到木佬佬。这样一来,有勿少内地渔民,到了这个季节,都来抲乌贼。在岛上搭个茅棚,临时住住,等乌贼汛一过再回去。日脚久了,有些渔民看看岛上土肥水清好开垦,岙多港深好抲鱼,索性拖儿带女全家搬来定居。依来,其也来,到岛上来定居的渔民越来越多了。

人一多,就嘈杂,有辰光难免还会发生口角,争争吵吵。安期生喜欢清静,这样哄哄闹闹的,他怨煞了,便从岛的东南面海边,搬到岛的西北角山上,找到一个向阳的石洞住了下来。啥人晓得,没过多少日脚,到西北角来定居的人也多起来了。呒办法,安期生只好离开这个岛,另找住所。

第二天,他雇了只小船,船靠在西山脚下的海边山嘴头——就是现在的稻篷村外山嘴。临走前,他坐在海滩的一

An Qisheng[1] Splashed Ink into Peach Blossoms

Once upon a time, Peach Blossom Island is a desert place.

One day, a lay Daoist named An Qisheng came to the island in a small boat. He found that the island was uninhabited, surrounded by the sea on all sides, with mountains at the east and west ends and a piece of flat ground in between. There were mountains, rivers and flat land, with warm climate and beautiful scenery. He liked it very much, so he settled down on the island, set up a furnace for alchemy, cultivated land to plant, and wrote poems and painted pictures in his leisure time, enjoying an easy life.

Every year when the peach blossom water gushed into the harbor, the squids would gather here and the tide would bring the squids up to the beach. So instead of going to the sea, people could catch a lot of squids there. As a result, quite a few inland fishermen came here to catch squids in this season. They put up a thatched shelter for a temporary stay until the squid season was over. As time went by, some fishermen found the island having fertile soil and clear water suitable for reclamation, lots of flat land and deep harbors easy to catch fish, so they brought their family to settle down. Seeing this, more and more of them came to live on the island.

As inhabitants increase, it was noisy, and inevitably squabbles

---

[1] An Qisheng, a legendary people recorded in some ancient classics, was a Daoist and cultivated himself to be an immortal.

四、舟山历史人物神话

块岩石上,看看山,望望海,唉!在这个岛上住了几十年,现在要离开了,真有点舍勿得!他触景生情,拿出文房四宝,磨好满满一砚浓墨,正想提笔写诗,小船老大在喊了:"赶快上船,再勿开船,潮水要错落了。"安期生呒办法,只好勿写,顺手拿起砚台,用力一泼,墨汁泼在岩石上,好像一朵朵盛开的桃花。直到现在,这里的山石中,还留着桃花形的花纹。这里有句话:"安期生墨一泼,桃花石头半山黑。"从那以后,这个岛就叫桃花岛了。

and disputes occured. An Qisheng preferred tranquility, and the noise bored him. So he moved from the seashore in the southeast of the island to a mountain in the northwest corner and found a cave on the sunny side to live in. Who would have thought that shortly afterwards, settlement also increased in the northwest corner? There was nothing he could do but leave the island and find another place to live in.

The next day, he hired a small boat, and the boat docked at the seaside spur at the foot of the western mountain, which is now known as the spur outside Daopeng Village. Before leaving, he sat down on a rock on the beach looking at the mountain, and the sea, thinking, "Alas! Having lived here for decades, I'm really reluctant to leave!" Moved by the scene, he took out the four treasures of the study and ground thick ink. When he was about to write a poem, the boatman shouted, "Get on board, or the tide will ebb." An Qisheng had no choice, but to stop. He picked up the ink stone and splashed. The ink sprinkled on the rock like blooming peach blossoms. Until now, there are still peach blossom shaped patterns on the rock. Here is a saying, "After An Qisheng splashed the ink, half of the stones on the mountain were black, covered with peach blossom patterns." Since then, the island has been called Peach Blossom Island.

46. 东福山

　　相传,秦始皇做了皇帝交关怕死,到处寻求长生不老之药,好让他永生永世做皇帝。

　　秦始皇身边有个方士,名叫徐福。这人一张嘴巴交关灵光,老是要在秦始皇面前讲大话。有一次,他对秦始皇讲,海上有座蓬莱山,是神仙住的地方,山上有长生不老之药,只要给他一千个童男童女,他就能够把仙药寻回来。秦始皇听了蛮相信,便命徐福带上童男童女,前往蓬莱仙岛寻求仙药。

　　这日,徐福的船队路过舟山洋面突然刮起风暴,海上的浪头,像小山一样,一个接一个向船队扑来,把船打得东倒西歪团团转,迷失了方向,随浪飘到一个无名小岛前。徐福站在舱板上一看,只见这个小岛树木茂盛,风景如画,好像一座仙岛。徐福心忖,现在船只损坏,淡水用尽,正好在这里修船充水,歇上几天,再做道理。他主意一定,便叫船队沙沙落了风篷,抛了锚,靠了岸。他们踏上小岛,发现山坳里还搭着座茅棚,里面住着一个长胡须老头。老头见有客人来,蛮高兴,连忙搬凳倒茶,又拿出烤熟晒干的乌贼鲞、黄鱼鲞、淡菜干招待客人。喝了老头的茶,吃了老头的海味,童男童女个个有了精神,大家就在岛上搭起帐篷,伐木的伐木,修船的修船,长胡须老头还带着他们到山上去挖井找水。小岛上一下来了介多人,闹热猛了。

The Dongfu Mountain

~~~~~~

Legend has it that Emperor Qin Shi Huang, fearing death in his late years, sought the elixir of immortality so that he could be emperor for all eternity.

Qin Shi Huang had an alchemist named Xu Fu who was a smooth talker, always swaggering to him. Once Xu Fu told Emperor Qin Shi Huang on the sea stood the Penglai Mountain, where the immortals lived so there existed the elixir of immortality. If the emperor could grant him a thousand virgin boys and maidens, he could find the elixir. Believing this, Qin Shi Huang ordered Xu Fu to take the young boys and girls with him and go to the fairy mountain Penglai in search of immortal elixir.

One day, when Xu Fu's fleet was passing by Zhoushan, a storm suddenly blew in the sea. The waves on the sea, like hills, rushed toward the fleet one after another. The ship went round and round, losing its way, and drifting with the waves to an unknown island. Standing on the deck, Xu Fu saw that the island was lush and picturesque, like a fairy island. Xu Fu thought to himself, now that the ship was damaged and the fresh water was exhausted, it was just right for him to repair the ship and replenish water. They could rest for a few days and then discuss new plans. Once he decided, he made his fleet lower the canvas, cast anchor, and pull in to the shore. When they reached the island, they found a long-bearded old man living under a thatched canopy in a col. The old man was very happy seeing the guests. He hurriedly moved the stool and

四、舟山历史人物神话

几日以后，船修好了，柴爿劈足了，淡水也充够了，按理说好开船了，可开船总要有方向呀！前几日，被风暴刮得呒头呒绪，现在连这个小岛叫啥名也勿晓得，在啥地方也弄勿灵清，船咋开开？还有，这几日，好多童男童女受了岛上蚊虫叮咬，忽冷忽热，浑身无力，生了冷热病，船上的药又治不好。徐福心事担煞，困也困勿着，半夜爬起，不想在帐篷门口看见一大把草药，拿来给病人一吃，没二日，病都好了。

徐福忖，这岛上只有老头一人，他帮助我找到了淡水，又送来了草药，是个好人，更是个奇人，何不再去向他请教行船的水路呢？来到老头茅棚，说明来意，老头告诉徐福，等天气雾蒙蒙，太阳出来的辰光，东边海面上常有岛影出现，朝东驶去，便是蓬莱仙岛。

徐福赶忙回去，做开船准备，第二日一早，海上雾气蒙蒙，等太阳出来辰光，果然看见东边海面上有一片模模糊糊的岛影。徐福辞别了老头，令船队起锚拔篷，朝东方这片岛影驶去。

后来，捕鱼人看到这个小岛上辟了路，挖了水井，好住人了，就三三两两在岛上搭起茅棚住下来了。因当年徐福东去路过此岛，所以将其取名为东福山。

poured the tea, and took out the sun-dried squids, yellow croakers, and mussels to entertain them. After drinking the tea and eating the seafood, the boys and girls all got refreshed. They set up tents on the island, chopping wood and repairing the ship. The long-bearded old man also took them to the mountains to dig wells for water. The island suddenly became very bustling having so many people.

A few days later, the ship was repaired, firewood was cut and fresh water was supplied. It was time to set sail, but they had no direction. They were hit by a storm a few days ago and now didn't even know the name of this island or where it was. How could they sail? Moreover, in recent days, many young boys and girls had been bitten by mosquitoes, which made them hot and cold alternatively, and weak all over. Worse still, the medicine on the ship could not cure them. Xu Fu was extremely worried and couldn't sleep. He got up in the middle of the night but found a handful of herbal medicine at the door of the tent unexpectedly. He gave it to the ill boys and girls and within two days, they were all well.

Xu Fu wondered, "The old man is the only one on this island; he has helped me find fresh water and sent me herbs; he is not only a good man, but also a remarkable man. Why not ask him the way to sail?" So he went to the old man's thatched tent and explained his purpose. The old man told Xu Fu that when the weather was foggy and the sun came out, there was often a shadow of an island on the east side of the sea. Sailing east, he could find Penglai Fairy Island.

Xu Fu hurried back and got ready to set sail. The next morning the sea was foggy and when the sun came out, he did see a dim shadow of island on the east coast. Xu Fu bade farewell to the old man and made his fleet lift the anchor and sail for the shadow.

Later, when the fishermen found that the island already had roads and wells and was suitable to live in, they put up thatched tents and settled there by twos and threes. Because Xu Fu passed this island in his eastward trip, so it was named the Dongfu Mountain.

五、舟山海洋生物神话

　　由于得天独厚的地理位置和特殊的历史原因,舟山的神话故事与海洋密不可分。位于东海大洋之中的舟山,美名"千岛之城",由206个岛屿组成,自然居民大多是以海为生的渔民,他们每日的作息与海洋是紧紧联系在一起的。舟山的本土神话故事大多与海洋相关,代表着舟山劳动人民每日观海而作的智慧和想象,也在漫漫的历史中逐渐演变为舟山的文化记忆,沉淀成文化价值,成为与外界文化交流时的特殊文化符号。这些故事也代表着舟山本地人对于海洋生活环境和海洋资源的原始想象。某些故事中的鱼类被赋予了独立的性格,从这些"人设"中也可以看出当地人们最朴实的价值观的形成,以及舟山集体无意识的形成。

47. 带鱼为啥没有鳞

带鱼本来全身长着银色的细鳞,亮闪闪咯,加上其细长的身条,在海里游起来,像一条白色绸带,飘来飘去,交关优美。

水晶宫里有许多舞女,是专门给海龙王跳舞的。这些舞女的舞,统是带鱼教咯,所以大家统称带鱼为舞师。当时水晶宫的第七代龙王,是个昏君,腐败猛。其每日吃参汤、燕窝汤,一边吃,一边还得有舞女陪伴着,跳舞给其取乐。

有一年,正好是这昏君八十三岁寿辰,在做寿的前三天,突然其一个圣旨下来,叫带鱼编一个舞,由八十三个舞女同时表演,为其祝寿。带鱼接到圣旨,不敢怠慢,日夜编排。到做寿那天,金锣银锣"喤喤"一敲,带鱼舞师就调排舞女表演,两个穿红衣裳的舞女最先走出,拉起手搭起了龙门。接着众舞女分九队出场,每队九人,每人穿一种颜色衣裳,九九八十一个舞女,手拉手、队连队翩翩起舞,缓缓旋转,从龙门下来回穿梭,像长龙起舞。众水族看得齐声叫好,拍手称赞,夸带鱼舞师有本事。谁晓得龙王看着看着,突然大怒,说:"九节连起来是条龙,龙咋好在女子腋下穿来穿去,这是有意对孤无礼,带鱼编出这样的舞,必有反心。将相听令,把带鱼的银鳞统统剥尽,关进牢房里,冻其三日,再处死刑。"虾兵蟹将听龙王圣口一开,不敢怠慢,马上照办。

龙王寿辰这日,正好是冬至,天气已经冷不过了。带鱼被

Why the Hairtail Is Scaleless?

The hairtail used to have so shining silver scales that coupled with his slender body he looked like a white ribbon fluttering gracefully when swimming in the sea.

In the Crystal Palace, there were many dancing girls who offered dances exclusively for the Dragon King. These girls were taught by the hairtail, so he was called the master. At that time, as the seventh reigning ruler of the Crystal Palace, the Dragon King knew nothing but dissolute profligacy. Day and night, he went on ginseng soup and bird'nest soup binges, during which there must be dancers accompanying him for entertainment.

One year, it happened to be the 83rd birthday of the wretched ruler. Three days before the celebration, his words came to the hairtail, asking him to choregraph a dance of 83 girls in expectation of some birthday congratulations. Upon receiving the decree, the hairtail didn't dare to procrastinate, and orchestrated all the day. On the day of the Dragon King's birthday, with the clang of gongs, two dancers in red came out first, as arranged by the hairtail, holding hands to set up a dragon gate. Then the 81 dancers came out in nine teams of nine dancers, each team wearing clothes of one color. Hand in hand, they came on the stage and rotated slowly, shuttling back and forth from the dragon gate. The long line looked just like a tumbling dragon. The aquatic community applauded in unison and clapped hands in praise of the hairtail's ability. However, the Dragon King gazed reflectively, and all of a sudden, he became

五、舟山海洋生物神话

剥掉鳞,浑身流血不止,眼看快冻煞啦。众水族都交关同情带鱼,舞女连夜织出一只雪白的纱罩,让他套起,想尽各种办法,偷偷把他放进大海,使他死里逃生。

从此,带鱼就没有鳞啦,身上只有一层白白的油霜,这就是当年舞女织的纱罩。而带鱼编的《穿龙门》舞,却传了下来,后来传到了人间,至今还有许多小孩常要玩呢。

furious, "These nine teams do form a dragon shape, but how could a dragon walk under women's armpit? The hairtail deliberately choregraph such a show to besmirch me. He must intend to rebel. Order! Strip him of all the silver scales, and froze him into the cell for three days before execution." The underlings didn't dare to hesitate and did it accordingly when hearing the Dragon King's order.

The day of the Dragon King's birthday was the winter solstice. It was freezingly cold. Stripped of scales, the hairtail bled profusely and was about to be frozen to death. The aquatic tribe all sympathized with the hairtail. The dancers wove a snowy white gauze cover overnight for him. They tried to sneak him into the sea by any means possible to save him from death.

Since then, the hairtail no longer had any scales but a white layer of cream, which was the gauze cover woven by the dancers. As for "Through the Dragon Gate", the dance choreographed by the hairtail, is handed down to the world and still played by many children.

五、舟山海洋生物神话

48.望潮吃脚手

　　望潮本是东海龙宫的太监,良心善猛。当宫女一点点事情做错,龙王要重重处罚宫女时,其总要出头为宫女说情。

　　一次、二次、三次,望潮说情的次数多了,龙王就起了疑心。龙王忖:侬一个太监,为啥待宫女介好?嗯,一定有私情。龙王越忖越气,就下令把望潮抲去,全身衣裳剥光,满头乌发剃尽,眼睛蒙住,赶出龙宫,让大潮元帅搁其到海涂里。

　　望潮在海涂里生活,苦猛苦猛。每到农历九月九以后,天气冷了,望潮吃勿住,就往泥涂洞眼钻进。在洞里辰光一长,呒告好吃,要饿煞,没办法,就吃自己的手脚。吃到第二年春

Why Wangchao Eats His Own Limbs?

Wangchao used to serve as a court eunuch in the East Sea Dragon Palace. With a heart of gold, when court ladies were about to be punished by the Dragon King for trivial mistakes, he always stood out and pleaded for them.

Once, twice, three times ... He interceded too much that the Dragon King became suspicious. The Dragon King thought to himself, "Why is a eunuch so nice to court ladies? Well, there must be some affairs." Thinking of that, the Dragon King became more furious that he ordered underlings to take him away, strip off his clothes and shave off his hair. Blindfolded, Wangchao was expelled from the palace and thrown into the tidal flat by Marshal Dachao.

The life in the tidal flat was really rough. After lunar September 9, the weather got colder. Wangchao found it hard to endure, so he went into a mud hole. So long had he been in the hole with no food around that he felt extremely hungry. Eventually, he had no choice but to begin eating his own limbs. By the next spring, all that was left was his round head. When the weather turned warm, the hands and feet started to regrow slowly. This is what the saying "On the ninth of September, it's time for Wangchao to eat his limbs" talks about.

When the court ladies found out about this, they took off their belts, on which they embroidered flowers and their names, and

五、舟山海洋生物神话

天,只剩个滚圆圆的头。待天气转暖时,才慢慢长出。"九月九,望潮吃脚手"就是讲这事。

　　宫女晓得这事后,就纷纷从自己身上解下腰带,绣一串花和自己的名字,送给望潮。望潮就把这些腰带缠在下身当裤子,以抵风寒。现在这些腰带已变成了吸盘。

　　望潮被大潮元帅搁到海涂后,就再也呒没回龙宫去。

gave them to Wangchao. Wangchao then wrapped these belts around his lower body as trousers to ward off the cold. Now these belts have been turned into suckers.

After being stranded into the tidal flat by Marshal Dachao, Wangchao never returned to the palace.

49. 乌龟壳为啥是破裂的

老早辰光,有一只乌龟住在海边头,其交关馋痨,一闻到香味,就要流馋痨水,一看到好吃的东西,贼形狗势专门要去偷吃。

有一天,乌龟和老婆没有事体做,到外头去白相。看见天上的喜鹊叽叽喳喳叫得热闹猛,看样子好像有啥喜事,乌龟就放大喉咙喊:"喜鹊妹妹!"天上喜鹊听见了就飞下来,停在乌龟面前,问:"乌龟大哥、大嫂,侬喊我有啥事体?"

乌龟连忙问:"喜鹊妹妹,侬这样子高兴,有啥喜事,是否讲给我听听?"喜鹊讲:"阿拉这样高兴,是要到王母娘娘地方喝喜酒去。"乌龟听后,嬉皮笑脸地拉拉喜鹊说:"侬把我也带去吧!"喜鹊也蛮乖,连忙对乌龟讲:"我是会把侬带去的,不过有一个条件,就是侬到天上后,不能独自行动,也勿要偷东西吃,阿拉吃啥,侬也吃啥,这条件侬做得到吗?"乌龟忖等晌有好东西吃,心里真笑煞,就一口答应:"能做到,能做到。"这样喜鹊喊来一批小姐妹,每人借给乌龟一根羽毛,一起飞到了天宫。

到了天宫里,大家统帮助王母娘娘做事体。乌龟开头也做得蛮卖力,后来闻到了香气,就懒得做啦,馋痨水流了出来。

其趁喜鹊勿注意,偷偷奔进了厨房,看桌子上摆着许多好下饭,头颈一弯,狠性命吃起来了。没一晌工夫,介多东西统

Why Are There Cracks on the Tortoise's Shell?

Once upon a time, there was Tortoise living by the sea. He is so gluttonous that he would salivate at the smell of aromas, and take some bites on the sly at the sight of tasty food.

One day, Tortoise and his wife had nothing to do, so they just hanged around. He noticed that the magpie in the sky was chirping gaily, as if there was something good happening. Then he called out loud, "Sister magpie!" Upon hearing that call, the magpie flew down and stopped in front of Tortoise and asked, "Mr. and Mrs. Tortoise, may I be of your assistance?"

Tortoise asked, "Sister magpie, what is your joy? Please fill me in." The magpie said, "I am so happy because I am going to the Queen of Heaven's palace to attend the wedding banquet." When he heard about this, he pulled the magpie, and gave a playful grin, "Take me with you!" The magpie was so kind, "It's alright so long as you comply with one rule. When you are in the heaven, you must not act alone or steal any food. Whatever I eat, you follow the suit. Can you do that?" On the thought of good stuff to eat later, he was so overjoyed to reply, "Yes, I can. I can." Whereupon, the magpie called on her sisters to lend Tortoise a piece of leather each, and put together, then they flew to the Heaven Palace.

When they arrived at the palace, they all helped the Queen of Heaven with her chores. At first, Tortoise worked very hard, but when smelling the aroma, he turned sluggish with his mouth watering.

　　　　　　　　　　　五、舟山海洋生物神话

被其吃光啦,后来连酒壶里的酒也被其喝光啦,桌子上只剩下一点乱七八糟的骨头。吃喜酒的辰光到了,总管喊:"各位客人请坐好,马上要喝喜酒啦。"仙鹤负责端下饭,其到厨房一看,下饭统呒没啦,只见乌龟肚皮吃得滚壮,连地盆也走勿过来,连忙告诉了总管。大家统气煞啦,一批小姐妹从乌龟身上把自己的羽毛拔去飞走了。乌龟真急煞了,一看只有一只喜鹊还在,就跪在地上连连磕头,要求喜鹊给其老婆带个信,把家里最软的东西拿出来,铺在地上,它要从天上跳下去。喜鹊看其可怜,就答应啦,可其把"软"字听成"硬"字了。小喜鹊飞到乌龟屋门口,对它的老婆讲了:"乌龟大哥要从天上跳下来,侬把家里最硬的东西拿出来铺在地上。"乌龟老婆就把家里最硬的红石板拿出来铺在地上,这辰光,乌龟从天上跳下来,刚好摔在石板上,其痛得气也喘勿过来,终算还呒没死,但从此以后,乌龟壳就破裂啦。

He sneaked into the kitchen without the magpie's notice. Seeing that there were many delicacies on the table, he could not wait to bury his head to gobble them up ferociously. All the food was consumed in no time, even the wine in the jug, and all that was left on the table was nothing but a mess of bones. As scheduled, the chief steward called out, "Please be seated, guests. It's time for the wedding feast." Fairy Crane was responsible for serving the food, but the scene in the kitchen astonished him when he went into the kitchen: all the food was gone, and Tortoise could not even make it to the floor due to his distended abdomen. He rushed to tell the chief steward. Everyone was furious. The magpie sisters all plucked their feathers off the tortoise and flew away. So desperate was Tortoise that when he saw that there was still one magpie left, he fell on his knees, kowtowing to her one after another. He begged her to bring a message to his wife that he required the softest thing in his house be taken out to get him from the sky. Feeling sympathy for him, she consented to the request. Unfortunately, she got the word wrong, mistaking "soft" for "hard". The magpie flew to Tortoise's door and said to his wife, "Mr. Tortoise is going to jump down from the sky, and he asks you to take the hardest thing in the house and lay it on the ground." Hence, no sooner had his wife took the hardest red stone slab in the house and laid it on the ground than Tortoise jumped down from the sky. He fell right on the slab, too painful to breath. Luckily enough, he survived it. But from then on, there are cracks on the shell.

50. 海鸥的传说

　　从前,舟山有一个蓬莱仙岛。岛上住着一个穷苦的渔家姑娘,名字叫渔姑。渔姑年纪只有十七八岁,生得好看猛,事情也交关会做。其织起网来比啥人统快,唱起歌来比啥人统好听。因此,岛上的小伙都想娶她当老婆。渔姑呢?心中早喜欢上了一个蛮有本事的渔人,名叫渔郎。

　　岛上有个渔霸,人家统叫其"害人精",想娶渔姑当小老婆。有一天,其趁渔郎枸鱼去的辰光,就派管家对渔姑说:"要是侬答应了阿拉老爷,侬这一生就吃也吃勿完,用也用勿完。"渔姑睬也勿睬管家,还把其骂了一顿。

　　管家回去以后,对渔霸讲了。渔霸听了,真气煞了,派人撕破渔姑家里的网,抢走渔姑家的东西,封了渔姑家的门。渔姑呒没办法,只好到海边等渔郎,等其回来想办法。

　　渔郎回来了,枸了一船鱼。渔姑对渔郎说:"阿拉还是成亲吧,省得渔霸再来找麻烦。"渔郎讲:"好吧,我先把这船鱼卖了,成亲的铜钿也好有了。"

　　渔姑和渔郎要成亲了。这天夜里,乡亲统来了,交关闹热。就在这辰光,渔霸带来一群人,把渔郎绑走,偷偷丢到海里去了,把渔姑抢到了其屋里。

　　渔姑被抢去后,渔霸三番五次来劝说,要渔姑和其成亲。

　　渔姑一直勿肯答应。渔霸呒没办法,就对渔姑讲:"渔郎

The Legend of Seagull

~~~~~~

Once upon a time, there was a Penglai Island in Zhoushan where a girl, named Lady Yu (Yugu), from a poor fisherman family. Lady Yu was a gorgeous and capable girl about 17 or 18 years old. She was more ambidextrous in weaving and better at singing than anyone else. Therefore, all the boys on the island wanted to marry her. But Lady Yu had long been in love with a capable fisherman named Fisherman Yu.

There was a bully on the island called "Pest", who wanted to make Lady Yu his concubine. One day, while Fisherman Yu was out fishing, the bully dispatched a steward, who said to Lady Yu, "You will be set up for life so long as you consent to my Lord's proposal." However, Yugu ignored the steward and scolded him.

The steward went back and told the bully what happened there. The bully was so angry that he sent his underlings to tear her nets, rob her of belongings, and seal the door of Lady Yu's house. Lady Yu was helpless, and had no choice but to come to the seashore, awaiting Fisherman Yu for a way out.

Finally, Fisherman Yu returned with a boatload of fish. "Let's get married," Lady Yu said to him, "just in case the bully comes back troubling us." Fisherman Yu replied, "Well, I will firstly sell this boat of fish to raise the money for marriage."

Lady Yu and Fisherman Yu were about to get married. That night, all the villagers came to congratulate them. What a lively and gay night! At that moment, the bully brought a group of men. They

五、舟山海洋生物神话

已经死了,侬再等也呒没用场,还是依了我的好。"渔姑一听渔郎已经死了,当场就昏了过去。

渔姑被救醒,渔霸又派人来劝说。渔姑讲:"要我成亲,得答应我一件事,给我一丈白布和一把剪刀。"渔霸怕渔姑寻短见,早就吩咐,凡是剪刀一类铁器勿准带入渔姑房中。现在见渔姑要剪刀,就问:"侬要剪刀做啥?"渔姑讲:"我要做孝衣,没剪刀咋做?"渔霸想了半天,答应了渔姑的要求。

渔姑穿上孝衣的第三日,渔霸喝得醉醺醺,摇摇晃晃来到渔姑房里。还没等其来到床边,渔姑就从枕头底下抽出剪刀,戳了过去。渔霸连忙一躲,剪刀戳进了其右眼。其痛得大叫一声,连忙逃了出去。

渔霸被渔姑戳瞎了眼睛,成了独眼龙。其又气又恨,叫人把渔姑捆在花园的亭子里,四周堆满干柴,点上了火,想烧死渔姑。谁料不管火多猛,渔姑身上的孝衣就是烧勿着。后来,火越烧越旺,烧着烧着,忽然渔姑人勿见了,只看到火中窜出

kidnapped Fisherman Yu, threw him into the sea secretly, and carried Lady Yu to the bully's house.

After Lady Yu was taken away, the bully came repeatedly to persuade her to marry him.

Lady Yu never agreed. Anxiously, the bully told her, "Fisherman Yu was dead. It is useless to wait for him. Why not be my girl?" Upon hearing Fisherman Yu's misery, Lady Yu fainted on the spot.

When Lady Yu was brought round, the bully again sent his underling to persuade her. Lady Yu said, "You have to promise one thing before I consent. I need about three meters, cloth and a pair of scissors." The bully had forbidden any iron tools like scissors into her room in case she would commit suicide. Now she demanded scissors, so he asked, "What do you do with it?" Lady Yu replied, "How can I make mourning clothes without scissors?" The bully contemplated for a long time, and eventually assented to her request.

On the third day of the mourning, the bully came to her room, drunk and staggering. Before he could reach the bed, Lady Yu pulled out scissors from under her pillow and poked him. The bully ducked hastily, but scissors were stabbed into his right eye. He screamed and fled away in pain.

With one of his eyes poked blind, he was now a one-eyed man. Angry and resentful, he had Lady Yu tied up in the garden pavilion, surrounded by a pile of dry wood. He lit the fire, with a view to burning her dead. However, no matter how fierce the fire was, the mourning clothes remained intact. Later, the fire escalated, but all of a sudden, Lady Yu disappeared. All that could be seen was a white bird flying out of the fire into the sky with a mournful sound, "Fisherman Yu! Fisherman Yu!"

Knowing that she was Lady Yu, people couldn't bear to see her depressed, so they said to her, "Fisherman Yu is still alive. He

　　　　　　　　　　　五、舟山海洋生物神话

一只白白的鸟,直冲天空,一边飞一边叫:"渔郎,渔郎。"叫得交关伤心。

　　人家晓得这是渔姑变的,勿忍心让其太伤心,就对其讲"侬的渔郎呒没死,被㧕鱼人救上来了。"结果渔姑每天去寻渔郎,不管风浪多大,总是在船旁边叫:"渔郎,渔郎。"㧕鱼人交关同情其,就拿点小鱼、小虾给其吃。因其经常跟着渔船在海上飞来飞去,人们就叫它"海鸥"。

was rescued by a fisherman." Whereupon, Lady Yu embarked on the quest of Fisherman Yu, regardless of strong wind and waves, always calling out from one side of the boat, "Fisherman Yu! Fisherman Yu!" Fishermen took pity on her, willing to feed her on some fish and shrimps. She is named Haiou (seagull) because she often flies around fishing boats over the sea.

51. 对虾的传说

　　老早辰光，海龙王有个囡叫蕊霞，其生得如花似玉，老龙王很喜欢其。

　　蕊霞十八岁那年，老龙王想给其选个老公。一出口，做媒人进进出出，接连不断。托塔天王、太白金星、护法神统为自己的儿孙来做媒，这可把龙王给烦煞了。其心忖：就一个囡，给谁好呢？在其忖勿出办法的辰光，乌龟军师"噔噔噔"地跑了进来，帮龙王出了个主意。其说："侬还是搭一座百花彩楼，让公主抛彩球。抛中谁，谁就是驸马。"龙王同意了。

　　第二日中午，公主慢慢走上百花楼，还吭没把脚立稳，下头许多声音传上楼来："公主，对准我抛，我阿爹是做官的。我阿爷是做官的。"统在报自己的牌子。公主看看一个也不中意，不知咋办才好。

　　龙王看公主介多辰光勿抛球，心急煞了，大声地对囡叫："抛！抛！"蕊霞公主被其阿爹吓了一跳，手里的彩球"骨碌碌"被吓落了。下面等着的仙子仙孙真笑煞了，跳呵，挤呵，统去抢彩球。这样一挤一拥，把百花楼的一根柱子"咔嚓"挤断了。眼看彩楼就要倒塌，下面的仙子仙孙怕压着，个个抱着头逃跑了。

　　就在这混乱中，有一个看热闹的后生一下冲到彩楼底下，背一弓，将快要倒下的彩楼顶住了，可其自己的背却被压

The Legend of Prawn

A long time ago, the Dragon King had a daughter named Ruixia. As fair as an orchid, she was a treasure of the old king.

When Ruixia turned 18 years old, the king wanted to select a husband for her. The news of it soon brought a gang of matchmakers, in and out one after another, and even Tota, the Great White Planet and Dharma Protector came to make matches for their descendants. The Dragon King was so annoyed that he thought to himself. "Which one is the best to entrust him with my daughter?" As he was contemplating, Counselor Tortoise trotted to him and offered an idea. Tortoise said, "We can build up a flower-decorated tower where the princess could throw an embroidered ball. The one hit shall be your son-in-law." The king consented.

The next noon, the princess slowly walked up to the Hundred Flowers Tower, and before she could stand still, she heard many voices from below, "Princess, throw at me. My father is an official. My grandfather is an official." People contended for her attention by making self-introduction, but the princess didn't like anyone of them, not knowing what to do.

The Dragon King was so impatient to see the princess keep the ball for a long time that he shouted at his daughter, "Throw it. Throw it." Frightened, Princess Ruixia lost her grasp of the embroidered ball. Fairies waiting downstairs were so overjoyed, and they jumped and shoved each other, just scrambling for the ball. One of the pillars in the Hundred Flowers Tower broke with a loud "click" due

五、舟山海洋生物神话

驼了。

龙王派人把后生叫来，一看，晓得其是东海的渔夫，背又驼了，就赏给其一条船和一些财宝。可是这个后生啥统勿要，只求和公主成婚。

这可把老龙王难煞了，心忖：我的囡怎么能嫁给一个驼背！乌龟军师见龙王不出声，又走到龙王耳朵边嘀咕了一番。

龙王连忙叫："请公主。"公主走出来。龙王对其囡讲："公主啊，这个后生要娶侬，侬要勿要其？要就点点头。"龙王呒没讲完，公主就点了点头，并且拔出一根金钗送给后生，送罢连忙羞答答地走进房去。

看这种情形，龙王和乌龟军师统傻了眼。可乌龟军师眼珠一转，又给龙王出了一个坏主意：假装答应后生同公主的婚事，让后生回屋里准备婚礼，而在后生回家的路上，将其害煞。

这后生人很老实，勿晓得是在骗其，就由乌龟军师陪着回屋里去。谁料行到海中心，突然起了乌风猛暴，恶浪把船给掀翻了，后生葬身于海底，变成了一只大虾。

这个消息传到龙宫，蕊霞公主哭得死去活来。后来，蕊霞公主晓得后生是其阿爹害的，就对其阿爹讲："这个后生为我压弯了背，侬却害死其，我也要以身相报。"于是，就当着其阿爹的面，腰一斜，就地转了三圈，也变成一只大虾，"唰"地跳出龙宫，游到大海找后生去了，再也呒没回龙宫。后生变成公虾，公主变成母虾，从此就成双成对地生活在大海里，自由自在的，很是快活。这就是后来的对虾。

to the disordered throng. Seeing that the tower was about to collapse, the fairies below scurried around, afraid of being crushed.

In the midst of this chaos, a young onlooker dashed into the bottom of the tower, arched his back against the staggering tower. However, he got himself humped.

The Dragon King sent for the young man and found out that he was a fisherman from the East China Sea and that his back had been humped because of this incident, so the king rewarded him with a boat and some treasure. But the young man wanted nothing more than to marry the princess.

The king found himself caught somewhere in between, and thought to himself, "How could my daughter marry a hunchback?" Tortoise noticed the silence, so he came up to the king, whispering something.

The Dragon King hastily called, "Bring the princess in." The princess turned up. He asked her, "Well, this young man wants to marry you, and what's your opinion? If you agree, nod your head." Before the Dragon King had finished, the princess nodded and pulled out a gold hairpin. She gave it to the young man and then hurried to her room sheepishly.

Both the Dragon King and Counselor Tortoise were dumbfounded, not expecting such a result. Pondering for a while, Tortoise came up with another evil idea that the king could pretend to consent to the marriage, send the young man home for wedding preparation, and then assassinate him on the way home.

The poor youngster, having no idea about the hoax, was accompanied by Tortoise back. When the ship sailed to the center of the sea, a storm suddenly took place and overturned the ship. As a result, the young man was buried at the bottom of the sea and turned into a prawn.

When the news reached the Dragon Palace, Princess Ruixia

五、舟山海洋生物神话

cried her heart out. Later, the princess fathomed out that her father was held responsible for his death. She said, "I owe him my life and his humped back. Now that you murdered him, I have to repay him with my life." Therefore, in the presence of her father, she rotated on the spot and turned into a prawn, swimming out of the palace in quest of the youngster. She never came back. From then on, the two prawns, the youngster and the princess, lived a carefree and happy life in the sea forever. They were what we termed as Prawn.

52. 海蜇的传说

　　相传很久以前,东海里有一条青龙精,常常出来害人。每到重阳节,青龙精就会腾空出现在天上,一阵乌风猛暴,害得人们无法安宁。这时巫婆和神汉说:"这是青龙精想要娶老婆了,只有将阿拉这里一个姑娘嫁给其才能平安。"当地的县官听信巫婆和神汉的话,以为真是青龙想娶老婆,就规定:每年重阳节,由巫婆和神汉将一个最漂亮的姑娘送给青龙精做老婆。

　　有一年,轮到一个叫海蜇的姑娘了,海蜇姑娘的阿爹阿娘哭得死去活来。海蜇姑娘却不哭,她十三岁了,很聪明,知道哭也呒没用。

　　一天,她一个人走到海边,在泥涂上挖出一个洞,又从海里捉来三条小鲨鱼,养在洞里。海蜇姑娘每天守在洞口,鲨鱼长大点,海蜇姑娘也就将洞口挖大些。夏天到了,海蜇姑娘还跳进洞里和鲨鱼一起洗澡,她们成了难

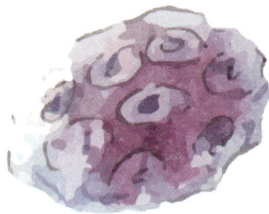

The Legend of Jellyfish

Legend has it that long ago, there was an azure dragon in the East China Sea, which often harassed people. Every Double Ninth Festival, the dragon would fly into the sky, engendering a violent gust of dark wind which would cause people much trouble. The witch and the wizard said, "The Azure Dragon must be in want of a wife. Peace can only be achieved by asking one of our girls to marry him." The county magistrate took them at their word that the dragon wanted a wife, hence he stipulated that every Double Ninth Festival, one most beautiful girl would be sent by them to the Azure Dragon as a wife.

One year, it was the turn of a girl named Haizhe. Her parents cried out, but she remained calm, for she was thirteen years old and smart enough to realize that crying is futile.

One day, she went to the beach alone. She dug a hole in the mud, where she kept three small sharks caught from the sea. Haizhe guarded the entrance every day, and would broaden the hole whenever the sharks grew bigger. When summer came, she jumped into the hole to bathe with the sharks, and they became inseparable friends.

The Double Ninth Festival approached, and the sharks turned mature. On this day, the Azure Dragon came out to harass people again.

Haizhe released the three sharks into the sea and then jumped into the sea herself. Upon seeing this, the dragon came down from

五、舟山海洋生物神话

分难舍的好朋友。

重阳节到了,鲨鱼也养大了。这一天青龙精又出来作怪。

海蜇姑娘就将三条鲨鱼放进海里,然后自己也跳进海里。青龙精看见了,就从天上冲下来,要吃海蜇姑娘。海蜇姑娘却被三条鲨鱼团团裹在当中。青龙精吃不到海蜇姑娘就和鲨鱼打了起来。后来青龙精战不过三条鲨鱼,被三条鲨鱼咬死啦。海蜇姑娘就这样为民除了一大害。

可是,海蜇姑娘自己呢,再也回不到陆地上来啦,后来,就在海里变成了一条扁扁的海蜇鱼。直到现在,鲨鱼和海蜇还是好朋友呢。

the sky to prey on Haizhe. Haizhe, however, was surrounded and protected by the three sharks. The dragon wrestled with the sharks in an attempt to continue his attack on her. Eventually, he was killed by the sharks. Haizhe managed to kill the evil for her community.

Our pitiful Haizhe herself, unfortunately, never made it to the land. Later, she turned into a flat jellyfish in the sea. To this day, sharks and jellyfish are still good friends.